Voice

Joseph Garraty

Ragman Press LLC

Dallas, TX

This one's for Matt Watson, for more than ten years of slogging it out with me in seedy dives, coffee houses on the edge of going out of business, and the occasional respectable establishment.

This book wouldn't exist without you, man.

ACKNOWLEDGMENTS

Special thanks to Evan Grantham-Brown, who reads all these things and makes them better.

PROLOGUE

The recording from the last Ragman concert is one song long. Half that, actually, since the song never reaches completion. The recording should have disappeared, should have been cleaned up by the police in the aftermath and filed away as evidence and never been heard again. It leaked out into the world, though, the way these things do, and the diligent and the curious can still dig up a copy if they want. Many do. Dumb kids at slumber parties, playing it like a game of Bloody Mary, trying to see who chickens out first. College kids, drunk or stoned at 3 a.m. Fans who followed the band from the early days and one day can't shake the need to *know*.

Most listen to it one time, and they turn it off before the end. *Well* before the end. Then they burn it, bury it, delete it from their hard drives or their iPods and go to sleep troubled and trying to forget that any such thing ever existed.

You can hear the crowd first. Rumblings, and a few shouts. It sounds like a good-sized crowd, maybe a couple thousand people. One voice—a woman's voice, high and clear—starts the chant: "Johnny! Johnny! Johnny!" In a matter of moments, everyone is chanting. There's a faint sound, maybe the drumsticks brushing the snare, and then a huge cheer goes up, dissolving the chant in a rush of noise.

Four clicks and then the rhythm section comes in— Danny T layin' it down on the skins, and Allen Sorenson on bass. It's a fast chromatic riff, low and rolling, and more than a little disorienting. You don't get a clear sense of whether the song is in a major or minor key, just a seasick feeling of rumbling motion. You can hear Danny's metal snare drum, a little too hot and with too much biting treble, cutting through the mix like steel teeth, and the scrape and rattle of the strings on Allen's big old Fender P-Bass are driving like a runaway eighteen-wheeler. It's impossible not to get caught up in the motion of the thing, even with no idea of where it's going.

Case comes in after a couple of bars. In the studio version of the song, the guitar tracks were doubled, but she's doing solo duty live. It doesn't matter. Her guitar sounds *huge*, even with just the one track—a Les Paul through a hundred watts of Marshall amplification, like the fist of God coming through a speaker cabinet. The sound is mean, distorted, heavy on the mids and snarling like a wild beast. She follows the bass part for an eight-count with the drums driving the tension up higher and higher, moves the figure up into an ugly harmony to make the tension even worse, and then there's a sleazy little run down into a slow, bone-crushing riff that comes from nowhere, like one of those grinding Black Sabbath steamroller riffs that destroys everything in its path. The transition is shocking, like plunging into a lake of cold, cold water or the sun being suddenly masked by brewing black thunderclouds. It raises gooseflesh on you when you hear it on the recording, and it must have had the same effect on the crowd experiencing it at the time. If you listen closely, you can even hear Danny say "*Fuck* yeah," just loud enough for his vocal mic to pick up.

The guitar drops out, and there's a lull. Then, just before where you'd expect the vocals to come in, there's this awful sound. A quiet, plaintive voice, desperate, and half-whispering, half-pleading: "Oh, God, please no."

Johnny Tango's voice. It cracks on the "e" in "please."

Then a quick inhalation and the vocals come in, and that's when you realize something is not right here, not right at all. The voice that comes out is nothing like a human voice, singing nothing like human words. It's vast and deep, oily and ravenous, and it pounds into your brain like a meat hammer. The pressure is crushing, mounting, thunderous, and you forget that this is a recording and you can turn it off at any time, you forget everything except that your brain is being pulped by a godawful, godless sound that shouldn't even exist, a sound like tectonic plates grinding corpses into fields of broken glass, and then, incredibly, the sound gets *worse*, and you open your mouth to scream, and—

Suddenly the noise stops and there's screaming everywhere. You haven't made a sound yet, but the air is thick with screams. The music on the recording has stopped, but the screams have only just started, and you listen in horror with your mouth gaping stupidly. These, too, are sounds that shouldn't ever come from human throats, but you can imagine all too well how they might. There's the sound of something exploding—for some reason you picture racks of lighting blowing apart—and a distant voice screams, "My eyes! Ah, my fucking eyes!" It's impossible to tell who it is, or even if it's a man or a woman, the voice is so distorted by pain and fear.

About then, somebody usually comes to their senses and flicks the Off switch, pulls the power cord, or simply yanks the headphone jack out of its socket. There will be a long moment of shocked silence. Maybe the guy who brought the weed to the party will wipe his mouth with a shaking hand and, face pale and eyes staring, say, "Dude, that's . . . that's sick." Nobody will argue. Nobody will say a word. The party is over. Everyone will leave without making another sound.

It's the screaming that gets everyone to pull the plug, and, in the bright daylight, if they ever bring it up again, that's what they'll talk about. Those awful screams. *God, wasn't that horrible? Oh, those poor people.*

They talk about the screams, but those are the easiest to forget. It's that voice, that VOICE, that sound of unthinkable speech in an impossible tongue that keeps them up night after night, driving some to the bottle and others to sleeping pills or religion. People scream every day. It's horrible, but screaming seems like a perfectly rational way of dealing with a difficult—but sane, you understand, definitely sane—world. It's *understandable.* It's *normal.*

That voice, though . . . No sane world would harbor such a thing. No rational world could accommodate it. And if it really exists, then there are cracks in the foundation of reality that no thinking being dares to contemplate.

Some rare individuals let the recording go to the end. There are another four minutes of screaming, pleading, shouting, and awful, maniacal laughter. After another thirty seconds, the crackle of flames begins.

If you listen closely, and turn the volume on your stereo all the way up, you can hear, at about seven minutes and twenty seconds, Johnny Tango's voice.

"Oh, God, I never . . ."

The recording ends there.

CHAPTER 1

"This band fucking *sucks*," Case yelled over the noise. Another night—another band—and maybe some of the fans would have shot her dirty looks, but this place was dead. Deader than dead. Probably nobody would have come out to hear this piece-of-shit band to begin with—just like the piece-of-shit band that was coming after them, Case thought bitterly—but the holiday guaranteed an empty room.

The bartender shrugged and put her glass down. "It's new band night. What do you want me to do about it?"

Case tossed back half the drink and coughed. New band night on Easter Sunday. What kind of dumbass would play new band night on Easter? Who would book such a stupid show? She shot a dirty look over at the ratty leather couch near the door, where the three other members of her own band were sitting, watching the current act with bland, glazed-over expressions. Damon was pulling on his goatee absently, which made Case want to go over and yank the damn thing out by the roots. The whole idea of new band night was to put asses in seats, prove to the club you could get people in the door so that they'd book you for a *real* date. So naturally, Damon had booked Easter fucking Sunday, ensuring they'd be playing new band night again next month. If the club gave them another chance.

She downed the rest of her drink. She felt like throwing the glass against the wall, but she put it on the bar instead. She turned around and put her elbows on the bar, watching the band onstage with her face screwed up in disgust, as if she were watching open-heart surgery. Or maybe a massacre.

Yep, they sucked. They had all the stage presence of limp pasta, and they couldn't play worth a fiddler's fuck, either. The guitarist watched his fingers stumble over the fretboard with the kind of intense concentration usually reserved for advanced math problems, and even the instrument itself was a horror show, some kind of godawful fifty-dollar pawnshop Charvel. The bass player at least looked comfortable on his instrument. It was a pity he didn't seem to know what key the song was in. As for the vocalist . . . Good God, the vocalist. He looked to be made entirely out of bones, so skinny Case thought she could see his ribs right through his shirt. He had a voice to match, too—thin, tiny, and scratchy, warbling like an anorexic basset hound. Case couldn't hear him very well, and she wasn't sure if that was because he wasn't projecting at all, or if the sound guy had turned him down to do him a favor. Save him some humiliation. It didn't much matter. Aside from the staff and Case's band, the only people in the bar were a bored-looking woman who had come in with the bass player and an aging ex-rocker guy in the corner who watched the band so seriously, sipping from a half-full glass of whiskey, that Case just knew he was somebody's dad. Empty room, and the vocalist still looked like he was trying to hide behind his mic stand.

She thought the band was supposed to be playing hard rock of some kind, but the guitarist and bass player were shitting all over the changes, and the singer had no balls. The only thing they had going for them was the drummer. If Case just tuned out everything else, the drummer had a tight little groove going. She found herself nodding her head along with that until the song ended.

"Two more songs, guys," the sound guy said. The singer flinched like he'd been shocked, and the band laid into something that sounded like a version of the Stones' "Sympathy for the Devil" that had been knocked down, stomped on, and finally kicked in the head for good measure.

At least everybody got a short set on new band night. Jesus.

Case got up to get her guitar. It wouldn't hurt to warm up a little before her set, she supposed. She slipped around the sound booth and went back to the "green room," an oversized storage closet that was packed with so much shit it was barely possible to walk in, let alone get your stuff out without a catastrophe. The little room was covered in peeling stickers and smelled distinctly of piss. She picked up her guitar case from the corner, extricating it from behind a stack of toms, and started to leave.

Damon met her at the door. Alcohol fumes and the scent of marijuana wafted off him, strong enough to burn her eyes. "Gonna rock this place, Steph?"

She exhaled very slowly. "If you call me Steph *one more time*, I'll break your nose."

"Ease up there, babe. Don't be like that." A slightly spacey smirk spread across his face.

"'Babe' was your last freebie, Damon. You ready to play this waste of a show or what?"

"Waste? Come on, we'll tear it up."

"Sure. We could have torn it up in the practice room. Less shit to move, and God knows we could use the practice. Same size crowd, too." She moved her guitar case to her other hand. "Just get your stuff and let's do this, okay?"

"Yeah."

She brushed past him, feeling his eyes crawling over her body as she walked away. *Prick.*

She only had time to stretch her fingers, and then the other band's set was over. Usually, this would mean a few frantic minutes of mutually stumbling over bodies and equipment while they got their gear offstage and Case's band got set up, but Case wasn't in a hurry. Her band was the last one playing tonight, and if they got cut off early— well, so fucking what? The sound guy didn't seem to care, either, taking his time to put everything in its place. He eyed Case appreciatively, but he at least made an effort to be subtle about it. She could tolerate that. Her customary stage getup was a pair of tight leather pants and a white tank top, and if not all the attention she got was welcome, most of it was, and it was manageable. Somebody had once told her, If you're going to be in the band, *look like you're in the band.* Good advice, she thought, but the guy who'd given it to her hadn't mentioned the extra baggage that came with it when you were a woman. Probably had no idea.

She supposed she shouldn't have bothered tonight. She could have played this gig in a bathrobe. *Ah, fuck that,* she chided herself. *We're here, and Damon's right about one thing—as long as we're here, we might as well rock out. It'll be like practice, only with better sound.*

They did the usual indifferent sound check—two notes each from the guitar and bass, ten seconds of whacking on the drum set, and Damon mumbling some third-grade joke about testes into the mic, and then they were on.

It was *loud*, and that should have helped. Despite the empty room, there was some adrenaline that came from just being onstage, and Case tried to push the bullshit nature of the gig out of her mind and enjoy playing. She let the first few bars of music—fast, driving—push her forward, and a nasty little grin curled up the corners of her mouth as she got into it.

Then Damon forgot the first verse—just didn't come in at all. The band played through it anyway, and Case went right into the chorus after that, assuming Damon would catch up then. The bass player, though, apparently figured they ought to repeat the verse and give Damon another chance. The result was a disaster, an aural train wreck as the two parts of the song plowed into each other at a hundred miles an hour.

The rest of the set—all five songs—went straight to hell from there. Case turned away and played with her back to Damon the whole time, certain that if she looked at him, she'd kill him on the spot.

The last song came as a mercy. The final chord died, the sound guy fired up some Van Halen through the main speakers, and Case put down her guitar and left the stage without a word. She headed toward the bar—the other guys could clear out their stuff first, and she'd take care of hers once they were out of the way. Meanwhile, if a drink had ever been in order, it was now.

"Screwdriver," she told the bartender, and she tossed him five bucks she couldn't really afford.

"Good set," somebody said.

She swung her head to the right and fixed a disbelieving glare on the singer from the last band. He had a small mouth and eyes that looked way too big for his head, and, astonishingly, he looked even skinnier up close than he had onstage. "Sure," she said. "I bet that's what they told Mick Jagger about Altamont, too."

The guy grinned, which went a long way toward making his eyes look almost normal-sized. "Nobody's dead here."

"Fuck. Nobody's here at all."

"Then no damage done. No problem."

She shook her head and went back to her drink. He had a point, she guessed, but that just aggravated her further.

"I have a proposition for you," the guy said.

"If this involves going back to your van, somebody's going to get hurt."

He laughed nervously. "No, nothing like that. I need a guitarist. You're good. I like your style. Very emotive. I've never seen anybody play the emotion *pissed off* so well."

"That's because I was pissed off."

Another chuckle. "Good reason. You want the job?"

"You have a guitarist." *Of sorts.*

"Not anymore. I fired him."

She turned back to him, surprised. "Really? When?"

"Just as soon as you say yes."

She snorted. "This is the worst come-on ever."

He rolled his weird eyes, still grinning. "News flash: Not everybody on the planet is out to fuck you."

"News flash: Between those who are out to fuck me and those who are out to fuck me over, I think just about everyone is covered."

He put his beer down. "What a lovely persecution complex you have."

"Persecution complex? *Emotive?* Did they just let you out of college?"

"Look," he said, steepling his hands in front of him and trying to look earnest, "I'm in a bad spot. I got the band booked for a show at some little college in West Texas. It'll be our first college show. I don't want to suck."

Case, by grace of what she assumed had to be divine intervention, kept her mouth shut.

"It's in two weeks," he said. "Pays two hundred dollars."

"Two hundred dollars for the band, or two hundred dollars a person?"

The guy blinked. "You, personally, will take home two hundred dollars after you play this show."

Shit. That was a good chunk of next month's rent money. Three nights of shitty tips. A professional re-fretting job for her guitar, if she threw in a little extra. She'd had gigs that paid more, but not often, and only when she played with cover bands.

"How the hell did you swing that?" she asked.

He shrugged. "I wrote a letter to the Student Activities Committee of every college I could find in a five-hundred-mile radius. Three hundred letters. These guys bit. Booked us, sight unseen."

The last bit of explanation wasn't necessary, Case thought. That they'd been booked without being heard was a given, or they wouldn't have been booked at all.

Two hundred bucks.

Still, something compelled her to be honest with the guy. "I can't save your band for you."

"Ouch. Don't hold back—tell me how you really feel," he said, voice dripping sarcasm. "I'm not asking you to *save* the band. Danny's pretty damn good, and—"

"Danny's the drummer?"

"Yeah."

"He *is* pretty damn good."

The guy nodded. "And Quentin will do all right, I think. He sometimes chokes when he gets in front of people, but he's solid. You'll see. We'll be a lot better with a good guitarist."

She almost said something nasty about the vocals, but she stopped herself. If he was going to pay her two hundred bucks, she ought to let it go. Besides, he looked so fragile with his tiny mouth and bug eyes. He might cry.

Somebody put a hand on her hip, and she whirled, arm already half-cocked back. It was Damon, standing too close as usual and weaving drunkenly. The rest of the band and the bony chick who'd come in with the bass player stood behind him. "Good fuckin' show, huh?" Damon said.

She lowered her arm halfway and took one step back, down the length of the bar. "Yeah, sure."

"We're all loaded up, and I'm gonna take off," he said. He took a step toward her.

"Great. Get the fuck out of here. And don't touch me again. Ever." She took another step back.

He didn't get the picture, or maybe he was just deaf. He took another step toward her. "C'mon, Steph—"

"Don't."

The note of menace in her voice must have been enough to break through the drunken fog in his brain.

"Who's this guy?" he asked, turning to the skinny dude.

"Fuck off, Damon," Case said.

The skinny guy, to give him credit, tried to calm things down. "It's cool, man," he said. "I'm John." He held out a hand.

Damon slapped his hand away. "Yeah. What the fuck are you doing here, John?"

"Just talking business."

Even Case recognized that as exactly the wrong thing to say. *Here it comes,* she thought.

"Business? What business do you have with my guitar player?" A light dawned in Damon's dim brain. "Oh— you're with the other band, the, the whatever-the-fucks."

"Ragman," John said. He swallowed nervously and pressed himself back against the bar.

"What business you got, Ragman?" Damon stepped toward John, getting right in his face.

"Just business."

Damon shoved him. It was a pathetic, drunken shove, but John staggered back.

This was going to get very ugly. Damon had sixty pounds or more on John, and John looked like the kind of guy who'd never been in a shouting match in his life, to say nothing of a barroom brawl.

"That's enough," Case said.

"I'll say when it's enough. *Steph.*" Damon sneered at her, and then he turned back to John and made his move. He was big, drunk, and slow, and the movement was telegraphed seemingly hours in advance. He stepped forward and dropped his shoulder back. John just stared, with no idea that he was about to get his face caved in.

Case never explicitly gave the order, but as Damon stepped into the wide, clumsy arc of his swing, her fist moved on its own, flashing out in a blur. Damon's head snapped back and blood flew through the air. He collapsed to the floor, moaning, with his hands clutching his face.

"Oww, fuck!"

Case gave the other guys a threatening look, but they obviously didn't want any more of this. The drummer leaned down and tried to pull Damon to his feet. "Come on, Damon. We gotta go," he said. Damon pushed backward, crablike.

"Hey," he said as the guys hauled him off. He scratched at the air with one hand. Blood covered the bottom half of his face. "You're gonna be at practice tomorrow, right?"

Case just shook her head, amazed.

She turned back to John, the skinny idiot who needed a guitarist. He stood there, shocked, his mouth hanging open and his eyes even wider than usual. Flecks of blood spattered his forehead.

"Looks like I need a band," she said. She crossed her arms and stared at him. "So I'm in. Call me Case. Got a pen?"

She wrote her name, number, and email address on the back of his band's mailing-list form, tore off the bottom, and handed it to him. "Your turn."

He wrote something on the paper and gave it back. She stared at it. John Tsiboukas. "How the hell do you pronounce that?"

"John," he said with a vague smile.

"Okay, then, John T. Send me directions to your practice room, and I'll see you there. If you can also send me some recordings of the songs, that'll go a long way." She started to go, then turned around. "Make sure your bass player knows his shit."

She left him staring after her and went to pack up her gear.

***

"Did I hear that right?"

John swiveled around on his barstool. Danny stood there, arms crossed and eyebrows raised, looking for all the world as if he were about to lecture a four-year-old. That's what big brothers were for, John figured.

"What did you just do?" Danny asked.

John grinned. "Found us a guitarist." His voice was hoarse from singing even the short set they'd played.

"Yeah? You might want to tell Seth that."

"Sure, no problem." John waved it off. "He'll be upset, but we all know he's not very good."

"He busted his ass to get ready for this show," Danny protested.

"I know he did. That's the sad part."

"That's pretty fucking rude, John."

John held up a hand. "I like Seth. He's a good guy. But we've been trying like hell, and—well, you heard him play."

Danny deflated, dropped his big hands to his sides. "Yeah. That was bad."

"Besides," John added, "she's *really* good."

"She's really *angry*, if that's what you mean."

"She's good. You know it." John tapped the side of his glass thoughtfully. "Kinda hot, too."

Danny gave him a serious look. "Careful there, bro. You know Rule Number One."

"No worries. I was thinking about presentation. She looks good onstage—should help get us some attention. Besides," he added, remembering the way she'd laid out the singer of her own band, "she'd probably break me in half."

Danny grinned. "True that. What did what's his name do to piss her off?"

"Invaded her personal space, I think."

"Note to self."

John laughed again. "No kidding."

"Well, looks like this place is all partied out. I'm gonna go get the car," Danny said. "See you out front?"

"Yeah."

Danny headed for the door. John nursed his beer, staring at the row of bottles at the back of the bar and thinking.

Stephanie Case. So that was her name. She didn't remember him—why would she have?—but he'd seen her band once before, playing some hole in the wall downtown. The band had been okay. She had been amazing. She played scorched-earth guitar, taking no prisoners and leaving smoldering ruin in her wake, and John had been enthralled. He'd watched nothing but her for the whole set, and then panicked and run like hell out of the bar before she got off the stage, afraid he'd say something unutterably stupid if she passed close enough for him to say hi.

And then she'd walked in just before his set tonight. He wished he hadn't recognized her. In the time it took him to place the face—and that had not been long at all—he'd gone from singing for the fun of it to singing for her, and he didn't need anybody to tell him how incredibly fucking stupid that had been. He'd tried to turn the performance up to eleven just for her, but his nerves had worked their peculiar evil, and instead of delivering a transcendent performance he'd been even worse than normal. What had he been thinking, that somehow he'd magically impress her and by the end of the set she'd be clamoring to join his band?

Actually, that was exactly what he'd been thinking, he admitted. A whole series of increasingly fantastic scenarios had slipped through his head while he tried to perform. None of them were realistic, but by the third song, he had known he was going to fire Seth. *He needed killin'*, as they said here in Texas. How he was going to convince Case to join up he hadn't had the foggiest clue. The friction with her own band had been a near-miraculous stroke of good luck, and then the invitation to play the college show had jumped into John's head while he was talking to her.

Yeah, and that had its own set of problems he'd have to navigate. He shook his head, put his empty bottle on the bar, and started toward the door. There'd be time to worry about all that later.

Outside, the street was dead—midnight downtown on Easter Sunday dead. The shops and clubs were mostly dark, and the parking meters stood, lone sentinels in front of empty spaces. The only movement was a plastic cup lid skittering along the sidewalk, blown along with a small cloud of grit.

To John's right, a man leaned against the brick wall of the bar, cigarette burning down in his hand. Tight blue jeans, white silk shirt unbuttoned at the throat, black cowboy boots. He gave off the vibe of an old rock-and-roll guy, his years long past. The kind of guy who'd missed fame and fortune by a hairsbreadth, the kind of guy you might catch at some hole-in-the-wall blues dive playing his ass off, and you'd walk away thinking, *Fuck! He's good! Why haven't I heard of him?* Maybe John *had* seen him somewhere—that might account for the vague sense of familiarity he got from the guy. The guy had been inside watching the set, but John couldn't help feeling he'd seen him somewhere else.

The guy gave John a thin smile and took a drag.

John nodded absently and looked down the street for Danny's car. Nothing moved anywhere.

"You don't have the money, do you?" the guy said. His voice was a low, hoarse whisper, the sound of an oily rasp dragged across wood.

John's attention snapped to the man. "What did you say?"

The guy took a step closer, and an awful scent, fishy and ripe with decay, hit John's nostrils, faint but foul beneath the smell of cigarette smoke. The guy grinned without humor. His face was sharp, angular, and though he was getting on in years, age had done nothing to soften those angles, and his grin was that of a hungry animal. Strings of greasy black hair, shot through with white, tumbled to his shoulders. "Don't get me wrong," he whispered. "I think you did the right thing. She's the piece you need."

"I don't know who you are, but—"

The guy narrowed his eyes, and John simply trailed off. What was that stink? Was it carried on the man's breath, or did he sleep in a trash bin behind a sushi restaurant? Christ! "There's the other thing, of course," the guy said, "but if you've got what it takes, I can help you with that." He trained his eyes on John's, and there was something dark and deadly in them. "And, Johnny my boy, I think maybe you do." He put his hand on John's shoulder and leaned in toward him.

John opened his mouth, grasping for some kind of reply, and Danny's car pulled up. The tires squeaked against the curb. The guy took his hand off John's shoulder.

Danny got out. "All right," he said. "Let's load up."

John glanced at him and then back to the guy, who was already walking away, the heels of his cowboy boots clacking against the concrete.

"Yeah," John said to his brother. "Sure."

***

They loaded the car in silence. Quentin and Seth had already taken off, so there was just Danny's drum set to load up—an appreciable amount of equipment, but at least none of it was very heavy. They crammed it into Danny's little hatchback and headed toward John's place. It wasn't far.

They pulled up outside the little shack John was renting, a tiny hovel with barely basic amenities stashed on a lot between a bunch of four-bedroom historic houses. The shack was a placeholder for the lot, and it was evidently so ungodly old that it had been grandfathered in despite the neighborhood's now-stringent neighborhood-association rules. It should have been bulldozed twenty years ago.

"You doin' all right?" Danny asked him, as usual. "Making ends meet?"

"I'm okay." John hopped out of the car without looking at him.

"Let me know if you need anything, okay?"

"Yeah, sure." John shut the door. "See you at practice," he said through the open window.

"Yeah. You bet."

Danny pulled away, and John walked up the sidewalk to his humble shack, set way back on the lot. He fumbled with his keys in the streetlight for a moment before finding the keyhole. The idea of locking the door was kind of a joke—a good hard kick would probably tear the door right off its hinges, and if it didn't, a good hard kick three feet to the left would almost certainly put a hole in the wall—but it was habit. That, and he was worried that if he made it *too* easy, he'd come in one day to find that a dozen homeless people had taken up residence.

He got the door open and went inside, not bothering to turn on the light. Electricity cost money, and the grungy yellow streetlight painting the blinds was bright enough for now. He walked through the small, empty living room and down the short hall to his bedroom. He threw his notebook on a shelf made of cinder blocks and scavenged lumber, already groaning under wobbly stacks of magazines, books, CDs, and DVDs—his whole exhaustive collection of rock history. The souvenirs of half a dozen college road trips and other expeditions were lined up neatly along the top shelf. A broken drumstick from a Steve Earle concert he'd driven three hundred miles to see. A ticket stub from the Rock and Roll Hall of Fame. A shot glass he'd smuggled out of the Whisky a Go-Go, that epic landmark of LA's rock scene, a place that had shocked him by turning out to be about the size of a large bathroom. He even had a stick of Elvis lip balm, all he'd been able to afford on his short trip to Graceland. One day he hoped to make a pilgrimage to Jeff Buckley's grave and collect a stick or a rock or a handful of dirt. Something.

It was a good collection of stuff, and he had visions of talking about it in an interview one day in the not-too-distant future when he was rich and famous.

John lowered himself to the mattress on the floor and sat against the wall. Usually he'd crack open his journal after a show and write down a few thoughts, but he felt a mean headache coming on. The shakes, too. He always had a post-show adrenaline high, even if they played just for the sound guy (which was typical), but his anxiety this time had been thrumming like a string that had been wound too tight, and his mind was so revved up now that he doubted he'd get any sleep tonight.

Stephanie Case was going to play in his band. Fantastic.

His stomach twisted and did an unpleasant flip-flop. What had that guy said outside the club? *You don't have the money, do you?* John didn't know how the guy knew that, but he was right on, eerily enough. Case thought she was going to make two hundred bucks, the guys thought the show paid two hundred bucks total, and the reality was that it paid forty dollars plus tips. John had been so excited about the possibility of playing a real show instead of new band night for a change that he'd guessed what the guys would accept for doing the show and put up the remaining one hundred and ten bucks to pay them himself. It would clean him out, but it would get them in front of a college crowd. At some level, he realized it was stupid and he never should have done it, but he *had* done it, and he had no intention of backing out.

Except now he'd promised Case the whole two hundred bucks—fifty of which he didn't even have, because that would have been his imaginary share of the take.

Tomorrow's problem, he thought. *Or the next day's.*

He swallowed and started to feel a little better. The show had sucked, there was no question about that—but somehow he'd managed to snag one hell of a guitarist.

Now he'd just have to figure out how to keep her.

CHAPTER 2

Practice was held in a rented practice room that was just like all the other rented practice rooms Case had ever seen. Four people and all their equipment were jammed into a room the size of a modest walk-in closet, one of dozens packed into the carved-up space of a defunct elementary school. The walls were lined with grey egg-crate foam that did nothing to dampen the sound of the speed metal band rehearsing in the next room. Why was it, she wondered, that there seemed to be a speed metal band next door to every practice room she set foot in? It was like a malign cosmic law, proof that there was no God.

At least there was no porn on the walls. That was a welcome change.

She arrived early, as she always did, reasoning that practice was supposed to start at seven, so she should get there beforehand and set up. Be ready to *play* at seven. It never seemed to work out that way, so she was pleasantly surprised when John and his drummer were there waiting for her. John had already made a spare copy of the key, which he handed to her without a word when she came in.

She paid the two of them little attention, setting up her gear while Danny set up and tuned his drums and John fiddled with the PA.

The bass player—Quentin, she recalled—walked in at about five minutes to seven and did an honest-to-god double take when he saw her.

"Uh . . ." he said stupidly, looking back and forth from Case to John like he had some kind of twitch.

Oops, Case thought. She leaned over her amp to plug in a cable, letting her hair fall across her face and hide her grin. *Somebody forgot to let Quentin know the score.*

John didn't seem to even notice. He gave Quentin, still standing in the doorway, a puzzled look and motioned him inside.

Danny caught it, though. He put his drum key down on the snare. "Aw, hell, John. You didn't call Quentin?" He didn't wait for an answer. "Quentin, this is Case. She's, ah, she's our new guitarist. Case, Quentin."

Quentin looked like he wanted to say something, but he cast her a nervous glance and let it drop. "Meetcha," he mumbled, and went over to his amp.

Case put on her guitar, a battered goldtop Les Paul that she wore slung as low as she could handle. It hung below her waist, which was a little awkward for her fretting hand sometimes, but it made things a hell of a lot easier for her picking hand. Besides, if it was good enough for Jimmy Page . . .

She tuned up, and, shockingly, the whole band was ready to go by seven.

First time I've ever seen that happen.

"Okay, we'll start with 'Aftermath' and see how it goes," John said. Danny counted it off almost before she was ready, but she jumped on it just in time.

It was an easy song, like all the songs John had sent her. Straightforward chord changes, no solo, no bridge, nothing fancy. It was an unfuckuppable song. Hell, the chorus had the same chord progression as the verse—it was like a meaner, less inspired version of "Knockin' on Heaven's Door," the same four chords for three and a half minutes. It was so easy that the real challenge was keeping her mind from wandering. She varied the rhythm a little bit, tried to syncopate it some, and threw in a few different chord voicings to spice it up, but it was like lentils—basically bland, no matter what you threw on top of it.

She looked around the room, watching and listening to the other musicians as her hands went on autopilot. Quentin wouldn't look at her, and he seemed to be trying to push himself into the wall. Danny was grooving, though. The song was so dull that the dynamics changes were the only thing carrying it, musically, and he pushed and pulled those through effortlessly. She found herself edging closer to him, embellishing a little bit around his rhythm, and the two of them eased into a back-and-forth that almost had a little *spark* to it. By the end of the second chorus, she was starting to feel good, and she lit into a solo that hadn't existed in the song before.

John sang the first few words of the verse before tapering off under her onslaught. She shot a challenging look at him, but he just nodded approval. Quentin didn't seem to know what the fuck was going on, but the chords were impossible to screw up, so he kept playing what he'd been playing. John came back in after one verse figure and Case slid back into the rhythm part. Danny shot her a grin, and she found herself smiling back.

They finished the song.

"That was . . . different," Quentin said. He was scowling.

"Yeah it was," John said. He looked terribly serious, but a light danced in his eyes. "Hell yeah."

After that, they practiced *hard*. John seemed to warm up some and get a little more comfortable, and while his voice was still thin and off-key, he didn't suck quite as badly as he had the other night. And it was clear that nobody outworked him. He rode himself mercilessly, having the band play the third verse of one song about fifteen times while he sang it over and over. He didn't seem to know what he wanted, just that each new attempt wasn't quite it. He was groping toward something, Case thought, trying one thing after another like searching for a light switch in the dark.

He didn't have the musical expertise to tell Danny or Case what to do, so he left them alone, but he got exasperated with Quentin quite a bit. "Jesus, Quentin, can you just remember the change for once? And I need you to back off there, I can't hear myself!" Quentin seemed to take it okay, but Case didn't know how he managed. She'd have simply walked out if John had treated her that way.

They practiced the same ten songs for over three hours, at the end of which Case and Danny were drenched in sweat and Quentin looked like he wanted to crawl under his amplifier and hide. John was so hoarse he could barely talk above a whisper. Case figured that couldn't be good for him—it had to be doing some damage, but whatever. It was his voice.

"Tomorrow night, seven again?" John whispered as they packed up.

Danny shook his head. "Can't do it. My—ah, I got stuff going on." He gave Case a sidelong look and then promptly looked down at his drum set.

"I can't either," Case said. "Gotta work for a living. Can't do Wednesday, either. Thursday should work."

John frowned. "Okay, then. Thursday."

Case put her guitar in the case. She wondered if she should take the amp, too, but decided against it. She'd just have to bring it back.

She was halfway out the door when she had an odd thought. *That's how a musician knows she's home. It's where she leaves her gear.*

She rolled her eyes at herself. "Thursday," she said to the room at large, and she left.

***

John was buzzed—that had been almost like real rock and roll! If they could tighten it up just a little before the show, it would be all right. For the first time in months, he felt like he was making progress.

His excitement dimmed a little when he saw Quentin staring at him, brooding like a storm cloud. "What happened to Seth?"

John looked away. "You know how it is."

"Not sure I do. How is it?" Quentin spoke quietly, but John could hear a low anger in his voice.

John sighed. He had worried so much about how to handle Quentin's cut of the upcoming show that he'd forgotten Quentin and Seth were buddies. Even if they hadn't been, Quentin didn't take surprises well. Great.

"She's good," John said. He could elaborate, but probably not in a way that would make Quentin any happier. He thought through a few options and decided to leave it at that.

Quentin stared at him for a long time before finally looking down. "Yeah," he said. He rolled up his cables, threw them in a bag, and headed toward the door. "See you Thursday."

John let out a breath he hadn't even known he'd been holding. That was one problem down. Not the one he'd actually been worried about, so it shouldn't have come as much relief, but he felt buoyed anyway.

"Hell of a rehearsal, huh bro?" he asked Danny.

"Yeah," Danny said. He had a distant look in his eyes, but he was still grinning. "That was all right."

"Thanks, Captain Understatement. That was better than all right, and you know it."

Danny shrugged. "We're getting there. Not there yet, but a hell of a lot closer. I don't know how you talked her into coming, but good call."

That was the opening—John doubted there'd be a better one. He braced himself. "Ah, about that . . ."

Danny's distant look got a whole lot closer. "Yeah?"

"I, uh, I had to make some promises to get her on board."

"Oh, Jesus. John, do you *ever* think before you open your mouth? Ever? What did you tell her?"

John looked at the ceiling. "I told her the pay for the college show was two hundred bucks."

"So?" It took Danny another second to put it together. "Oh, *fuck*—"

"I told her that *her* pay for the college show was two hundred bucks," John said, cutting him off.

"Yeah, I got it. Quentin is going to murder you in your sleep."

John tried on a weak grin. "So, I was wondering if maybe I could borrow fifty bucks."

"To pay Quentin," Danny said flatly.

"To pay Quentin."

"I ought to beat your ass," Danny said, but by the tone of his voice John knew that the argument was already won.

"I ought to let Quentin murder you in your sleep. I ought to *help*."

John's smile widened. He couldn't seem to stop it.

"So I'm out fifty bucks, because I don't get my cut, and then I'm out *another* fifty bucks because I have to pay for Quentin. Is that about right?"

John tried, unsuccessfully, to wipe the smile off his face. "Yeah. I'll pay you back."

"Yeah, right. Pull the other one." Danny sighed and scratched his close-cropped scalp. "I'll spring for it this time, but we're gonna split four ways, evenly, after this."

"Cool," John said. "This'll work out great—you'll see."

"It better," Danny said. "Gina's gonna be pissed," he added to himself.

"Gina," John echoed. "Your—ah, *stuff* you gotta do tomorrow night?"

Danny didn't say anything.

"Don't *you* forget Rule Number One," John said.

"Don't worry about me," Danny snapped.

John let it drop.

CHAPTER 3

He can hear the sound of the crowd. On the other side of the curtain, like a beast with ten thousand heads, the mass of people chants his name: Johnny! Johnny! Johnny! The stamping of their feet vibrates up through the stage, up through the soles of his feet, into his belly, his heart.

His throat. Their voice is his voice now, raw, thunderous, and powerful.

He looks to the left and to the right, and a sneer—a pure rock-and-roll sneer, a Billy Idol sneer—no, an Elvis sneer—pulls his lip up. Case is to his right, as always, but her goldtop Les Paul has been replaced by a guitar the color of blood, so deep and rich it seems almost to be dripping. To his left stands the bass player. John doesn't recognize the man, but he's strangely unconcerned. The bass player gives him a nod. All clear, he seems to say. Danny is ready behind him, just waiting for the signal.

He looks around one more time. The crowd is frenzied now as the stage lights come up.

Standing off in the wings, just past the mystery bass player, is Bob Dylan. Highway 61 Bob Dylan, his face smooth and unlined, his hair frizzed out in a thousand directions, his eyes hidden behind black plastic sunglasses. Robert Plant stands next to Dylan, shirt hanging open, arms folded. Dylan tips Johnny a nod, but Plant has a fuck-you expression on his face. Impress me, *his face says. His eyes are black and flat, like sharks' eyes.*

Behind both of them, an aging ex-rocker, his lined face all harsh angles and deep creases. He cocks a finger at John and grins.

Johnny tears his gaze away. He raises his hands, and the curtain starts to rise. The noise of the crowd rises with it, the chant breaking into numberless cheers.

The band starts, and the stage sound is loud, louder than the crowd, louder than the bellowing voice of God at the instant of creation. There are no other sounds in the whole universe.

Johnny steps forward, leaning the mic stand over, inhaling deeply before the first word.

The thick, rancid scent of decaying fish rolls into his sinuses and down his throat, and he chokes.

***

John woke with bile already racing up his throat. He jolted awake, bolting for the hall, but it was already too late. He didn't make it even close to the bathroom, but he was lucky enough to get clear of the mattress before his dinner came forth in one great convulsion, splashing the floor and spattering the walls.

He fell to his knees, choking and retching. His hands shook like mad, and he balled them into fists, using them to support his body as he leaned forward and spasmed.

That awful smell . . .

He knew it was just a dream, but he couldn't shake the sense that that horrible smell had been there, right there in the room with him in the seconds before he threw up. Now there was just the acid stench of vomit.

Smell or no, the dream kept coming back. It had been a couple of weeks since the show, two weeks since he'd talked Case into playing with the band, and it was a similar dream every night, with slight variations on the theme. Sometimes the curtain rose and John sang. In those dreams, his voice sounded glorious, but the crowd had turned to corpses. Sometimes they were still and dead, and other times they were living corpses that jeered at him and charged the stage just before he awoke. Often, he never sang at all—that stink choked him, or the equipment wouldn't work, or worse. Once, Robert Plant had stepped forward and cut the bass player's throat before the band had started playing.

Those were bad enough, but the worst was the simplest: The curtain rose, the band played, and he sang. He sang as he never had awake, as he knew he never could, and the crowd, enthralled and enraptured, sang with him. He woke from that dream with a sense of loss so deep that he wept.

That guy really got to me, he told himself for the tenth time. He had to stop thinking about the guy from the show, the one lurking in the wings in his dream. The guy had creeped him out, and he couldn't leave the memory alone, like picking a scab. *He called me Johnny.* Maybe John had announced himself onstage—he couldn't remember. The guy could have overheard someone talking to him. There were plenty of explanations for that. *But he knew about the money.*

Yeah, and there was no good explanation for that. There was nothing to be done about it, though, and John tried to push it out of his mind.

He finished coughing and went into the bathroom to rinse out his mouth. It was still dark out. He'd have plenty of time to clean up the floor, do a little writing, and take a shower. Definitely take a shower. It would be a cold shower, since he'd stopped paying the gas bill in order to free up the cash to take a voice lesson twice a month, but he was getting used to cold showers.

After that, there would be nothing to do but wait a few hours. The show was today, and Danny would be by early in the afternoon to pick him up.

Yeah, the show. No wonder I've been having these dreams. It's just stage fright.

He repeated it like a mantra while he scrubbed the floor. *Just stage fright.*

***

Case had been busy in the two weeks since agreeing to play the show with the band. She'd picked up a few extra shifts at Applebee's and split most of the rest of her time, as usual, between practicing and looking for another job. The Applebee's gig sucked worse than Steely Dan, and the sooner she could get out of that, the happier she'd be. At least the schedule was flexible—she had no problem trading a shift to free up the Saturday for the college trip. Weekend shifts were easy to get rid of, since there were more customers and better tips.

Probably not two hundred bucks' worth of tips, though.

Practice had gone as well as could be expected, given what they had to work with. Quentin had tightened up considerably, and she had worked out her parts to her satisfaction. Danny was solid as always, and John—well, there was nothing to be done about John. He was what he was. Still, she didn't think they were going to humiliate themselves, and that was a good first step.

Case turned in to the parking lot of the practice building at around two in the afternoon, bleary-eyed and squinting at the sun. She'd lost track of time the night before and ended up playing her guitar until the small hours of the morning—unplugged, so as not to aggravate her neighbors, with whom she already had a tenuous relationship—and she was barely awake. She had picked up an enormous coffee at the 7-Eleven on the way, and it was already half gone. She'd have to piss something fierce in an hour or so, but that was better than falling asleep on the road.

Danny's hatchback pulled in next to her as she was getting out of her car. John got out and stretched.

"Nice day, huh?"

She stared at him through half-lidded eyes. "You look like hell."

"Didn't sleep much," he said. "I see you're extra cheerful today."

"Let's load up."

They started moving the stuff, packing it into Danny's hatchback and into her little Toyota in any way they could get it to fit. Nobody had a van, so they'd agreed to take two vehicles, and she had insisted that she drive one of them. They seemed like good guys, but she hadn't known them long. She'd keep control of one of the cars, thank you very much. She had some doubts about whether her ten-year-old Corolla would make it the three hours to Wichita Falls, Texas, and back, but she'd take her chances.

Quentin showed up before long. He went inside to get his bass rig, and John stopped her from following.

"Just a sec," he said.

"Yeah?"

"I'm riding with you, if that's all right."

"Not with your brother?"

"Nah," John said. "Quentin—well, honestly, you stress Quentin out."

She shrugged. "Whatever. You ride wherever you want."

They finished loading, and she watched as John situated himself near her passenger-side door. Sure enough,

Quentin took in the situation and looked relieved as he headed toward Danny's car.

She finished her coffee in one long swallow, and then they were off.

***

Highway 287 was a boring road all the way west. John said he'd stay up to keep her company, but he didn't even make it ten miles. He slumped down in a position that made Case's back and neck hurt just to look at and started snoring shortly thereafter. She turned up the CD player.

The next time he was conscious was when they stopped to hit the restrooms. John grabbed lunch at a roadside stand, then picked at it, taking a few bites of his cheeseburger before wrapping it back up in the paper and throwing it out.

"Nerves," he explained sheepishly. Case shook her head.

John fell asleep a few miles later and didn't wake up until they were rolling into Wichita Falls, a little after five in the afternoon. He started jittering, tapping his foot, and folding his notebook right away, and Case figured his nerves were cranking up already. She hoped he wouldn't puke.

"There," he said. "That's the college."

"Midwestern State University," Case read off a sign. "Home of the Mustangs."

John leaned forward. "Cool."

Case nodded. She drove through campus, looking around at the buildings. Students walked between classes, but they didn't walk very far.

"This is a very small college," she said with some asperity.

"I told you it was, didn't I?"

She pulled over to the curb, stopped, and put the car in park. John pressed himself against the car door.

"John?" Her voice was pitched low and felt tight in her throat.

"Yes?"

"Look me in the eye and tell me that this college is going to pay us eight hundred dollars to play for a couple of hours."

He squirmed. Case saw a frantic look in his eye, and he looked out the window like he was half-thinking about making a run for it. "I never said that," he said.

She ground her teeth. "You told me, very clearly, at least twice, that I would personally take home two hundred dollars from this gig."

"That's true," he said.

"It better be. If you stiff me, I will pull your balls off."

John nodded hastily. "I won't stiff you, I swear. I never lied to you—I told you you'd get two hundred dollars, and you'll get it."

She faced forward and put the car in gear. Before she pulled away from the curb, something else occurred to her. She turned back to John. "How much is the total pay for the gig?"

"Six hundred," he said, too fast. She gave him a flat look. "Forty dollars," he mumbled.

"Forty dollars," she repeated.

"Yeah."

She closed her eyes. When she opened them again, John had a stupid, sickly grin on his face. "You dumb fuck," she said. "If—and I stress *if*—I stick with this band for any length of time, you are never allowed to handle band finances again. Got that?"

John nodded. "So, since now you know about the forty, do you suppose that maybe—"

"Don't even joke about that. Just shut up, John."

He shut up.

***

"This is a fucking cafeteria," Case said.

John glanced nervously at the two girls from the Student Activities Committee, who were in turn looking nervously at Case, as if she might go off or something. The four of them stood in the basement of the student union, in a little corner area full of ugly, varnished yellow tables and benches.

"It's not really a cafeteria," John said. "It has more of a, I don't know—coffeehouse vibe."

Case didn't bother to address that. She walked over to the tiny platform that constituted a stage and made a show of inspecting it. The drums would fit on it, just. She put her hands on her hips. "Where's the PA?"

One of the girls—John thought her name was Charlotte—pointed at a big green Rubbermaid box in the corner. Case walked over and pulled a snarl of cables out of it and looked inside. She dropped the mess on the floor and then picked up a speaker that was about the size of a toaster. The look on her face could have curdled milk.

John walked to the box, trailing the nervous committee girls. There was a second toaster-sized speaker in the box and a cheap combination mixer and power amp.

"I, uh, guess these are the monitors?" he said hopefully.

Case gave him another of her withering stares. She could communicate an awful lot with silence, John had noticed. Mostly disapproval. And anger. She was very good at anger.

John had a sinking feeling. "Those are the mains, aren't they?"

"What do you mean?" Charlotte asked.

"Yes," Case said, ignoring her. "Those are the main PA speakers."

"No monitors? At all?"

"You figure it out."

Danny and Quentin showed up then. Danny took in the place in one glance. His forehead wrinkled up and his mouth tightened in that way it did when he was trying not to laugh. He was being a good sport, but that only pissed John off.

Quentin looked like somebody had punched him.

"Well, let's get the gear in," Danny said. He chuckled. "I'll get the roadies started and make sure the tour manager has security on standby. Looks like it's gonna be a rowdy gig."

Case grinned, and it looked like there was actual humor in her smile instead of just spite. That made John feel even worse—this wasn't much of a gig, but it was still important, dammit! His guts were churning; he was worried about the equipment, about whether anybody would show up, and above all about his own performance. Was it too much to ask for them to take it seriously?

"I'll start unloading," he said, and he stalked out.

***

They put the little speakers up on chairs that were themselves on top of tables they'd dragged to the sides of the "stage." There were, in fact, no monitors, so they angled the speakers in toward the center to try to give John a fighting chance to hear himself. If he moved so much as half an inch forward, squalls of screeching feedback rent the air, but if he moved back a step, he couldn't hear himself at all.

Not that he could hear himself that well in any case. The speakers were small and not nearly loud enough to get over the drums. At first, John just turned the amp up louder, but the speakers started to distort, putting out an ugly, compressed sound that fuzzed out whenever he got loud. That wouldn't work, so he tried fiddling with the equalizer to find some way to get the vocals to stand out more in the mix.

After twenty or thirty minutes of this, Case pushed him out of the way and cranked the amp up until well past the point of ugly distortion. John grimaced. His voice sounded like it was coming out of a megaphone and going through a fuzzbox at the same time.

Case listened for a moment and then nodded. "That's not a bad sound for you."

"Thanks."

She shrugged. "It makes you sound mean. Can't understand a damn thing anyway, so you may as well sound like you've got some attitude."

He wasn't sure the speakers were going to survive the experience, but the sound definitely had attitude. It made the feedback problem even worse, though, until he found the one spot where the mic could stand without shrieking all the time. He resolved not to touch the mic stand the whole night. That would be awkward—he had no idea what he'd do with his arms, and he suspected he would look like a fucking tool, but those seemed like the least of all available evils.

It was a good thing they'd arrived early, because sound check took over two hours. They finished up less than twenty minutes before the show was supposed to start. A handful of curious students had already taken up some of the chairs toward the back.

Behind them, standing in the very back corner, stood an aging ex-rocker, hair hanging lank around his face, his eyes narrowed in a steady, measuring squint.

What the fuck is he *doing here?* John's nerves, already frayed from the gathering crowd and the stress of sound check, sizzled with unwanted extra voltage. His stomach heaved and twisted, and he excused himself. It was all he could do not to run to the bathroom, and as soon as he got around the corner, he *did* run. He made it to the toilet just before his meager lunch came up.

He washed his hands and rinsed out his mouth. His hands were shaking even worse than they usually did before a show. He stared at himself in the mirror for a minute or more, working up his courage, and then he went back out.

The guys—Case included—were waiting just to the side of the stage.

"All right," he said, trying not to look at the crowd, or past it to the man appraising them at the back of the room. "Let's go."

***

The performance turned out to be a good time, much to Danny's surprise. They made a few embarrassing fuckups at the beginning, but the crowd had a good attitude and didn't seem to care. About thirty bored college kids had showed up, probably because the entertainment options in Wichita Falls, Texas, were pretty thin, particularly for the under-twenty-one crowd. They weren't the most animated crowd he'd ever seen—mostly they just sat at the tables and nodded their heads—but they clapped at the right parts and didn't run off, so that was cool.

John didn't seem to know what to do with his hands, so he jammed them in his pockets and left them there the whole time. He looked like a flagpole or a stalk of corn, and Danny felt bad for him. He sang as badly as Danny had ever heard him, and between songs, he made awkward, garbled jokes into the mic and shuffled his feet a lot.

That was a shame, but it would be okay. It was obvious that the students had come out because they were bored, but that they stayed because of Case. She was smokin' tonight, playing like a woman possessed. Danny had been worried before the show—she had seemed more than a little put out at the venue, and really pissed at John, doubtless for one of the ten thousand reasons John usually pissed people off—but Danny had cracked a few jokes and gotten a smile out of her, and once the music started she loosened up a lot. She was a hell of a player, and it was hard not to watch her move once she got into it. Danny stared, just like everyone. At one point, she turned around in the middle of a song and happened to lock eyes with him. It felt like a spark—no, *lightning*—jumped from her to him. He flushed and almost lost the beat. She turned away in an eyeblink, and maybe it was wishful thinking or just his distractedness, but he thought that she fumbled the next chord.

During the last song, she got up on one of the tables and played her solo to raucous cheering. This was probably the loudest it had ever been in this room, Danny thought.

They got a hell of an ovation when they finally finished up, a little before ten, and the four of them stared at each other in bemusement and surprise. Danny gave Quentin and John a high-five each, and then held up a hand for Case.

"That's really lame," she said, but her eyes were bright and she was smiling.

"Come on."

She slapped his hand hard enough to sting his palm.

A lot of the students hung out while the band tore down, and while most of them wanted to talk to Case—she was not incredibly receptive to this, Danny noted, answering in monosyllables—a few of them were musicians who wanted to talk shop with Danny and Quentin. Danny chattered happily about snare drum heads and bass pedal tension, Neil Peart and Mike Portnoy and all the usual drummers-only topics, and before he knew it one of the kids invited him and the rest of the band to a party off-campus.

That was when he noticed that John was gone.

CHAPTER 4

"Fucking Christ," John spat as he kicked open the doors exiting the student union. The air had grown stifling and oppressive inside, and he wanted nothing more than to get out, to get as far away from this building as possible. He'd tolerated it as long as he could, but as the mob formed around Case and zit-faced college kids lined up to talk to Danny—and a couple of cute college girls stood giggling and talking up Quentin, for fuck's sake!—he'd stood, alone, just in front of the stage, waiting for any sort of acknowledgment. None had come. One kid gave him a sheepish nod and half a smile as he walked past, trying to get to Danny. When John had finally stalked off, nobody had even noticed.

"What a goddamn disaster."

Outside, a soft breeze blew over him, but instead of cooling him down, it made him unnaturally aware of his clammy, sweaty skin.

The scent reached him before he saw the man—cigarette smoke covering something nastier, more elemental. John turned, and though he knew what he would see, he still gave a start when he saw the old guy, the ex-rocker, leaning against the wall as he'd leaned against the bar two weeks before.

"What are you doing here?" John asked.

The guy exhaled a cloud of smoke that curled and writhed in the air. "Your band did good tonight, Johnny," he whispered.

Those few kind words blunted the edge of John's misery, and he started to relax. "Thanks. I appreciate that."

"Not you, Johnny. The band." The guy looked directly at John, his eyes gleaming black caverns in his skull, and the corners of his lips curled up. "You sucked."

"Hey, asshole, I—"

The guy flicked his cigarette to the sidewalk and walked toward John. "Yeah?"

John looked down. "I wasn't asking for your opinion," he muttered.

Cold, damp fingertips touched his chin and pushed his head up to meet the man's eyes. "It's not gonna get any better, you know. They're good. Your guitar player is *real* good. She's gonna get up on stage and shake her ass, and you're gonna be left outside, watching them clamor for her attention every time."

"That's . . . that's not really fair," John said. "She works hard."

"The band's got the magic, Johnny. Believe me, I know. They're gonna be the real deal. How long do you think it'll be before they figure out you're holding them back? Half a dozen more shows? Maybe a dozen, at most? You looking forward to starting over when they shitcan you?"

"They can't fire me," John protested, but he heard the whine in his own voice. "It's my band. Danny's my brother, for Christ's sake."

An awful sound clawed its way up from the man's throat, as if he were coughing up jagged metal hairballs. It took John a second to recognize it as laughter.

"Sure," the guy said. "Sure."

"What do you want from me?" John shouted. "I'm doing the best I can, dammit! Did you follow me all the way up here just to make me feel like shit? You've got that much time on your hands?"

"I'm telling you how it is, Johnny. And like I told you before, I can help you. If you've got the guts for it."

"How are you going to help me? You can't even fucking talk." That got another hideous laugh from the man, so John kept talking to drown it out. "And what do you know about me? How did you know my name? How did you know about the money? Who the hell are you, anyway?"

The guy put out a pale hand. "Call me Douglas. I've been looking for you for a long time, Johnny. You're going to do great things."

John reluctantly shook the man's hand, then pulled away, fighting the urge to wipe his hand on his pants. The wind picked up, and without the cigarette masking the smell of decay, John's stomach rolled over. "Yeah, I'm off to a hell of a start."

"Everybody was nobody once."

"Most of them stay that way."

"Come with me, and I promise you won't." The man's words hung heavy in the air, the whisper seeming to echo and scrape in John's ears. This seemed like such a crock of shit, and yet—

The door to the student union swung open behind him, letting the yammering of the small crowd out into the night. It seemed to violate the silence somehow, and John clenched his fists.

"Hey, there you are." It was Quentin. "We're going to a party, come on." Quentin's eyes glanced over at Douglas, then quickly back to John. "Come on," he repeated.

Douglas spoke before John could answer, his nasty whisper carrying on the night air. "You having a good time, Quentin? Meet some nice girls in there?"

"Come on, John."

A lurking green anger flared to life in John's heart. "Answer the man's question," he said. "You meet some nice girls in there?"

Quentin reached one hand back and rested it on the door handle. "Yeah, I guess so. You coming or what?"

"Nope. You have a good time." He turned to Douglas. *This is crazy!* part of him thought. *You don't know this guy from Adam!* But it was burned raw by the sudden release of anger. "All right. Let's go."

Douglas nodded and started walking. After a moment's hesitation, John followed.

Quentin rushed forward and grabbed his arm. "Are you nuts? Who the hell is this guy? What do you want with him?"

John shook Quentin's hand away. "Just business. Go have a good time. I'll call you later."

Ahead of him, Douglas was still walking, boots tapping a regular rhythm on the sidewalk. John rushed to catch up.

He could feel Quentin watching them until they turned the corner.

***

"Get in," Douglas said.

John stared, openly gawking at the sleek black car parked at the curb. He didn't know from cars, but this one was forty years old if it was a day, and yet it was so pristine it glistened in the moonlight. It had a hungry look to it, poised to leap though it wasn't even running yet. "This is your ride?"

"Yeah. Nineteen-seventy Charger. They don't make 'em like this anymore. Get in."

The car started with a throaty growl, and John barely got in before Douglas peeled away from the curb. The lights of Wichita Falls, Texas, faded in the rearview mirror, and in a surprisingly short period of time, they were in the middle of nowhere. No streetlights, no house lights, no lights of any kind other than the stars and a fat, pale moon. This country seemed somehow slippery in time. Away from the road and the power lines, it could have been yesterday, or a hundred years ago. Maybe two hundred. Perhaps the illusion would disappear in the daylight—there'd be a tractor in the fields, airplanes overhead, something—but right now he couldn't shake the feeling that he had invaded an earlier era. The few houses they passed with their electric porch lights seemed to shrink against the surrounding darkness.

John's cell phone rang, and he jumped. He took it from his pocket, looked at the small screen. Danny. John turned the phone off.

"Where are we going?" he asked at last.

Douglas's face was ghostly in the light from the dash. "You've heard of Robert Johnson?"

"Yeah. Blues guy."

"*The* blues guy. He inspired Muddy Waters and Eric Clapton, Jimi Hendrix—all those guys. You know the story they tell about him?"

"Sure. Everybody knows that one. He went down to the crossroads and sold his soul to the devil." John tried to laugh, but it died in his throat.

Douglas nodded. "He was nobody once, just like everybody else. Just a kid living on a plantation who wanted to play the blues more than anything else. He worked like hell, but it came slow." His mouth twitched in a smile that was gone a second later. "You know how it is.

"He heard stories, though. If you wanted something bad enough, you went down to a certain crossroads at night, and you waited. There was a price to pay, of course, but there's always a price to pay."

"Nobody gets out alive," John muttered.

"Yeah." Douglas pulled a pack of cigarettes from his pocket, separated one from the pack, and stuck it in his mouth. He offered the pack to John, but John waved him off. Douglas pushed the round knob of the car's cigarette lighter into the dash. *Wow,* John thought. *You don't see those anymore.*

Douglas continued, his hoarse voice sharp over the rumble of the engine. "So, one night, Robert put his guitar in the case and went for a long walk. Down to the crossroads. He waited around, and before too long he heard the sound of footsteps on the packed dirt behind him.

"He turned around, and there was a man there—a big man, in a black suit. The man didn't say anything. He simply held out his hand. Robert put the case on the ground and took out his guitar. He looked from the guitar to the big man's hand and back, and then he handed the guitar over.

"The man in the black suit tuned the guitar. He played just six notes, one for each string, and twisted the tuning pegs until each string seemed to sing all by itself. Then he handed the guitar back and walked off down the road."

The lighter popped out of the dash, and Douglas lit his cigarette. The tip glowed redly in the darkness.

"When Robert woke up the next morning, he was the best blues player the world had ever known."

"Cute," John said. "He didn't exactly live happily ever after, though."

"Nope. He died when he was twenty-seven."

"Like Kurt Cobain," John said.

"And Jimi Hendrix and Janis Joplin."

"And Jim Morrison."

The man grinned. John shuddered and stared out the window. A possum glared up at him from the side of the road, its eyes reflecting an eerie, baleful yellow-green, its thick, grotesque rat tail curling around behind it. *What the hell am I doing here?* he asked himself without much conviction. *This guy's nuts.*

The possum slipped off into the ditch. The car streaked by, and Johnny tried not to look into the darkness after the creature. He was suddenly convinced there would be other things out there looking back.

"So we're going to Mississippi," John said. The sarcasm tasted like dust in his mouth.

"No. There are other places where the world is thin. I think I know all of them by now." Douglas stared forward still, his eyes shrouded and blank. "But we are going to the crossroads. How's that grab you, Johnny?"

John turned back to the window. Douglas was nuts, he knew. But suppose John took him seriously. Suppose they were headed to the crossroads. How *did* that grab him?

The coffin was inevitable. Even at twenty-two, John knew that. You lived your allotted span and then they dumped you into a hole. And after that? He found it difficult to credit an eternity full of harps and angels and hosannahs. Nothing in the world he'd seen suggested that such was likely, while the alternative seemed evident in every headline, every atrocity, and every petty act of duplicity around him every day. John had never believed much in God, and he didn't see any reason to start now.

The devil, though? That guy had his hand in everything. Might as well take it when it was offered and get the most you could out of your threescore and ten.

Or even one score and seven?

Yeah. Even that.

"Just drive," John said.

***

It was nearing midnight when Douglas slowed the car and turned onto a poorly marked side road. A sick tension hummed to life in John's head, not exactly audible but just at the edge of sensation, like the shrieking noise he sometimes heard when somebody left an old television on.

Ahead, in the headlights, he could see a line perpendicular to the road, halfway up a low rise. A road.

Douglas slowed the car down as they approached. The road crossing theirs was another badly kept asphalt road. Aside from the drainage ditches to either side and the slight rise ahead, the ground was featureless. High grass, wet with dew, rippled in a slight breeze.

The tension in John's head ratcheted up a notch. This place felt really bad in a way he couldn't adequately describe, but it also felt . . . not quite right. Like two notes that were supposed to be in harmony, except one of them was out of tune.

Douglas turned the key in the ignition, and the car growled once before going to sleep. "Here we are."

"I . . . think this is the wrong place," John said slowly. "It doesn't feel right."

"Smart kid. But this is as far as I go." A spasm of something—pain? sorrow? regret?—crossed Douglas's face, and then it was gone. "What's up ahead is . . ." He exhaled heavily. "It's not for me. Not anymore."

John waited for an explanation, but Douglas stared ahead, silent and waiting.

There seemed to be no more delays to be had or excuses to make. It was time to go on ahead, or tell Douglas that, sorry, this had all been a waste of time, and can we please go back now?

John grabbed the door handle and pulled. The door swung open smoothly, and he got out. Stones ground into the pavement under his shoes. He took half a step, then turned around. "Hey, kill the lights, would you?"

The headlights went dark.

There was no noise here. Nothing. No crickets, night birds, or even wind. He couldn't bring himself to slam the car door in that oppressive silence, so he pushed the door until the dome light went off and left it like that, unlatched. Now that he was out of the car, he could see that the high grass here looked strange, wrong. It was too dark, almost black, and oddly twisted, with ragged edges along the blades. It seemed to conceal something horrible, and he moved to the center of the road.

He took another step, and that faint, awful dissonance ratcheted up in intensity, humming in his head, in his belly, in his chest. Two notes, sickeningly out of tune, pulsing and thrumming. It set up a resonance, an ache in his bones, and he thought if he stayed here for any length of time, it would slowly tear him apart. His heart would rupture; blood would blossom in his brain, seeping into his tissues even as his life drained away.

Don't do this! the rational part of him begged. Or was it the frightened part? He couldn't tell (*maybe because there's no difference right now*), but it didn't matter. The decision was made.

He started walking rapidly, almost running. He had to *go*, had to get where he was going before he lost his nerve. He had no doubts anymore, or at least none he dared contemplate, but he thought that if he slowed down for one second, if he flinched from the task he'd set himself, *fear* would set in, wrap its crooked, clutching fingers around his brain stem and squeeze. He'd slow down, stop, and turn around without ever consciously giving his body instructions or permission—fear would do that for him.

That kind of fear had been his secret reason, the reason he'd never told anybody, for dropping out of school. That, and Danny. He remembered Danny and all his rock star dreams from high school, the fire he'd had then. Danny had practiced like hell, night and day, until their father had finally told him he'd have to soundproof the garage or knock it off entirely. Danny had taken a break for three weeks while he figured out how to do the soundproofing, and then he'd done it—roping his little brother in for assistance, naturally, helping him hold up big sheets of heavy five-eighths-inch drywall and trying to nail it in place while keeping it from slipping. Once that job had been complete, Danny had gone right back to practicing like hell.

Then Danny had gone to college. There were bands, but there were also girls and schoolwork and a part-time job, and each time John talked to him, it seemed a little of the fire had gone out. Danny still played—still *loved* to play, maybe more than anything—but all those other considerations, all those other demands on his time added up. When he graduated, he found a job and moved to Dallas with Gina, and the drums had still been in storage when John visited four months later. He'd gotten them out eventually—"I still gotta play!" he'd told John one day— but he moved from one lackluster band to another without seeming to care whether they had any prospects or not. He needed to play, he said, and play he did, but there wasn't anything special to it.

When John had begun the slow crawl out of his introverted cocoon in college and started singing, Danny's lesson for him couldn't have been clearer. It would have been so easy to finish the degree, get a nice, safe, cushy day job that took care of bills (and luxuries, like hot water), and play music on the side, just like his big brother. But then, too, John had known that if he compromised even slightly, he would have flowed like water down the path of least resistance. With the rent paid and food on the table, would he have ever pushed himself to get onstage, to face down his stage fright night after night, or would he have simply gotten used to it? *It's okay,* he would have told himself. *I'll work on it later. No rush.* He had known the outcome of that, thanks to Danny, and so, before the fear could paralyze him and guide him back to the path of least resistance, he had swept away all other options.

His parents had screamed blue murder, of course, and even Danny had called to ask him what he was thinking. He'd tried to respond with calm assurance—"This is my calling. This is what I'm supposed to do"—and while he believed that was true, it wasn't the whole reason. Truth was, he didn't want to let the fear get its hooks in, let that time slip away as if it were of no real importance—that's what made the decision for him. And no matter how much his parents yelled and protested, once the decision was made, he took the next step and the next without daring to stop and reconsider or even talk about it.

His actions now were just a logical consequence of that first decision. *Well,* he thought, *sort of a logical consequence.* If he really stopped to think about it, his destination didn't seem all that logical at all. In fact, it seemed more likely that he was rushing toward a dream, a nightmare that had taken root more deeply than it should have instead of being flushed out by his subconscious in the usual house-cleaning process dreams were supposedly part of. It seemed *very* likely.

It didn't matter. The decision was made. Perhaps this was a waste of time—but perhaps it was not.

This isn't worth it! That thought nearly got him to stop, it seemed so out of place. What had all his sacrifices been for, if this wasn't worth it? What did his life mean? He thought of the shouting crowds of his dream. It would be madness to give that up, to walk away, to go back to a dysfunctional band where he would always be in danger of being abandoned, of being left to carve out his future by himself, talentless and afraid, of singing to empty rooms and trying like hell, breaking himself against nature and the inevitable, trying and failing and failing and *failing* to reach somebody, anybody.

His foot hit the ground, and the other one after it. As he walked, the dissonance coalesced into a terrible, gut-scraping sort of harmony. There was a slight rise ahead, and he pounded up it without slowing or looking back.

The strange tension got worse as he crested the rise, more dissonant and wrong, and yet . . . it *pulled*, too.

He reached the top of the rise, and he saw it.

"There," he said, and his breath went out of him in a rush.

***

The crossroads were ahead, marked by an old, dead tree, gnarled and crooked. It hung over the smudge of road, black on grey, a lone sentinel watching over this haunted place, shielding itself from harsh moonlight with outflung limbs. The tree looked ancient, and the bark had fallen away, leaving only smooth wood that gleamed like bone in the moonlight. Hadn't they executed criminals at crossroads? Or had they buried them there? He couldn't recall, but the stout branches of the tree stretching over the road looked plenty strong enough to support a hangman's noose. How long had that tree grown there? He didn't want to think about it.

The awful tension fell off as John got closer, but it resolved itself into an even greater sense of wrongness. It was, he thought, as though the notes were now tuned correctly, but they made the ugliest chord imaginable.

He walked on, and the strange chord screamed and wept, weird harmonies humming somewhere not above or below his normal hearing but just *outside* it somehow. He'd never experienced anything like it, and as he stood in the moonlight at the center of the crossroads, he understood that there was power here—strange and unearthly power, something that transcended normal human experience. Something that demanded not just respect but awe.

The wind gusted, and the branches in the old tree clattered together like a handful of teeth. John turned. He didn't like having his back to that tree. Anywhere else he looked, he could see as far as the moon would let him, but anything could be hiding behind that tree. He stared at it. It was only fifteen feet from the edge of the road opposite where he stood, but the thick crosshatched shadows thrown by the moon through the branches shrouded much of the tree in darkness. Was that a humped figure pressed up against the trunk, dark in the deep shadows, or was it simply a burl or a sawn-off branch that had long since healed over? It couldn't be a person. Surely he'd have seen them when he walked over. Surely, he thought, surely, but his heart pounded harder all the same.

"Hello?" he asked. His voice sounded small and flat out here, out in this open space with nothing to reflect it back at him. He took a hesitant step toward the tree, never taking his eyes from the hump. Another step, and the wind picked up again. "Is someone there?" He chided himself for asking such a stupid question—if someone *was* there, they'd already shown that they weren't going to answer. He suddenly found the presence of mind to wonder that if someone was there, and they weren't the type to answer, then what possible good could they be up to? Why the hell was he approaching? If someone was lurking there, he ought to be running back to the car as fast as his skinny legs could carry him.

Nonetheless, he took a few steps closer. Now he stood at the edge of the road near the tree. That was as far as he would go. He felt a strong reluctance not to step off the road. He was tempted to laugh at himself—this wasn't a fairy story, for God's sake!—but he couldn't find it funny at all.

"Hello?" he said again, stupidly. He didn't speak loudly, though, and he couldn't hear his voice over the pounding in his ears, the hammering of his heart.

The wind gusted again, harder. It pushed some of the branches aside, and for one split second, the moon shone on the sawn-off branch that came off the tree's main trunk, the branch that John had gotten all worked up over.

He let out all the air in his lungs in one rush and almost started laughing. Then he heard a sound, faint over his own pounding heart, and he froze.

A footstep.

That's your imagination, John. You worked it a little too hard in the last few minutes, and now it's fucking with you.

Another footstep from behind him, sand crunching on the asphalt. Closer this time.

Don't turn around, part of him begged. *Please don't turn around.*

John turned around. There was somebody standing there, not ten feet away. John tried to scream, but terror had frozen his throat. He stared, eyes bulging and mouth open.

"Nice night," the man said. His voice was deep and warm, good-humored and somehow calming. John's scream dissipated, turned into regular, if somewhat rapid, breathing. The man waited patiently. He stood with an easy slouch, his black shirt open to the third or fourth button. In his left hand, he carried a battered guitar case, and silver rings glittered on his fingers. Dark hair spilled from beneath a cowboy hat and curled across his cheek. The brim of the hat cast his eyes into deep shadow.

"Uh. Yeah. Beautiful." John's voice was hoarse, his mouth dry. He seemed to have recently swallowed a pound of ash. He coughed.

"You okay?" the man asked, grinning.

John nodded.

"Didn't mean to startle you," the man continued. "You looked like someone I used to know." Had John thought his voice pleasant? Maybe it was, on the surface, but something oily churned and slithered underneath it.

"I, ah, I get that a lot."

The man just grinned again. He was closer, now, close enough for John to see the neatly trimmed, pencil-thin line of beard edging his jaw, flowing into a tidy, short goatee. The man put down his guitar case. John's eyes darted to it, then flicked away.

"You play?" the man asked.

"No. Not really. Uh, no." That was the best John could do for an answer. Terror had split his brain into a dozen fragments, each handling a different problem badly. One fragment was gauging the distance to the car and screaming *RUNRUNRUNRUN!* over and over again. Another was warning him that his bladder was dangerously full and telling him it would be best to dump it *right now*. Still another was frantically supplying rational explanations for the apparition before him.

That last was easy to ignore. He knew what—*who*—was in front of him, whether he wanted to fully come to grips with it or not.

"Too bad," the man said, disappointed. "Music is good for the soul. I gotta admit, I'm surprised. You *look* like a player."

"I don't—I mean, I sing," John said.

The man's grin widened, showing teeth unnaturally white in the moonlight. "Ah. There you go. Best instrument of all, the voice." He took on a conspiratorial tone. "How's that working out for you?"

John didn't answer.

"I might be able to help you out." The man's teeth parted slightly, and his tongue glistened. "But I don't get the feeling you're all that serious. I look at you and I see a skinny kid, kind of goofy-looking, a little awkward. I bet you haven't gotten laid in a long time. Be honest with me, Johnny—this has nothing to do with music. It's really about pussy, isn't it?"

John flinched. "No. Uh, no sir."

The man showed his teeth again. "Oh, Johnny. I have seen your dreams, Johnny. You can't lie to me."

How had the man gotten so close? He was only an arm's length away, close enough that John could have reached out and touched the collar of his shirt, if he'd wanted to do something so utterly insane as that.

"No," John whispered.

"I have seen your dreams, Johnny. I've seen the women you dream about, flesh sweat-slick and soaking wet, writhing in ecstasy beneath you, legs wrapped around your body, nails gouging furrows into your skin."

John was sweating now. As the man spoke, John saw images in his mind's eye—his own fantasies paraded before him, furtive, frantic fantasies that lasted only a few minutes and left him feeling guilty and dirty and spent afterward. He saw a woman's body laid bare, impossibly perfect, his mouth pressed to her breast. He saw her straddling him, his hands grasping her narrow waist, her back arched and mouth open, every muscle quivering. He saw her on all fours, kneeling on a bed covered in red satin, cords standing out on her forearms as she clutched the sheets in her fists and screamed. He screamed too as he bucked and thrust behind her. In the darkness around the bed, vague figures shifted and laughed and watched, and he did not care. He saw her turn, push him onto his back, and take him in her mouth. The images were *too* clear, more detailed than any dream or recollection he'd ever had. He could see the fine hairs along the back of her neck, sweat droplets on the side of her face. He could almost feel her—no, he *could* feel her! He could feel her hand wrapped around him, feel the skin of her fingertips. She climbed on top of him again, and he could feel the touch of naked flesh along his body, pliant yet firm. He could smell her now, too, as he could taste the sweat on his upper lip.

Standing on a back road in Texas, John trembled, but not in fear. He was distantly aware that he was so hard it hurt.

"You can't lie to me," the man said again. "I have seen your dreams." He paused, and this time he did laugh. "Isn't this what you want?"

John opened his mouth, but nothing came out. His mind was blank. He felt flushed, tense, unfulfilled. He wanted to answer the man and couldn't even think of what answer to give.

"Well?"

The vision dimmed, and the faint pressure, the feeling of skin against John's body eased. *No, wait! Don't make it stop please don't stop oh God don't ever let it stop.* He felt like he would have given anything for just a few more minutes.

Anything? a nasty, seductive voice in the back of his head asked. *Really?*

"No," he said. Somehow. His voice came out as a dry squeak, and he thought saying that word might have been the most difficult thing he'd ever done. "No." Insanely, he added, "Thanks anyway."

The man took one deliberate step closer, and the image—vision—evaporated. John's shoulders slumped, and exhaustion swept through his body. Sweat stung his eyes, cold in the breeze. He tried to back away but managed only a little shuffle.

"What have we here?" the man asked. He laughed again. "Maybe I misjudged you. Maybe you're more serious than I thought." The man took a few steps around to John's side. The moon caught him at a different angle, and for a second John could see the flesh of his neck, maggot-white and pulsing. Then the man turned, and his skin seemed normal once more. The stink hit John then, that same decaying-fish smell that clung to Douglas, only a hundred times worse, choking and foul. *What, no brimstone?* John thought crazily, even as his knees started to shake and the pain in his bladder doubled.

"What is it you want, Johnny? What else do you dream about?" The man leaned closer, almost whispering. John looked forward, not daring to turn his head, not daring to look into the eyes below the brim of the hat. If he saw them, he would go crazy. He would die, right here, right in the crossroads, and his spirit wouldn't be able to find its way home. They'd find him with his eyes wide and staring, his hair white.

Johnny wondered if he would actually be able to talk, or if the words themselves were locked in his frozen throat. His tongue was leaden, shot full of novocaine, a block of wood.

The man waited.

Johnny opened his mouth, and incredibly, his voice *did* emerge, thin and creaking. "You . . . You know what I want."

The man stepped forward, and that foul scent swirled around Johnny, thicker than ever, worse than he could ever have imagined. His guts clenched.

"Immortality," the man said. "Of a sort. You wish to enthrall and captivate, to open the hearts of men—not to mention the legs of women—to enrich yourself and ensure your place in history with nothing . . . more . . . than the sound of your voice." The man had circled around him, taking a step on each word—*nothing, more, than*—and now he stood before John again. John stared at him, unable to look away, and yet unable to see the man as clearly as before. The air shimmered in front of him, and the man's image shifted and blurred. John saw nothing more than a man in a black shirt, decked out in silver rings—but he got an impression of something else, something with squirming maggot-white flesh and cold, implacable eyes.

This time, John's voice did desert him. *This is it,* the nagging voice whispered. Was it the voice of prudence or fear, rationality or cowardice? Was there a difference? Was there any way to tell? *This is your last chance. You can stop this right now. You can stop something terrible, something* unspeakable, *from happening.*

John looked at the man, stared into the blackness where the man's eyes should be, and he nodded.

"Say it," the man said, and traces of that grinding, metallic sound surfaced, sharp enough to draw blood. "Say *yes.*"

"Yes," John said, and his voice was the voice of an old, old man, weak and wheezing.

"And will you pay the price?"

As though from a great distance, John heard himself speak again. "Yes."

The man held out his hand and waited.

John's guts roiled. *Don't do this!* he thought, but he knew it was way too late for that.

"Take my hand," the man said.

John reached out. His hand passed through the weird shimmering area in front of the man, and the image wavered. John caught another glimpse of sickly pale, pulpy soft flesh before his eyes darted away. He tried to concentrate on the top of the man's hat, certain that he didn't want to see any more than he had already.

Shocking cold seized his hand as he pushed through some invisible barrier.

The man pushed toward him. In John's peripheral vision, the motion looked strange, like the man's elbow bent in the wrong place. John had a moment to wonder about that, and then he found the man's hand. It was cold, the touch of an earthworm or a corpse ripe with decay. The fish stink was gagging-thick, a horrid miasma that swirled around John's head until he was dizzy and sick with it.

Then the touch was gone.

John collapsed to his knees in the road, weeping and trembling, his limbs convulsing in wretched spasms.

When he finally had the strength to get up, the man was gone.

CHAPTER 5

It was late the next day when Case dropped John off in front of his house. It had been a bad day of travel. John had met Danny at the party sometime around three in the morning and tried to smooth things over. Danny had been a little pissed, but he'd get over it. Quentin gave him a dirty look and continued to drink. John had been too wired to sleep, so he walked most of the night, coming back to the party around dawn just in time to meet Case. She'd slept in her car after getting bored with the party, which meant she hadn't slept worth a damn either. The two of them tracked Danny and Quentin down and declared they were leaving.

Just past a speck of a town called Henrietta, Case's car had started to overheat. It had taken them forever to find a mechanic that would work on it on Sunday. Once they finally did, it turned out to be a simple matter of replacing the serpentine belt.

That little adventure had eaten up most of the day. The sun was going down as John got out of the car.

Case didn't even comment on the place. She watched him shoulder his backpack.

"Practice Tuesday?" she asked.

"Yeah," John said, pleasantly surprised. He'd been worried the whole way home that she was going to wash her hands of Ragman after the strange way the weekend went down. "See you then."

She nodded and drove off.

John let himself in. Though the sun hadn't quite set yet, it was dark inside already. The dank scent of mildew hit him, which meant it must have rained while he'd been gone. The corner of the living room flooded when it rained a lot, and it always stank for a few days afterward. There was a smell under it this time that wasn't normally there, though, something fishy and rotten. Dread coiled in his belly.

He turned on the light. The small living room and kitchen area were empty, as always. Nothing looked out of place, but that smell was definitely not typical. He left the living-room light on as he walked through the little house. He flipped on the bathroom light and a cockroach ran for cover. There was a tiny lizard, too, pink and translucent, in the bathtub. For a moment he entertained the idea that the lizard might be the source of the smell, but he reluctantly discarded it. Little lizards were forever getting in through cracks and gaps in the siding, and they never stank up the place like this. He ignored the lizard, left the bathroom light on, and took the three steps down the short hall into the bedroom.

The stink was worse here, and there was no kidding himself that it had come from something natural. There were no new discolored spots on the ceiling, no wet spots on the stained beige carpet. He walked over to the far wall, where the tendrils of plants had worked their way inside the house. A handful of them grew there, some creeping as much as a foot up the wall. He'd always felt reluctant to touch them, but he left them alone there nonetheless. It wouldn't have surprised him at all if there was a leak here, but the slab was high enough off the ground that it was above any pools outside. In any case, the carpet was dry.

A rustling sound caused him to jump, startled, before he recognized the sound of the high weeds out back scraping against the walls. He let out a nervous laugh.

John walked back through the house one more time. The back door in the combined living room and kitchen was locked and bolted. As far as he knew, that door was unopenable anyway—the structure had shifted over time, and the door was wedged tightly in the frame. The window next to it gave him the creeps, though. All the other windows in the house were shrouded with blinds, ugly but functional, and he rarely opened them. The small window above the sink had no blinds, no curtains. It was simply a blank eye looking out on the man-high weeds in back, the same miniature forest that scratched and scrabbled against his bedroom wall. Looking out on the back—or looking in on the living room.

John backed away from it, back into the hall. He felt stupid, but he had a sudden horror of looking out and seeing a face, maggot-white with unblinking eyes, looking back at him. He watched the window as he stepped backward, terrified that something would appear. The only thing that could be worse than that would be if he turned away . . . and something watched him from behind.

Nothing so much as glimmered in the window, and once it was gone behind the corner, he went back to the bedroom.

Still nothing here but that too-familiar stink. It swelled, as though riding a hidden air current, became thick and gagging. Then it was gone.

"Jesus," he said. He hoped that stench wouldn't follow him around, clinging to his skin the way it did to Douglas. What the hell was it, anyway?

Whatever. It was gone now, and hopefully it would stay that way. Now that he was *well* away from that awful place in the Texas countryside, he was anxious to try singing and find out if he got what he'd bargained for.

He started to power up his iPod, then hesitated. It would be too easy to let the sound in the headphones give him a place to hide. He should do this a cappella.

Maybe I should wait, anyway. I'm tired—I probably won't sound any good, just because of that. And I'm not warmed up. And I'm still a little hoarse from the show yesterday.

He shook his head. Excuses, all of them. He had to put it to the test eventually, didn't he? What was he afraid of? That his voice would be the same as always, and this whole adventure had been a waste or a delusion—or that it would really be different?

Fuck it. Here I go.

Wait! What should I sing?

The answer came to him as though it had been ready and waiting. "Rust," a song he'd written when he was getting ready to quit school. He'd never played it with the band, because it still felt way too personal, but it was exactly right for tonight.

He took in a deep breath, filling his lungs—and then, just before he started to sing, he felt something in the back of his mind push forward. The sensation was so weird, so alien, that he stuttered and almost stopped, but the air was leaving his lungs already, rushing out, waiting to be shaped into sound.

He opened his mouth and let the song come.

"Down along the ditches
On a road headed out of town
I'm walking with my collar up
My neck bent, my head down

They say if I leave the world will kill me
But if I stay, I'll go to rust"

It sounded like the same old John—almost. He thought the pitch sounded steadier, the sound maybe just slightly clearer, though the difference was so small it could have been his imagination. *Or maybe stark raving terror followed by a few hours of steady paranoia and exhaustion is good for the voice.* He tried the second verse.

"The warnings come fast
Like lights and screaming sirens
They say it isn't time yet
For me to walk among the violence

"Out there in the real world
Where the swinging hammer sings
Where 'You get what you pay for'
Doesn't mean a damn thing

"If I leave the world will kill me
But if I stay, I'll go to rust"

The lyrics gave him a sudden chill. *You get what you pay for doesn't mean a damn thing.* Christ. That was not the sort of thing he wanted to be thinking right now. Not one bit.

He wasn't *sure* if his voice was any better, but he thought so. Trying to dismiss the second verse, which had turned suddenly eerie on him after years of singing it, he sang the rest of the song through to the end.

"Before I file off the sharp edges
Before I hit the assembly line
Before I listen to another word
From a voice that isn't mine

"Down along the ditches
On a road headed out of town
I'm walking with my head held high
Face to the wind, and collar down

"If I leave now the world might kill me
But I won't stay here and go to rust
Go to rust
Go to rust"

Now he was sure. His voice *was* different. It was stronger, and there was something else in there, underneath, something powerful that coiled and stretched and waited for release. His singing voice wouldn't win any awards yet, but he thought that might be a whole different story if he could figure how to let that *something* loose.

John sang until late in the night.

CHAPTER 6

Case woke up already late for work. She'd had awful dreams all night, and it had taken until five or six in the morning for her to drift into a slumber that was actually restful. Either she'd forgotten to set the alarm, or she'd turned it off in her sleep and then forgotten about that, but in any case she was twenty minutes late for work when she picked her head up off the pillow and squinted at the clock.

She swore, got up, and checked the closet. It was empty. Of course. She had planned to do laundry this morning before work. She grabbed some clothes off the floor at random. It was only after she'd gotten her T-shirt on that she thought a shower might be a good idea. She froze in the act of putting on her jeans, thinking. Show up even later, or skip the shower?

"Fuck it," she said. She pulled her jeans on, finger-combed her hair, and took off.

I'll be glad if we ever make any money off the band, she thought as she drove to the restaurant. She'd heard of a couple of local acts that pulled in over a thousand dollars a night— that was a lot of hours she wouldn't have to wait tables.

That made her think about the show, and she sighed. They were a long way off from a thousand dollars a night.

Gonna have to change a few things, I think.

She was still thinking about what to do with the band when she arrived at the restaurant. She rushed inside and headed to the back to get her stupid apron and name tag.

"About time," her manager said as she walked past him. He had a tray in his hand and sweat on his face. "Good thing for you we're shorthanded today, or I'd send you right back home."

She nodded without slowing down and went back to suit up.

The lunch rush was in full swing. They gave her a couple of tables that had been waiting too long, pretty much guaranteeing she'd get lousy tips. *It's my own damn fault,* she reminded herself, but that didn't do much to put a smile on her face either.

The one good thing about the lunch rush was that she was too busy to be bored. Her manager hadn't been kidding—they were shorthanded today, since two other waitstaff hadn't shown up besides her. Busy was good, though. The final tally for lunch was two fucked-up orders, one spilled lemonade, and forty-six bucks in tips. Could have been worse.

By two, things had calmed down. Usually by the end of a busy shift she felt surly and hostile at the world, but this time she felt all right. She chalked that up to relief that she hadn't gotten fired, and that she'd made a little money despite showing up late.

At the end of the afternoon, she hung up her apron. A couple of the other servers were talking nearby. Case didn't pay them a lot of attention. She overheard something about a mugging, or at least a frightening encounter in a dark alley. One of the girls was complaining about the dangers of moving to the city, and Case allowed herself a little grin. *Welcome to the jungle,* she thought, and she turned to go.

"I was really scared," one of the women said. Case had worked a lot of shifts with her before, but couldn't remember her name. Work was a place you went, made your money, and got the hell out, not a social convention. She never seemed to have anything to say to these people anyway. Case brushed past her, and she didn't seem to notice. "I don't know, I'm thinking about taking karate or something."

Case stopped in midstride. "Oh no," she said. "Krav Maga."

The two women stared at her in surprise. The one who had been mugged—or threatened, or something; Case hadn't been paying attention—gave her a funny smile. "Huh? Was that English?"

Case was almost as surprised as they were. "Actually, no," she said. "It's Hebrew, I think."

"Hebrew for . . .?"

Case blinked. "I don't know." She felt awkward. This conversation hadn't been on the schedule, and mostly she just wanted to go home. "It's a martial art, a really nasty one developed in Israel. If you're serious about learning self-defense, start there."

"How come?"

"Karate's not all that practical. It'll keep you in shape, but it's not really about self-defense most of the time. It's become a tournament sport, and you're not going to square off in an alley and fight for points. Besides that, there's a lot of punching and kicking—it relies on strength quite a bit. You're what, five-two, one-ten?"

The woman looked confused for a moment, but she caught up. "Something like that," she said.

"Yeah. Even a little skinny man will have a big advantage on you in both reach and overall strength, particularly upper-body strength. If you go toe-to-toe with him in a straight fight, you *will* lose."

She felt like she'd just given a speech, but the woman looked curious rather than annoyed. "I knew it couldn't just be as easy as it looks in the movies."

"Not even close. A typical woman is not likely to win a fair fight with a man. So you learn Krav Maga."

"So it's Hebrew for 'knee him in the groin and run,' then?"

Case laughed. "Actually, that's part of the training. Krav Maga isn't a strength-based martial art. It's about knowing where and how to attack to do the most damage. It teaches you how to hurt somebody badly enough that they leave you the hell alone, and quickly enough that you don't get hurt too much in the process."

The other woman nodded, looking impressed. "I'm Erin," she said. "This is Danielle."

"Case."

"Where'd you learn all this?"

Case shrugged. "My old man. He wanted to make damn sure I could take care of myself, so he taught me a lot of stuff himself. I liked it, so I did a little martial arts for a while." She had done more than a little—she had trained for years, until she'd broken a finger in a tournament fight. That had brought both martial arts and guitar playing to a terrifying halt, and she'd spent weeks praying her finger would heal straight. After that episode, she'd done most of her training solo, just to keep in shape.

Case paused and looked from one of the women to the other. "I can show you a few things, if you want."

Erin smiled with genuine enthusiasm, and Danielle, though skeptical, nodded. "Let's go."

"What, now?"

"Sure. We're just about ready to leave."

Case checked her watch. She had a couple of hours before band practice, and she was in a lot less hurry to leave than she had been. "Yeah, okay."

***

Case had a surprisingly good time. The three women went to the parking lot in back of the restaurant, and she taught some of the basics—how to break a hold, how to escape a choke, and, yes, how to kick someone in the groin effectively ("Use your whole shin, not the tip of your toe"). Erin jumped right in, asked a lot of questions, and seemed to take it very seriously. Danielle was more reluctant. She gave the impression that she thought this was all faintly foolish, and she kept looking around as if she was afraid somebody would see her. At first, Case wanted to yell at her. *Don't you see, this stuff is important!* But she let it go. If Danielle wanted to be somebody's damsel in distress, that was her problem. If she was lucky, there would always be somebody there to rescue her.

Before long, Danielle was sitting on the sidelines, fanning herself with her hand. Erin was asking for more, demanding that Case show her a certain move over and over again.

Case eventually gave up, laughing. "You'll have to practice it by yourself for a while. Keep trying." She watched Erin go through the motions a few times. The shadows, she realized, were getting long. She checked her watch.

"Hey, I've gotta go," she said. "I'm gonna be late for practice."

"That's hardcore," Erin said, panting. "Out here with us for two hours, and then you're going to train somewhere else?"

"Band practice, actually."

"Oh. A woman of many talents. Cool." Erin wiped her forehead with the back of her hand. "You going to be around tomorrow?"

"Yeah. Double shift."

"Cool. See you then."

Case left smiling.

***

"Have fun," Gina said. She didn't look up from the legal brief she was poring over, just wrinkled her brow and stuck her pen back in her mouth.

Danny leaned over and kissed her, pen and all, and he was rewarded with her laughter. She put a hand on his chest and playfully pushed him away. "Go on, get outta here," she said, affecting a Brooklyn accent. "Ya botherin' me."

Danny laughed. "You bet," he said. "Need me to pick anything up on my way back?"

"Nope. I think we're all right."

"Okay. See you later."

His grin faded as he went out to the car. Gina was a first-year associate at a big local law firm, so she was always working. He had mixed feelings about that. On the one hand, she never complained about his practice schedule or his late-night shows. On the other, she never had time to do anything with him anymore. She'd never been the partying type and didn't really care for rock music or cigarette smoke, so it was no big deal that she never came out to his shows, but he wished she had time to do *something* with him. She'd had more time in law school, it seemed like.

Oh, well. There was nothing to be done for it. She was the woman he loved, and that was that. No couple was perfect.

He swung by and picked up John. He usually parked at the curb and went up to pound on the door, but tonight John was waiting out on the sidewalk for him. Danny pulled up, and John shouldered his backpack and got in. He looked good, and he wore a smirk Danny had learned to recognize over the years. *I know something you don't,* it said.

"What's up?" Danny asked.

"Nothing. Couldn't be better."

"Uh-huh," Danny said, but John didn't say another word, just looked out the window and tapped his foot with the music on the radio.

They got to the practice room early so Danny could set up, since he'd just dropped off the kit after getting back and gone home. The drums and hardware were still on the floor in the corner.

John paced while Danny set up, and it sounded like he was singing quietly to himself. He jumped when the door opened.

Case came in with Quentin just behind her. While everyone else went through their normal rituals of setting up, she just stood her guitar case up in front of her, crossed her arms, and watched. Danny whacked the floor tom a couple of times, decided it was tuned well enough, and looked at her.

She looked back at him, and he felt that familiar tingle in his gut. She always seemed to be evaluating him with that look, and try as he might, he kept wondering if he was coming up short. He didn't think so. Sometimes that look was positively hungry. He thought of Gina, and he was glad there were other people in the room.

"What's on your mind?" he said.

Case spoke slowly. "What did you all think of the show the other night?"

"It was all right," Quentin said.

"Jesus," John said, and the grin faded from his lips. He scuffed the floor with his shoe. Everyone waited for a moment, but that seemed to be all the contribution he wanted to make.

"I thought we did a good job," Danny said. "We were tight, and we played well. The crowd seemed to like it."

Case shook her head. "There isn't shit going on in Wichita Falls. I think that crowd would have turned out for somebody belching into a microphone in four-four time."

"Why don't you tell us what *you* thought of the show, then?" John asked.

"I'll tell you what I think—I think our material needs some fucking help."

Danny winced and looked to John. Sure enough, John had stood up a little straighter, cocked his head, and put his hands on his hips. He'd never been particularly receptive to criticism.

"What do you want, Case?" John asked. "If you don't like the songs, then what are you doing here?"

She raised her eyebrows and gave him a bland look. *You done?* it asked, as loudly as if she'd shouted. He broke eye contact.

"John," she began, and she took a deep breath. "Most of these tunes are four chords long, because you wrote them on an acoustic guitar, and you only know how to play a dozen chords total. We've worked them up quite a bit, but they're boring as fuck to play, and they're boring to listen to."

"Whoa, there!" Danny cut in before John could react. "I think what she means to say is that we've done all we can do with the songs as they are. They're good songs and all," he shot a warning look at Case, though he was virtually sure she wouldn't get it, "but we might want to try some other things."

John made a face. "Like what?"

"I've got a few ideas," Case said, "but you guys will have to help. Right now we're a hard rock band trying to play what is basically folk music, and it's like eating steak-flavored ice cream. Either one might work on its own, but together they're a disaster." She looked around the room. Danny caught her eye and nodded.

"Go on," he said. John glared at him.

"I've got some ideas for rearranging the existing tunes. The lyrics are good, and we can use them to start with. You're gonna have to be flexible though, and try some new things. Some of it's going to be a lot more difficult than anything we've played together so far, so we're going to have to bust our asses. Eventually, I'm going to bring some new stuff I've been working on, and you, John, are going to have to write the lyrics. It'll be a partnership."

"Not exactly like Lennon and McCartney," he said.

"More like Elton John and . . . what's his name."

"Bernie Taupin," John said angrily. "The guy who writes the lyrics is Bernie Taupin."

She shrugged. "Well, what do you say?"

The room was quiet. Danny could see John's face, fuming and hurt. There was no trace of his former good cheer. Case wasn't exactly Captain Diplomacy, and she hadn't pulled any punches. She probably *thought* she had, but that didn't change the effect. John had started the band, and he'd put his heart into it, and here she was telling him that it wasn't good enough, that he'd have to give up some of that ownership if he wanted it to succeed. It had to sting, and Danny felt bad for him.

Even so, Danny knew Case was right. He'd have more fun playing some more interesting music, and probably there would be more of an audience. He looked at the other three people in the room. John and Case were engaged in a staring contest, and Quentin was trying to make himself small enough to disappear.

John's never going to forget this, Danny thought. *Maybe he'll forgive me, but he won't forget.*

"I think we should give it a try," Danny said.

He didn't know if he expected an explosion or what, but he relaxed considerably when John nodded.

"Yeah," John said softly. "Let's try it."

"Oh thank God," Quentin said.

Everybody turned and looked at Quentin. There was a pause, Quentin flushed red, and then everyone in the room burst out laughing.

***

"All right," John said, a grin slowly emerging on his face. "I wanna warm up with 'Circular Firing Squad' first."

Quentin raised an eyebrow. That was a tough song, at the low end of John's range and with a few large-interval jumps that he struggled with. He usually bitched like crazy if anybody wanted to run through it early—said he needed four or five songs to warm up to it.

Case shrugged. "If that's what you want."

"Hell, yeah. Hit it." Half John's grin broke free, twisting his mouth into a smirk.

Quentin shrugged and nodded at Danny, then Case. *Ready.*

Case stomped her distortion pedal, unleashing the screaming squall of feedback that started the song.

Danny and Quentin came in together, tight and on cue. Quentin's fingers rambled up and down the fretboard, and the low rumbling from his amp shook his chest. This was the best—that feeling of being locked in to the rhythm with Danny, the thunderous thud of the kick drum and the way it meshed with the throbbing bass when they were really on. Quentin smiled, nodding his head with the beat.

John hit the first line right between the eyes. He nailed it, maybe for the first time ever, and it sounded so good even Case looked up at him with a grin. He sounded *good*. The whole band sounded good, and Quentin played harder, getting into the groove.

By the second verse, though, that good feeling had started to sour. Something wasn't right. John didn't sound this good. John *never* sounded this good. He wasn't performing flawlessly by any stretch of the imagination, but he was on pitch a lot more than usual, wasn't fading out on the low notes, and there was a presence, an edge in his voice that cut to the heart of the song like a straight razor. It sounded *like* John, but it didn't sound like *John*.

Quentin looked searchingly at John's face, and John grinned with a crazy glee as he went into the chorus.

> *"If it's nobody's fault*
> *Then it's everybody's fault*
> *If it's everybody's fault*
> *Then it's mine*
>
> *"But if I'm goin' down*
> *Everybody's goin' down*
> *Said I'm not goin' down alone this time*
> *I'm not goin' down alone this time*
> *I'm not goin' down alone."*

He ended the first chorus with a feral howl—a *perfect* feral howl, one that seemed like it belonged there in the song, had always belonged there, and they'd only been playing half the song until now.

Quentin eyed the door. He could run. *Wait, what? Why the hell would I do that?* He didn't know. All he knew was that something was badly off in this room.

He missed the next change and stopped playing entirely. Danny and Case each stumbled to a halt in their own time. Everyone looked at him.

John was the only one he could see, though.

"You sound different," Quentin said.

"I sound— Oh!" He chuckled. "My singing, you mean? I think the voice lessons are starting to finally pay off. A bunch of stuff just *clicked* over the last couple of days, you know? I'm flattered that you noticed!"

Quentin stared at him. What else could he say? He didn't have any reasonable explanation for why John's voice bothered him so much. It just felt . . . creepy. That explanation felt lame even inside the privacy of his own head. "Never mind," he said. "Can we just start the song over?"

***

After the warm-up, Quentin calmed down a little. He still didn't know what was wrong, but he wasn't going to let it get to him. Hell, maybe John really did finally "get it," like how sometimes you woke up in the morning suddenly understanding how to do quadratic equations or whatever. That explanation was about as satisfying as a hearty breakfast of air, but it was all he had.

They tackled Case's new arrangements next. It was rough at first, but Quentin saw the potential immediately. Case brought a sleaziness, a swagger to the music that had been missing. Quentin had never learned new music very quickly and he struggled to keep up, but he didn't feel too bad about it this time—even Danny was having a hard time remembering the new rhythms and parts to songs they'd been playing in a different configuration for months. They walked through the parts slowly at first, Case laying out the new arrangements, and then, as they learned, they strung them together until it almost sounded like music.

John wasn't holding anything back. The new arrangements had an attitude lacking in the old four-chord beaters, and once John got over his initial, automatic distaste for each new piece, he really tried his damnedest to get into it. For the most part, he succeeded, bringing a new ferocity to the music. At one point he let out a primal yell that seemed to come all the way up from his heels. Evidently, John hadn't expected that himself—the look on his face was so comical that Quentin had to look away to keep from laughing.

By the end of the night, three and a half hours of practice, they'd worked through three songs. The songs weren't ready for performance yet, but they'd sparked something, and all four musicians in the room looked at each other with satisfaction. They packed it in for the night with a feeling of new possibility.

"Be right back," John said. "I gotta get a drink."

Case hoisted her guitar case and was almost out the door when Quentin spoke.

"Hey," he said, looking from Case to Danny and back. "You guys think John's okay?"

"Huh?"

"I mean—he went off with that weird old guy the other night, and he's been acting funny. Do you think maybe—I don't know. He's on drugs or something?"

"I don't think so," Danny said, his voice hard.

Quentin felt heat rise to his face. "Yeah. You're probably right," he said. "Sorry to bring it up." He rushed out of the room, head down and bass in hand.

***

"That was strange," Danny said. He grabbed his sticks and went to catch up with John. Case stopped him on the way out the door with a hand on his shoulder.

He turned to her. His heart rate seemed to have doubled instantly.

"I don't know what Quentin's deal is," she said, "but he's on the right track. What *are* we going to do about John?"

His mind was sluggish, and the first answer that came to his mind was *he doesn't have to know*. What came out was "Huh?"

"You know. He gets fucking terrified every time he's onstage. The first time I heard him, I thought he sounded like an eight-year-old girl. He's getting better, he really is— in here. The other night onstage, though? He sounded like an eight-year-old girl."

Danny swallowed. She was so close that he could see green flecks in her brown eyes, so close that he could smell her sweat. It was sharp, biting, and yet somehow intensely enticing. He looked down at her hand, then back to her face.

She took her hand away and let it relax by her side, but she didn't look away.

"Yeah," he said, his voice husky. "It's a problem. I'll . . . I'll think about it."

He practically ran to catch up with John.

CHAPTER 7

"Ow, shit!" Case yelled and dropped the short stick she'd been holding.

Erin looked at her with concern. "I'm sorry! Are you okay?"

Case grinned. "Yeah, fine. Just surprised. I didn't expect you to hit me that hard." They had been practicing knife disarms, and Erin had chopped down on Case's wrist *hard*.

"Sorry."

"Don't be sorry. If you're going to do it, do it like you mean it. Just don't forget that control is important, too." She shook her hand. "Hope I can still play tonight," she said, smirking.

Erin's eyes widened. "Oh God. I'm really sorry."

"I'm kidding. It's okay. Really." Erin didn't look convinced. "We probably ought to get some arm guards or something, if we're going to keep this up. Let's take five and get a drink," Case said. She went over to the shade near the side of the building, sat on the asphalt, and opened the bottle of water she'd left there earlier. Erin sat next to her.

Training had been going well, Case thought. It had only been a few weeks since they started, but Erin was an avid student, and she had clearly been practicing outside of their informal classes. Danielle had gotten bored after the second or third session and stopped. Case had thought Erin would lose her enthusiasm shortly thereafter, but it hadn't happened yet. Erin was tough and had a great attitude, and Case had found her surprisingly easy to get along with.

"You're learning fast," Case said.

"Thanks. I've got a good teacher."

There didn't seem to be anything to say to that. Case drank some water and handed the bottle to Erin, who accepted it gratefully.

"Band practice tonight?" Erin asked.

"Show tonight, actually."

"What kind of music do you play, anyway? No—wait. Let me guess. Death metal." Erin made horns with her left hand, stuck out her tongue, and did a little mock head-banging.

Case made a face. "No way." She took the bottle back. "I hate metal. We play hard rock."

"Like Nickelback?"

Case gave her a look designed to wither flowers and kill cockroaches.

"Not like Nickelback," Erin said.

"No. More like the New York Dolls or Motörhead."

Erin tightened her lips and shook her head. "Sorry. Not ringing any bells."

"How about Led Zeppelin? Guns N' Roses?"

By way of response, Erin opened her mouth and belted out a couple of lines from "November Rain." It was horrifying. She was even worse than John on one of his bad days. Or maybe it was just that she didn't have a bunch of loud instruments drowning her out.

"You hate me," Case said. "That's the only possible explanation."

"Sorry, Sensei," Erin said solemnly. Case growled, but Erin ignored her. "I am a humble student, seeking only knowledge. You hate metal, but you play hard rock. I didn't know there was a difference."

"It's all in the attitude," Case said. "I want to play music that says 'Fuck You' to the world."

"'November Rain'?"

Case glared at her. "There are other— You know what? Forget I said Guns N' Roses, okay?"

"Done. But heavy metal isn't fuck-you enough for you?"

"Metal isn't fuck-you at all. The whole metal scene is a club for crybabies who want to all wear the same black T-shirt and feel like they fit in somewhere. Metal is where misfits and fuckups go to feel safe. If you only want to be exposed to your own kind, you play metal, and you never have to run the risk of pissing somebody off."

Erin rolled her eyes. "Do you have to overthink everything?"

"I wouldn't have said I overthink anything. Somebody once told me I ought to have 'Poor Impulse Control' tattooed on my forehead."

"Somebody didn't know you very well," Erin said.

Case looked away. "Yeah."

The silence stretched, but Erin spoke up before it got awkward. She was good at that. "So what's the name of your band?"

"Ragman."

"Cool. Tell me when and where you're playing, and I'll drag out all my friends so they can find out what real fuck-you music sounds like."

For once, Case didn't have a smartass remark handy. She felt absurdly touched at Erin's offer. "Hey," she said. "Thanks."

"Don't thank me yet, because I'm about to kick your ass," Erin said, and she got up. "You ready for another round?"

"Are *you* ready for another round?"

Erin bared her teeth. "Bring it, bitch."

"Bitch?"

"You heard me."

Case laughed, drank the rest of the water in one swallow, and stood. "All right. Let's go."

CHAPTER 8

John leaned over the table and whispered to Danny. "Dude, we have an audience."

"I know," Danny said. "What's up with that?"

John didn't have any idea what was up with that, and he wasn't sure which surprised him more—that Case was over talking to a group of half a dozen girls that had just come in, or that a couple of Quentin's buddies had shown up. Quentin didn't have buddies. The idea of Quentin slamming back a beer and yelling at the Cowboys on TV with a bunch of guys seemed incomprehensible. Nonetheless, there they were.

And Case . . . that was more than incomprehensible.

"When did Case get friends?" John asked.

Danny laughed. "She's probably had them all along. She's not the Antichrist or anything."

"Bullshit. Case with friends . . . that's an inversion of the natural order of the universe, as far as I can tell."

"They don't even seem to have fangs or anything," Danny observed.

"No, they don't." In fact, they looked alarmingly normal, like any group of young women dressed for an exciting Wednesday night out on the town. "That doesn't freak you out?" John asked.

"Can't say that it does."

"And what do you mean, 'she's probably had them all along,' huh? Like she's been waiting until we're *worthy* or something?"

Danny gave him a patronizing older-brother look. "You have to admit we've come a long way since she started. Can you blame her for waiting?"

"Hmph." John drummed his fingers on the table. He supposed he ought to simply be grateful to have an audience for once—an audience that was actually there to hear them—but now he was even more anxious. He bounced his leg.

"Don't think about it," Danny said. That was the problem with brothers—they knew you too well.

"Can't help it."

Danny nodded knowingly. "I got an idea about that."

Case walked up before he could elaborate. She was smiling, and John thought she might have been happier than he'd ever seen her, at least when she wasn't playing. "Look at that," she said. "We have fans."

"Don't remind me," John said. He swallowed. "No pressure or anything."

She didn't bother to hide her disdain. "You gotta get over this, John. Even playing to a handful of people is better than playing to an empty room, and they're not going to come back if we suck. So man up."

"Thanks. Thanks a lot. That's a hell of a pep talk, Case. They ought to use you to talk suicides down off buildings. 'Would you just fucking jump already? You're holding up traffic, asshole.'"

Anger flared in her eyes, but before she could say anything, Danny held up his hands.

"Look, I was just thinking about this," he said. "I've got an idea. It might help, or it might be completely retarded, but hear me out, okay?"

John hesitated. Usually when Danny said an idea might be completely retarded, it turned out to be, well, completely retarded. John still had a scar from one of Danny's suggestions involving a very small bicycle and a very high hill when they were kids. There had been a spectacular crash, of course, a trip to the emergency room, and nine stitches.

Still, it had been a hell of a ride.

"All right. Let's hear it."

Danny grinned, and Case pulled out a chair and sat down.

"We need to make up an alternate persona for you."

"What the hell are you talking about? Like Bruce Wayne or something?"

"Something like that," Danny said. He continued before John could protest. "Think about it. You get onstage and you're worried about all kinds of things. Are you going to sing well? Do you look like a jackass? Are you going to say something to embarrass yourself? Is this socially acceptable?"

"I wouldn't say I'm worried about what's socially acceptable," John said.

"I think you are. The front man of a rock band has to behave in a way that would be downright strange if he acted that way normally, and I don't think you ever forget that you're the same guy once you get offstage."

"That's because I am."

"I don't think that's the way everybody sees it. Even if they do, it doesn't matter. You're practically expected to be eccentric and over-the-top onstage. Reckless, even."

John frowned. "And how is adopting a stage name going to help?"

"Stage *persona*. You pretend to be somebody else when you're up there. Somebody who doesn't give a fuck. The persona gets all the attention and the social disapproval, and you can walk away scot-free after the show."

"Sounds like bullshit to me," John said. "When did you get a psych degree?"

"It's not bullshit. Marilyn Manson used to piss off people by the thousands, but do you think anyone gives a shit what Brian Warner thinks?"

"Who the fuck is Brian Warner?"

"Marilyn Manson, when he's tucked into bed at night and the makeup has all been washed off."

"I'm not giving myself a blowjob on stage," John said.

Case gave him a c'mon-let's-be-realistic look. "I think that was an urban legend. If the man could suck his own dick, he'd never have left the house."

John changed tactics. This whole conversation was making him uncomfortable. "It all sounds so hokey," he said.

Case narrowed her eyes. "I don't know. I think there might be something to it."

"What, you too?"

"I read an interview with Buckethead once where he said the mask and all that crap—the whole persona—helps him loosen up onstage. It's just like Danny said. He can do whatever he wants, because the character takes the heat. I think he said that the irony was that, because of the character, he could act more like himself than he could if he was just, you know, being himself."

"Who the fuck is Buckethead?"

"A guitarist," Case said.

"Who plays with a bucket on his head," Danny offered helpfully.

"And a mask."

John considered this. He felt cornered, and that wasn't fair, but the idea had its own seductive charm. For twenty-five minutes, the whole short set, he could step out of his own life and pretend to be somebody who wasn't fucked up and overtired and insecure. He looked at the group of girls chattering over by the bar, and acid squirted into his stomach.

"Yeah, okay. What the hell?" he said. "How do I start?"

Danny blinked. "Huh. I didn't think you'd bite, so I haven't really gotten that far." Typical. Like most of his stupid ideas, he hadn't thought it through to the end.

"I'll be right back," Case said, getting up.

"Wait, where are you going? We're on in twenty minutes!"

She didn't bother to answer. John watched, nonplussed, as she went right past the guy working the door and left the club.

"What the hell was that all about?" he asked Danny, bewildered.

"I don't have any idea."

They tossed around a couple of ideas, but the ideas were all pretty lame, John thought. Makeup and masks were right out. "This is not fucking KISS," he told Danny. "And if you're gonna make me do all that shit, you have to do it too." Danny backed off after that, but he didn't have much else to offer. The conversation petered out, leaving both of them staring at the table.

Case got back after a few minutes and threw a heavy bundle in John's lap.

"It's big on me," Case said, "and you're skinny, so I think it'll fit."

John unfolded and held up a black leather motorcycle jacket. It was old and beat-up, covered in buckles and zippers, but he had to admit it exuded cool all by itself.

"I'm going to feel like such a poser in this thing," he said.

"Fake it till you make it," Case shot back.

He started to put the jacket on, and Case put a hand on his arm. "Wait," she said. "John Tsiboukas is not badass enough to wear that jacket. Tonight you're . . ." She bit her lip, thinking.

"Johnny," Danny suggested.

John twitched like he'd been burned. *I have seen your dreams, Johnny.* "I don't think—"

"It's perfect," Case said. "Can you think of a more rock-and-roll name than Johnny? Johnny Ramone, Johnny Rotten. Johnny Winter. Johnny Thunders. And all those songs from the fifties and sixties. It's classic. Yeah, that's it."

John thought of Douglas, and the—the man at the crossroads, and he shivered. Still, Case had a point. It was evocative, and he couldn't see a crowd of people chanting *John, John, John,* unless they had to get in line for the toilet.

"Maybe," he said.

"Yeah," Case said. "Johnny . . . Johnny Tango."

That didn't impress him at all. "Tango?"

"Yeah. Military alphabet for T."

"Sounds kind of, well, pussy."

She grinned, sharklike. "Nobody'd tell Johnny Tango that to his face."

Before he could argue, an image formed in his mind. Johnny Tango. He wore a motorcycle jacket, greased his hair back, and kept a switchblade in his boot. He said *motherfucker* a lot. He called his friends *motherfucker* in an amiable sort of way, he called the guys he fought with at the bar *motherfucker* right before he worked them over, and he used it as an all-purpose expression of rage and frustration. *Ow! Motherfucker!* was the kind of thing he said when he pinched his fingers while working on his car. He liked cars. He drove an old car, one of those giant tail-finned boats from the fifties, white and cherry red, and turned a wrench at a local garage to keep himself in cigarettes and beer. It was a caricature, sure, but for pure rock-star attitude it sure beat the hell out of a nervous part-time Starbucks barista whose house smelled like fish.

John put the jacket on. It fit perfectly. Danny gave him a nod.

The sound guy came over. "You guys are on."

John looked up at him, then back to Case and Danny. He tried on a nasty grin. "All right, motherfuckers. Johnny Tango it is."

***

John was already sweating by the time they took the stage. It was July, and he was wearing a heavy leather jacket. His momentary bravado was fading even as he went up the stairs on the side of the stage.

I feel like a moron. I look like a moron. Case is right—John Tsiboukas is not badass enough to wear this jacket.

No, he wasn't. He ought to take the damn thing off right now. It was making him even more self-conscious, and Christ knew he didn't need any help with that.

John stopped on the stairs, hidden from most of the crowd by the giant speaker stack. Case, Quentin, and Danny were already at their instruments.

His palms were slick with sweat, and he felt like he was going to die in that heavy jacket. He tried to shake it off;

this would not be a good time for Johnny—the *real* Johnny, Johnny the alter ego, Johnny the attitude—to take a night off.

Fuck that noise, he thought, mustering a sneer that felt completely false. *Johnny never takes a night off.* The bravado rang hollow, and his throat felt tight.

He peered around the speaker stack. There were so many people! Even with the lights glaring in his eyes, he could see the shapes and silhouettes of the crowd, reflections in eyes and off glasses and bottles.

What if I can't sing? What if it's gone now? Terror gripped him, and it seemed like his throat must have sealed itself up.

Either Case jumped the gun because she, too, had a case of nerves, or she was simply being hateful. She laid into the opening riff of "Burn" without even checking to see if anyone else was ready. It was hot, fast, and greasy—a hell of an opener, if they didn't fuck it up. Quentin and Danny were more ready than John had given them credit for—or maybe Case *had* checked, and he'd just missed it—but they came in right where they were supposed to.

It was a solid start, and John's terror cranked itself up. *Don't fuck this up, don't fuck this up, don't fuck this up.*

He almost missed his cue. The opening figure was nearly wrapped up, and there he was, standing like an idiot on the side of the stage. He forgot all about ditching the jacket, crossed the stage in a few quick strides, and made it to the mic just in time to hit the first line. *What if I can't sing?*

He was out of time. He opened his mouth and sang.

> *"Light it up!*
> *Light it up, baby*
> *Let the fireworks fly*
> *They say we all gotta die*
> *But I'm goin' up like a rocket tonight"*

To his horror, the words came out flaccid and half strangled. He knew they weren't his best lyrics, not by a long shot, but they were all he'd been able to fit to the rolling, tumbling, sleazy riff Case had brought to the group, and if they weren't going to stand up on their own, he'd have to sell them.

And he wasn't selling them. There was a spotlight in his face, so he couldn't see the crowd, but he didn't need to. He could imagine the look of mild boredom on the faces of Quentin's buddies and the group of girls who had come to see Case, to say nothing of the other bands and the people who had come to see them.

Fuck that, he thought. *Johnny Tango doesn't give a damn what those people think. He* means *this shit.*

Now he felt the push, that weird sense of something pushing forward in his mind that he'd gotten so used to over the last few weeks. Had it been there at the beginning of the song, and he'd been too tense to pay it any attention? He didn't know, but it was followed, as always, by that questioning feeling—only this time, the feeling came as an actual voice, quiet but sure, a ragged whisper in his head, as clear as if it had been piped through headphones despite the volume of the band.

Now? it asked.

He flinched, startled, but then relief flooded him. He hadn't been abandoned or cheated. He could do this.

Yeah.

John grabbed the mic with both hands. The black jacket seemed to suck up the light, suck up some energy in the room and transfer it to him. He belted out the second verse with something that could almost be mistaken for confidence, his voice steadier and stronger than ever, and he even gave it a little swagger at the end.

> *"They're watching me*
> *They're watching me, baby*
> *Waitin' for the flash*
> *Waitin' for me to crash*
> *But I'm burnin' up before I hit the ground"*

He looked to his right. Case was doing her best Slash impression, her legs in a wide stance while she held the guitar almost vertical. Her fingers flew over the fretboard. She spared him a grin, though, and an almost imperceptible nod.

He flashed a sneering half-smile back at her and hit the chorus:

> *"Get it hot enough, and everything burns*
> *And baby I'm ready*
> *Ready to burn every*
> *Everything down tonight"*

He was feeling it, now. He threw himself into the last line of the chorus, tearing the words from his throat so violently that his voice cracked and broke on the word *tonight*.

For once, he didn't care. The attitude was right, and Johnny Tango was all about attitude. So it wasn't pretty— big fucking deal. Johnny Tango didn't give a damn about pretty, unless you were talking about chicks or cars, and, truth be told, it was optional as far as chicks were concerned.

There was a space in the music after the first chorus, a spot where the guitar dropped out for a few bars before roaring back in for the next verse. Sweat poured off John's face as he stepped up to the mic during the lull, and, without even knowing he was going to do it before the words came out of his mouth, he shouted at the crowd.

"Is it hot enough for you, motherfuckers?"

And by God, a few people in the bar yelled back at him. Quentin was so surprised, either by John or by the crowd response, that he flubbed the transition back to the verse. He recovered quickly, though, and they rolled into the third verse without a major disaster.

John could hear part of his mind yammering at him from the back. *John, what are you doing? You're acting* crazy! *What are they going to think? They're going to know you're a fraud.*

He hesitated for just a fraction of a second before blowing it off. *John ain't home,* he thought, *and Johnny don't give a fuck.*

They plowed through the rest of the song, finishing it to real, enthusiastic applause and a couple of shouted "Yeah"s. John looked over his shoulder at Danny, who was smiling like a fool. Danny cocked a finger at him, and the meaning couldn't be clearer—*Nice job, bro.* John couldn't help smiling a little in response.

They burned through the rest of the set. They hit "Rust," "Twenty-First Century Blues," "Walkin'," and "Changing Gears" in succession, and they pretty much nailed all of 'em, John thought. Danny and Quentin were as tight as they'd ever been. Case went off to wherever it was she went when she performed, and she must have found something pretty goddamn good there, because her extended solo in "Walkin'" was so smoking hot it even got John's attention, and he'd seen her play it two or three times a week for months. He remembered to call her out at the end of the song—"Give it up for Case on lead guitar!"—and she flashed him a grateful smile while her little cheering section went crazy.

For his part, John never quite hit the intensity in the rest of the set that he had during the last half of "Burn," partly because he couldn't keep his nagging conscience silent. The other thing, the voice, strained and flexed, but the part of him that got awkward in public and was perpetually afraid of embarrassment held it back, always telling him to back off a little, don't get too close to the edge—there was no telling what you'd see down there, and what if you slipped? He couldn't keep it silent, but he kept it quiet, and that was a good start.

He knew it wasn't perfect, not by a long shot, but he felt proud of his performance for maybe the first time since he'd gotten up, shaking and terrified, on an open-mic stage.

Not a bad night's work, he thought as the last note rang out.

***

They cleared their stuff off the stage in the customary frantic rush while the next band set up, stashing the gear in the side room. Case slapped Quentin on the back as they walked out of the storage room together. "Good show," she said. His eyes widened, startled, but he managed a smile.

"Yeah," he said. "Yeah, it was." He scurried off toward the table his friends were sitting at, and Case made for the bar.

"Case!" Erin screamed.

She's louder than my fucking amplifier, Case thought with amazement. "Erin!" she yelled back, much less loudly.

"You're awesome!" Erin rushed forward, arms outstretched for a hug.

"Whoa, there!" Case held up two hands in self-defense. "I'm all sweaty, and I stink like a pig. Trust me, you don't want any of this right now."

Erin stood there for a moment, at a loss for how to proceed. "You're awesome!" she shouted again after a few seconds.

Case laughed and slid around her to the bar. She ordered a Jack and Coke and turned around to find herself surrounded by a semicircle of women—Erin's friends.

"When are you going to teach me to play guitar?" Erin asked, way more loudly than necessary. She wasn't wasted yet, but it sure looked like she'd had more than one, and they were working already.

"Right after I show you how to break a man's arm using only two fingers."

"You can do that?"

"*I* can do that. I don't know about you yet." There was general laughter. That helped Case to feel at ease, but she still felt a little boxed-in and awkward. She had just met these women, except for Erin, and she didn't know what to say to any of them.

That turned out not to be much of a problem. They asked her some questions about music that were easy to answer, and Erin—talkative, excitable Erin, God bless her—smoothed over everything else, dragging the conversation all over hell and gone without so much as a backward glance.

Case had started to feel pleasantly extraneous to all this noise when she happened to catch a glimpse of John and Danny. The two brothers were sitting back at the same table they'd started the night at. Danny was talking to somebody—a fellow drummer, Case guessed from the Zildjian shirt—but John sat apart, disengaged and quiet. He'd been watching her and the people with her, Case thought. He looked quickly away, but she saw the resentment on his face.

Well fuck him, she thought, angry at first. But she looked back at him, and this time she saw the pain under the resentment. The anger died away as fast as it had flared up, and she thought she understood now. He'd really outdone himself tonight, gave a performance that she hadn't thought was in him, and probably neither had he. And it looked like nobody had even noticed. *That sucks. He deserves better than that.*

"Hey Erin," she said, inadvertently cutting the other woman off in midsentence.

"What's up?" Erin asked. She didn't seem to notice the interruption—just hopped right off one sentence and onto the next, like they were all trains that would get her where she was going.

"You should meet John . . . ny. Uh, Johnny." What was the protocol for stage names? she wondered. Did he go back to being John right after getting off the stage, or was he supposed to wait until he left the building? She had no idea, but he was Johnny now, and she guessed he'd stay that way for the rest of the night. "The singer," she added for clarification.

"Cool," Erin said.

Case led the group over and made introductions. She didn't remember most of the names, but once Erin was introduced, she did the rest. Erin had a talent, Case realized, one that she herself lacked and didn't understand—she drew John and Danny and the other guy into the conversation effortlessly, and before long the whole group was talking as if they'd known each other for years. The next band started playing, but the group just talked louder.

Case sat back, watching and listening with a low anxiety building in her stomach. The conversation was all right, but the room was too loud, and something nagged at her, a feeling like low voices in the next room talking about her or . . . or somebody watching her.

"What is it?" Danny asked her, the fourth time she looked over her shoulder. "Expecting someone?"

"No," she said. This was ridiculous. Rather than take surreptitious glances behind her all night, she turned around and studied the crowd directly.

She saw him immediately. He sat at a table alone, and even though there were a fair number of people in the club, he had space on all sides. A young man, unshaven, with short, spiked hair and a black silk shirt. He could have been any twentysomething out for the night . . .

Except for his face. His head lolled forward and his mouth hung open. A thin shining cable of drool connected him to the table.

And he was staring at her. If you didn't look closely, he seemed like he was wasted, ready to pass out and hit the floor any minute now, but his eyes were fixed on her, crafty, clear, and unwavering.

When her eyes met his, the slack came out of his face and a slow grin stretched his mouth. A *hungry* grin. She could see his teeth gleam from across the bar. The tip of his tongue, pink and wormlike, slid across them.

"What the fuck?" Danny asked. He was leaning around her, looking at the guy.

Case moved.

"Hey, wait!" Danny said, and he put his hand on her shoulder. She found that she didn't mind, but he'd better not try to stop her. "What are you doing?"

"I'm going to go talk to that creep."

"I'll do it."

She didn't even respond to that statement, just started walking.

Case got to the table with Danny right behind her. The two of them loomed over the creep, who twisted his head sideways and looked up at Case with narrow eyes, crinkled at the corners like he was laughing about something.

"You got a problem?" she asked. That much seemed self-evident now that she was close up. Was he fucked up on something? PCP, maybe?

He leered at her, pulling the corners of his mouth wider than seemed natural.

"You've got three seconds to wipe that smile off your face before I do it for you. And maybe do a little impromptu dental work while I'm at it." She thought she sounded tough, but something told her to get away from this guy. He wasn't just creepy. He wasn't . . . right. At all. He should never have been let out of the house by himself. Or the institution.

"Ready to burn, ready to burn, ready to burn," he crooned in a cracked voice. Goose bumps ran all the way up Case's arms, over her shoulders, her neck.

Case stepped back and automatically checked the distance to the exits.

All at once, the guy slumped and fell across the table, knocking his plastic cup over and spilling its contents everywhere. Case jumped. The sharp scent of alcohol filled the air.

The guy sat up, and Case jumped again, this time cocking her arm back, ready to nail him if he so much as looked at her funny.

He *did* look at her funny, but not in the way she expected. Confusion clouded his eyes. He held himself upright, unsteady in the manner of drunk people everywhere, and that eerie, strangely boneless lolling was gone.

"I think I'm a little fucked-up," he said. He slurred the words to near-unintelligibility. "Nah. I'm *really* fucked-up. Can I just . . . "

Case never found out what he wanted to do. He passed out, hitting the side of the small table and knocking it over as he fell to the floor.

"Anybody know this guy?" she asked, looking around the room.

Nobody would claim him.

"Christ," she said. "This is not my problem."

"I'll get the bartender," Danny said. "He probably deals with this all the time."

"Yeah. Great."

Danny walked off. The guy on the floor rolled over and made some muffled noises. He'd be all right, Case thought. *But remind me not to take whatever the hell he's been taking.* She suppressed a shudder.

Over by the bar, Danny had managed to get the bartender's attention, and back at the table, the crowd that had accreted around Erin happily chattered away. It seemed like a good time for Case to throw her things in the car and get out. Any pleasure she might have taken from socializing was gone.

She headed toward the storage room without waiting for Danny to get back and started moving things. She loaded the heavy stuff first—if some asshole decided to make off with her gear between trips, he'd look pretty funny trying to carry her fifty-pound speaker cabinet down the street.

On the third trip, she nearly ran into Danny on the way out of the storage room. He was a big guy, and he filled the doorway—she would have seen him coming if she'd been looking up instead of trying not to bang her guitar case on any of the clutter in the room.

"Hey," she said. He was close, and his nearness made her stomach do weird things. She didn't understand it—he wasn't her usual type. *No tattoos, and he hasn't even been to prison once,* she thought sarcastically. But when they were playing music, they shared moments that were so intense it made her face feel hot and her breath come in gasps. Lately, those moments had been coming even when they weren't playing music.

This is stupid. It wasn't like she'd missed the gold band on the third finger of his left hand, the gold band that said *Keep off, bitch!* to everyone who happened to see it. She ought to avoid him when they weren't onstage or practicing. This was like playing chicken, she thought, and she didn't know if she was teasing him or teasing herself or just behaving like a stupid, self-destructive sixteen-year-old who didn't care who got hurt.

Who would it hurt? He hasn't mentioned his wife, and she doesn't seem to be here tonight. You don't know his situation.

She met his eyes and again felt that magnetic pull, that force that urged contact.

"The bartender's got everything under control, but I gotta tell you—that guy kind of freaked me out," Danny said. "You all right?"

"Yeah. I'm good. He's not the first wasted creep I've ever met," she said, though she'd never met one quite like that.

"I guess not." Danny stood awkwardly, filling the doorframe. Was he waiting for her to say something? "Hey," he said after a bit. "That was cool. What you did for John. I think you made his night."

"He deserved it. He put it on the line for a change, you know? He played a kickass show." She heard him talk, and she made the right words in answer, but the words were camouflage for the real conversation.

"So did you," Danny said.

Oh boy. That warm, light-headed feeling rolled through her, and, sure enough, her face felt hot. *If this room had a door . . .* But the room didn't have a door, and she wasn't going to invite him out to the car, and this conversation needed to be over. She needed to get out of here right now. "We all played a good show," she said. "See you at practice."

She hurried to rush out, but of course there wasn't much room in the doorway. She ended up squeezing past him before he had time to get out of the way. Most of the length of her body moved against him, one breast brushing his side, his elbow. That brief contact seemed to last a slow, agonizing hour, seemed to burn her body everywhere he touched her. She heard him gasp and thought dimly that she might have done the same.

Then she was past him, and she didn't look back.

CHAPTER 9

Danny woke up with the sun screaming through the curtains, battering its way into the room, clawing at his face. He groaned and pulled the blanket over his head.

Wait a minute, he thought. *Something's not right here*. His mind was sluggish, slow machinery moving on rusty rails. There was the light—God, the sun was bright!—and there was warmth, weight, *presence* next to him in the bed.

He pulled the covers off his head and checked the bed. Gina was lying there next to him, wide awake with her head propped up on her hand and a grin on her face.

"Hold on," he said. "Thinking."

"Take your time."

"What time is it? It feels late."

Her smile widened. "You're getting warm."

Then it clicked. She worked way downtown, and she usually left early to get ahead of the traffic and get some work done before the phone started ringing. She was *never* home when the sun was up this high. "You're supposed to be at work."

"I'm terribly sick," she said. The smile didn't leave her face, and now a wicked gleam in her eye joined it.

Danny picked his head up and blinked. "You don't look sick."

"*Terribly* sick," she repeated. She coughed a few weak, bogus coughs into her hand.

The sun was much too bright, he realized. Too bright for her to be here, sure, but also too bright for him to be here. "What time is it?"

"A little after ten."

"Oh, shit. I gotta go." He started to get up, but she barred his way with her arm.

"You're not going anywhere. You're terribly sick, too."

"Oh? Does my boss know?"

"Yes indeed. He says to rest up."

Danny laughed, finally understanding. "Oh, I don't know if I'll be doing much of that," he said, and he reached for her.

***

He made breakfast afterward, French toast and eggs. He'd proposed eating in bed, but Gina had wrinkled her nose. "It smells like sex in here."

He couldn't argue with that, and while the scent was pleasant enough, or if not exactly pleasant then pleasantly evocative, he could see why she thought it didn't mix well with breakfast. She came out to the dining room in a robe. He plucked at it, trying to get her to take it off, but she wasn't having any of that. "Later," she promised, laughing. "I'm trying to eat here."

Danny sat down at the table with her with a dopey smile on his face. He'd slept well, breakfast was served, and the sex had been fantastic. The release had been more than welcome, but the sense of togetherness, of actually spending some time with his wife for a change, was even more so, and if, for just one moment toward the end, he'd imagined Case's athletic body instead of Gina's curvier figure, he would push that as far down in his subconscious as he could manage and not think of it again.

He was busily not thinking of it again when Gina asked, "How was the show?"

He concentrated on cutting his French toast. "Pretty good," he said neutrally. "Probably our best yet. If we're not careful, we're going to sound like a real band pretty soon. John really put his back into it this time."

"He's getting over his stage fright?"

Danny was touched by the question. He so often felt that she merely tolerated his nattering about the band that he was grateful that she remembered. "Yeah. He really is." He popped a forkful of French toast into his mouth. "I'm proud of him."

"Good for him," Gina said. She'd met John on a few different occasions and had told Danny he seemed like a bright kid, though it was tragic the way he was wasting his potential. Danny got out of those conversations as fast as he was able, before he said anything to disparage his own nice, stable, well-paid, boring-ass employment in the cubicle farm. He half-agreed with Gina, and half-admired his brother for having the balls to check out of the whole tiresome system, but the one time he'd supported John's position he'd gotten a surprisingly excoriating lecture from Gina on social and familial responsibility. John's decision to squander his potential was apparently a big nasty loogie in the face of the entire social structure that supported his way of life, and he was refusing to hold up his end of the bargain by contributing in any meaningful way. Danny had listened, eyes round as bottle caps, while Gina unloaded on John and ungrateful deadbeats like him. Danny had backpedaled so fast it felt like he'd strained something, trying to get as far from that conversation as possible. There seemed to be an implicit judgment there on his own priorities—that they were only *just* in line, and he'd better not let them slip. He had avoided any conversations in the same vein ever since. It was enough that Gina seemed to like John okay, despite the fact that she thought he was one step above a tapeworm, and Danny had left it at that.

With that recollection firmly in mind, he decided a change of subject was in order.

"How come you decided to play hooky today?" he asked.

"You know. All work and no play."

Danny smiled. "I thought all work and no play makes you partner by the time you're twenty-eight."

That drew a laugh from her. "It does, but it also makes you very, very tired sometimes."

Danny looked at his wife in the sun through the kitchen windows. She *did* look tired—one good night's sleep wasn't enough to undo months of straining under the yoke—but she looked happy, too, and he felt a surge of emotion.

"I love you," he said softly.

She reached over the table and took his hand. "I love you."

Her hand was small and white against his own big, clunky hand, fingers narrow and straight where his were thick and squared-off. It was an odd-looking match, but it seemed just right to him.

"This was a good idea," Danny said.

***

"Hey there, rock star! How ya doing?"

Case shook her head, but she grinned. "I don't know how you can be so goddamn cheerful at this hour, Erin."

"It's ten-thirty!"

"It is, and you should be hungover and hating life right now." Case pulled her apron off the peg and started tying it around her waist.

"Oh, I never get hungover," Erin said. Case didn't see how that was possible, but since nobody could be hungover and that loud at the same time, she supposed Erin was telling the truth. "I didn't black out, either," Erin added accusingly, "but I sure didn't see you leave. What's up with that?"

"That's, um, a long story." *Huh,* Case thought. *A month ago I'd have told her "none of your fucking business" and left it at that. Must be getting soft in my old age.*

Erin raised an eyebrow. "Does it have something to do with your so-very-cute drummer?"

Damn. That social radar or whatever it was that Erin had was a serious danger to others. "I'll tell you about it later, okay?"

"Okay, but I'm gonna hold you to that. I know you're planning to wear me out in training and hope I'll be too tired to remember, but it'll never work. You don't stand a chance."

"I believe that."

"Good." Erin clocked in.

"Hey, thanks again for bringing your friends out. That was cool."

"No problem. We had a good time. Did you get enough people out to get booked for the weekend?"

"Not even close," Case said.

"That sucks. Don't worry, though—the word is out now. You just make sure to tell me when the next one is, and I'll do the rest."

***

The restaurant was crowded for lunch and then emptied out in a hurry, and Case's shift seemed to fly past. She and Erin clocked out a little after three and headed for the gym where they practiced now, ever since the manager at Applebee's had told them that a few patrons had raised questions, and he didn't want to see them fighting in the parking lot anymore. As long as they got to the gym early enough, or late enough, there was always a room available. It didn't always have nice cushy mats on the floor, but any floor at all was guaranteed to be a step up from the hot, dirty asphalt of the parking lot.

Despite Erin's warning, Case worked her extra hard that night. Maybe she'd forget to follow up her earlier question, and maybe she wouldn't, but Case had frustrations of her own to work out, and the exercise felt good. Movement and exhaustion had a way of clearing the head, and she could certainly use that.

They collapsed to the floor after about an hour. Case sat leaning back on her arms with her legs outstretched in front of her. Erin lay flat on the floor, eyes wide and staring at the ceiling.

"You tried to kill me," Erin said breathlessly.

"You're still alive, aren't you?"

"Parts of me aren't sure. Check back later." She exhaled. "But that doesn't get you off the hook. Your escape act last night and your friendly teddy bear of a drummer. What's the story?"

Case sighed. This could all have been avoided if she'd had the presence of mind to stop by and make some excuses last night, but she'd been so rattled after her run-in with the wasted guy and the following encounter with Danny that she'd gone straight out to the car and kept going. Probably it really wasn't any of Erin's business, but she found herself talking anyway.

"I didn't mean to ditch everybody," Case explained. It sounded pathetic even to her. "I just don't like to hang out with the drummer—Danny—any more than I have to." She stared straight ahead at the mirror on the other side of the room. It was easier to talk without looking directly at Erin.

"You don't like it, or you don't think it's a good idea?" Erin said. "Because it looked like you liked it just fine. You guys are electric together onstage. Yowza. Chemistry, baby."

"It's that obvious?"

"I think the whole room could feel it. You know he can barely keep his eyes off you the whole time you're playing?"

Case closed her eyes. "No. I didn't know that."

"It's true," Erin said. Her cheerfulness was really starting to get irritating. "And sometimes you'd give him one of those smoldering looks and you two would lock eyes—so hot."

"You've got to be kidding. '*Smoldering*'?"

"Would I make that up? Besides, you know. You were there."

"Great," Case said. "Now I feel like I've been performing some kind of sex act onstage. Thanks."

Case said nothing else. Not only were her hormones dragging her around by the pelvis, but evidently it was obvious to anyone watching. Just fucking fabulous.

"So what's the problem?" Erin asked. So much for silence. "Is there a band rule that says you can't jump on the drummer? You guys are consenting adults."

Case finally turned and looked at Erin, giving her an incredulous stare. "You noticed all this, and you missed the fucking wedding ring?"

Erin gave a short laugh. "Huh. You know, I did. That's kind of funny when you put it like that."

"Yeah. A regular riot."

Erin chewed her lip. "Have you asked him about it? Maybe they're into kinky stuff."

"Jesus Christ," Case said. "Not Danny. No way. Other than getting smashed every once in a while, he's a choirboy."

"And you don't think choirboys are into kinky stuff? I swear, they're the ones you gotta watch out for."

"Jesus Christ," Case said again. It was less satisfying this time. "No. Not Danny. I know everything there is to know about the kind of boys you gotta watch out for, and Danny is not one of them. Believe me."

Erin was quiet. Case could see her calculating, turning the problem over in her mind.

"I guess you ought to avoid hanging out with Danny any more than you have to," Erin said after a while.

Case nodded. She took a drink of water and swirled it around her mouth. She was tempted to spit it on the floor, but she got up instead, crossing the room to spit it into the water fountain. She came back and sat again. "A year ago, I think I'd have just taken what I wanted, and damn the consequences. It wouldn't have been the first time."

"Maybe you're less of a stone-cold bitch than you used to be," Erin said. The smirk on her face took most of the sting off the words.

"Maybe that's it," Case conceded.

"Or maybe you really care about Danny."

Case recoiled. "Jesus, Erin. That's about as funny as a fork in the eye."

Erin only shrugged. The two women sat in silence, each with her own thoughts. Outside the room, the normal clanging and banging of equipment went on and on.

"You're too easy to talk to, you know that?" Case said.

"It's a gift."

***

John served up another low-fat half-caff mocha blah blah blah what-the-fuck-ever with somewhat less than the usual Starbucks-approved amount of good cheer. The show last night had been great, and he'd even gotten enough sleep for a change, but the comedown was a bitch. For twenty-five minutes onstage, the gears of his own personal universe had meshed for once, and he had been propelled forward into . . . into what? Into something that felt like his real life, he thought. Making music that moved people.

It hadn't moved many people, sure, but it had been a start. It had rankled at first that he'd pushed himself up to a new level—with the help of the band and Johnny Tango—and nobody had really given a damn. Then Case's friends had come over (and he was still grappling with the world-altering implications of that unexpected phrase, "Case's friends") and told him how much they'd enjoyed the show, and suddenly he'd felt like he hadn't been wasting his breath after all. They hadn't been bullshitting, either, or at least he didn't think so. They'd really had a good time, and though they had been there mostly to see Case, he'd gotten the sense that they'd really appreciated his performance, too.

For a moment or two, all had been right with the world.

And now he was making six-dollar coffees for hurried people with BMWs and no brains again.

Talk about a hangover.

He poured some tea into a plastic cup and set it on the counter, then turned to the guy working the shift with him.

"Drew," he said, "can you imagine Ian Anderson working the assembly line in a factory?"

Drew was maybe a couple of years older than John, but apparently not enough older. He blinked. "Who?"

There was something to be said for remembering your audience, John thought wryly. He tried again. "Daughtry," he said. "Can you imagine him pumping gas somewhere for six bucks an hour?"

Drew nodded. "Yeah. Totally. That's probably where they should have left him."

John couldn't help but laugh. "Bad example. How about Fred Durst?"

Drew narrowed his eyes and tipped his head toward the ceiling, thinking hard. "No," he said finally. "I can only imagine him in prison."

"Fair enough," John said, laughing some more. This might have been the only non-coffee conversation he'd ever had with Drew, and the guy was funnier than John had expected. "Come on, work with me here. One more time. What about Madonna?"

"I can imagine her doing *lots* of things," Drew said. "And she probably has."

More laughter. "You're not making this easy on me."

"Sorry, man," Drew said. His grin said he was anything but. "Where are you going with this?"

"Haven't you ever seen somebody, a musician or an actor or someone like that, and thought *Yeah, that's what this person is supposed to be doing.* Like it's impossible to imagine them doing anything but what they're doing. Like they were made for it."

Drew shrugged. "Not really, man. But I know some people who feel that way."

"Yeah?"

"Hell yeah. Everybody who walks in the door here takes one look at me and thinks, *Damn. That man is* made *for brewin' up a badass Cinnamon Dolce Latte.*"

"You have no culture."

"Not a shred." Drew turned to the woman who had just walked up to the register. "Welcome to Starbucks," he said. "Would you care for a Cinnamon Dolce Latte?"

"Uh, no thanks."

Drew glanced at John and shrugged.

John shook his head and went in back to make sure they had enough cups. A faint muttering sifted up from the back of his mind, dark, incomprehensible murmurings, but he paid it no attention.

***

Quentin bit back a curse, closed his eyes, and grimaced, covering his thumb with his fingers. With his other hand, he held on to both the top rung of the ladder and the heavy framing hammer he'd mashed his thumb with. Warm blood trickled from his fist.

Better a thumb than a finger, he thought, though really any abuse of his fretting hand was a drag.

"Hey! Pay attention up there, for Chrissakes! You all right?"

Quentin opened his eyes. Cesar, the foreman, was looking up at him with concern.

"I'm gonna come down for a minute, okay?"

"Yeah, fine."

Quentin slid his hammer into the loop on his belt and clambered down the ladder, leaving spots of blood on every other rung.

"Let's have a look," Cesar said. Quentin showed him the thumb—the nail was torn half off, and the wound under it welled with dark blood.

"Nice one. Come on. There's a first-aid kit in my truck." They walked over, and Cesar dug the white and red box out from behind the seat. He handed Quentin a bottle of peroxide and a roll of gauze.

"Thanks," Quentin said.

"Where's your head today, man? Jimmy said he about had to throw a two-by-six at you to get your attention a little while ago, and now this." Cesar gave him a fatherly frown. "If you're out of it today, you should go home."

Quentin shrugged and opened the peroxide. This was going to hurt like a bastard. "No, it's cool," he said.

"Stay out too late last night?"

"Yeah. That's it." Quentin gritted his teeth together, screwed up his face, and poured the peroxide on his thumb. It hissed and spat and burned like hell. Pink foam spilled onto the earth. "Yeah," Quentin said again. "Just didn't get a lot of sleep."

That was part of it, sure, but it wasn't the whole story. He'd seen the old rocker, the one that hung around John like a fly buzzing around roadkill, at the show, and hadn't been able to get him out of his mind since.

About halfway through the set, Quentin had seen him from the stage. The guy hadn't been looking at the band or watching John at all—instead, he'd been turned half away from the stage and watching the faces of the crowd, his glance moving from one to another every few seconds. Whatever he was looking for, he didn't find it, and he left at the very end of the set, slipping out the door as the band tore down. Quentin didn't think John had even seen him.

The guy bugged Quentin. He had the sleazy manner of the kind of guy who'd sidle up to you in a crowded club and ask if you needed a gram, maybe half a gram, but his eyes were too slow, too attentive, and he wasn't as jumpy as the dealers Quentin knew. The drug dealer vibe wasn't *quite* right, but that's all that Quentin could figure him for. That would explain John's odd behavior lately, too.

And the voice? How do you explain that?

"Shit, I'm just tired," Quentin said.

Cesar nodded. "Go home, kid. It ain't worth getting hurt out here for fifteen bucks an hour."

Quentin wound the gauze around his thumb. "Yeah. I guess you're right."

CHAPTER 10

The stage was huge, almost the width of the whole building. It was just the kind of stage John would have loved to play on, he thought wistfully. One day. The place was packed, maybe a thousand people and standing room only, just like it would be for him one day. For now, though, he was only a spectator, jammed in next to a bunch of sweaty bodies and jostled this way and that by hard elbows and rude shoulders. Still, excitement crackled through his body. He was in the very front, pressed against the rail in front of the stage. Best seat in the house, so to speak. He couldn't wait for the band to get started, even though he couldn't precisely remember who he'd come to see. A heavy rock band, he was sure—the drum kit, Ampeg bass amp, and Marshall JCM800 guitar amp attested to that. The guitar amp was a little weird, though; he would have expected a big speaker cabinet in a venue this size, one big 4x12 at least if not two, but there was only a small cabinet on the floor.

It looked familiar. So did the drum kit, now that he was looking, and his excitement soured with a sense of low dread, like a low bass note that was felt more than heard. He stared at the kick drum, stupidly trying to figure out where he'd seen it before.

He was still staring at it when the crowd around him cheered and surged forward, smashing him against the metal rail. He pushed back, and the space around him, maybe three feet on every side, cleared instantly. None of the cheering, screaming fans touched him now; they avoided him, they wouldn't look at him, even though they kept cheering and waving and pressing against each other. He dimly thought he'd have to hang on to that trick for future shows.

The beat kicked in, and the first chords of the song started.

That's funny, he thought. That sounds like "Burn." That humming sense of dread doubled, acquiring some evil harmonics, and he felt his head turning back to the stage.

No, he thought, all excitement gone. I need to leave here. I don't want to see this. I have to go! He couldn't stop himself looking, though, his head turning and his eyes opening wide to take in the whole stage.

His brother was sitting behind the drum kit. He looked good, too—happy, thrilled to be playing as he pummeled the floor tom and snare. Case was there, too, playing a Les Paul the color of blood (and why did that seem familiar? he was sure he'd never seen it before)—and fuck! Even Quentin was there, way on the right side of the stage, nodding his head and teasing deep, rumbling notes from his bass.

This was bad, this felt wrong. This was the thirteenth floor, aces and eights, the black spot, every omen of dread and cursed luck he could think of. Where was the singer? He, John, should have been on that stage—but there was nothing he wanted less at that very moment. He wanted to run, to turn and plow through the crowd behind him, leave a trail of spilled beer and irate people all the way to the door, and his fucking legs wouldn't move.

The song moved to the chorus figure, and still nobody was singing. Nobody onstage, anyway—the crowd around John shouted the words (those shitty goddamn lyrics) at top volume, breaking into even louder cheering as Case turned and locked eyes with Danny across the stage. There was a kind of feral, bestial hunger in her eyes—and in

Danny's, too. She walked toward him without breaking eye contact, swaying her hips slightly as she went. The crowd went nuts.

Do it! *a woman just behind and to the left of Danny shrieked, her voice many times louder than the thousands of watts of amplification in front of him.* Doooo iiiiiit!

Case walked behind the drum set and reached out with her right hand, seizing the front of Danny's shirt. She hauled him out of his seat and pressed her lips to his, mashing his lips against his teeth so hard that blood trickled down his chin. Her guitar was gone—John had no idea where it had gone—and her entire body was crushed against Danny's. Danny kicked the drum set apart without breaking from her embrace, and then it, too, was gone.

Only Quentin was still playing, grooving along to his bass line with a sadistic grin on his face. The crowd roared, shouted, and screamed, and John suddenly knew that this was a part of the act they all expected. This was what they'd come to see.

Case backed up, pulling Danny with her to the front of the stage. Then she turned, spun, and threw him to the ground, tearing frenetically at his clothes. His T-shirt shredded away, his pants tore into strips that she ripped away and threw into the audience.

God, please no, please I don't want to see this, I don't want to watch this.

Then Danny was naked and Case was straddling him, still fully clothed. From John's vantage point, so close to the stage, he could see everything—the blood on Case's lip, her hard nipples, Danny's erect penis crushed against his body and outraged.

Come on, girl! *somebody shouted behind John. John turned (*I turned! I can turn! Maybe I won't have to see any more!*) to tell her to shut up, that was his brother for God's sake, but he couldn't tell who'd said it.*

*His head turned back to the stage of its own accord (*No! No no no!*) and his face contorted into a cry of horror. Case's skin had gone pale, all maggot-white and pulpy, and jagged, ragged teeth filled her mouth. She threw her head back and howled, and the crowd howled* *with her. Then she leaned down as though she was going to whisper something in Danny's ear, but instead she took the ear in her mouth and pulled, tearing it slowly off Danny's head. She teased it, worked it as John stared and the crowd yelled, pulling the ear away along with a ragged strip of flesh that went all the way down Danny's neck to his collarbone before it tore free.*

Yes! *Danny screamed as blood spurted from his wound. John could hear him as clearly as if they were the only two people in the room.* Oh, God yes!

Case tore the strip of flesh away and threw it into the crowd. John could see the ear, whole and intact, still hanging on the end of the strip as it sailed into the audience. Droplets of blood fell on John's face, in his hair.

Then Case bent down again and stopped with her mouth hanging open inches from Danny's face. Saliva dripped onto Danny's skin. Case looked up from below her eyebrows at the crowd, a wordless query.

NO! *John screamed, but the crowd screamed louder.*

Case sank her teeth into Danny's cheek just below his eye—his eye, for God's sake, his fucking eye—*and pulled.*

***

John woke with a scream still dying on his lips. Darkness surrounded him, wrapped around him, thick and heavy like wet black felt. *Stinking* wet black felt. The smell had come like a fog in the night, caressing him, seeping into his pores—that awful smell, the smell of fish guts rotting in a Dumpster, of rotting logs half submerged in stagnant water, the murky, musky smell of semen and spoiled milk and mold—and now it was everywhere.

There was a sound, a faint tap on the wall by the door, and then he knew: *Something was in here with him.* That was where the stench had come from—a man, or something like a man, clad in a black silk shirt and a cowboy hat, a patient, ironic grin on his face, mad eyes shrouded in darkness. He was standing there, maybe close enough that one step would bring him to Johnny's very bedside.

You can't take me now, John thought. *You can't! It's too soon!* No sound escaped his lips, though—he didn't dare make a noise. His chest burned from holding his breath, his shoulders shook from terror. He'd screamed just seconds ago, he *knew* he'd screamed, the sound had scoured his throat and was still ringing in the air, and yet now he was terrified to make the smallest sound, not even daring to breathe. There was that *thing* there, that thing that was not a man, and though it must have heard him, John felt sure that it was waiting, silently laughing, for John to make one more sound. To call it to him. Then it would take that single long step, and it would reach out and touch John with one clammy hand, and John would die.

Or worse.

John's chest burned and burned, and swatches of dark color, purple and noxious green, flashed in his vision. He had read that you couldn't kill yourself by holding your breath—your body would *force* you to breathe eventually, and what would happen to him then, when he sucked in that unwanted, involuntary gasp of air?

He would have to move before then. Run, though the room was small, and the laughing *thing* was standing in the hall. Where would he run? Where *could* he run? Where? It didn't matter—he had to get up, had to run, had to do something now, before—

There came a faint scratching sound from near the hall.

Terror gripped him again, and he froze. His heart pounded like a maul in his chest, in his ears, in his head.

John sprang up from the mattress, scratching and scrabbling at the wall for the light switch, suddenly convinced that *light* was the answer, light would dispel the thing, or light would reveal it and he would be stricken insane at the sight, but either way he'd no longer have to sit scared in the dark, waiting.

He hit the light switch with his hand just as he hit the wall with his body. He felt the switch click, but the room stayed dark.

Oh God, it got the lights! John thought, semi-coherently. He bounced off the wall, skidded back on the damp carpet, and huddled on the floor with his arms over his head, waiting for the inevitable touch, that cold clammy slick slimy touch that would kill him or drag his soul screaming from his body.

A minute passed, then two. Nothing moved. Nothing could be heard above John's own ragged breathing.

There was a sudden sound, a mad fluttering that traversed the room, followed by a faint *click*. A tapping sound on the wall near the window.

He knew that sound. It was a water bug, Texas's answer to the cockroach. Bigger, of course, because this was Texas, and if that wasn't bad enough, the damn things flew. Particularly at night—and they made a *tap* when they landed on a wall. His house was infested with them.

He remembered, then, why the lights hadn't come on. He hadn't paid the electricity bill yet, and they'd cut him off yesterday. That's why there was no tiny glow from his charging phone, no faint green light from his digital alarm clock.

It was only then that he understood that he was alone in his house and had been all along. It was the smell, that awful fucking smell, that had fired up his overheated imagination.

And the dream.

Yeah, the dream had been a doozy, too. No wonder he'd woken up screaming.

Fucking Danny. Fucking Case, too. It wasn't hard to figure out where that goddamn dream had come from. The band had played another show last night, really kicked ass, and John had really gotten into it. He'd never performed so well in his life. Even Case had slapped him on the back afterward and told him he'd played a "great fucking set." That had been so unanticipated he'd actually stood there for a few seconds trying to figure out if he'd heard her correctly.

"Uh, you, too," he'd said. And she *had* played well, but he'd been half afraid she was going to leap over the drum kit in the middle of the set and fuck Danny's brains out right onstage. He wasn't alone, either—the entire universe could see the two of them making googly-eyes at each other all night.

It made for another layer of intensity in the show, but there was nothing good down that road. It wouldn't be like Danny to get it on with Case, but greater men than Danny slipped up all the time. John worried constantly, to the point where he was afraid to leave the two of them alone. *If Danny* does *fuck this up—no pun intended—he'll feel so guilty* I'll be lucky to see him again, let alone Case.

And then Ragman would go spiraling down the drain.

John had reminded Danny of Rule Number One about five times, but all Danny ever said was "I got it under control." John sure as hell hoped so.

All of that aside, it had been a great show. Quentin's buddies had come out again and brought a few friends, but what really did it was Case's friend, Erin. She'd brought the same girls that she'd brought the time before, and they all brought a friend, and some of the friends brought friends, and it was just like a chain letter. The guy at the door counted thirty-one warm bodies that came to check out the band, and that was enough to nail down one of the vaunted weekend spots. John knew it wasn't much, but it was something he'd been working at for almost a year, and there was a sense of triumph.

At the end of the night, they'd all gotten good and drunk and hired Erin to manage the band's publicity. John thought that might have been the only good decision ever made by a bunch of drunk people—he suspected that Erin could single-handedly pack Shea Stadium if given enough lead time.

As long as Danny didn't fuck up Rule Number One, it looked like they were on their way.

***

At the next practice, the four of them were still stoked from the show. Danny and John got there first, as usual. Danny didn't know how he looked himself, but John hadn't been able to clear the grin off his face since Danny picked him up, and Danny felt much the same. Quentin came in, also fully equipped with a dumb smile, and hummed while he plugged in. Case was actually bopping her head to music only she could hear, but from the few bits of lyrics Danny could hear coming out of her mouth, he had a strong suspicion that she was jamming along with "Changing Gears," the one song left in the set that she professed a mild dislike for. (To be specific, she had said, "This song draaaags. It moves like old people fuck." Danny was afraid that he would never cleanse his mind of the image that had conjured.)

"All right guys," John said when they were all ready. "We rocked that last show. The one next month is more than twice as long, though, so we have to figure out what we want to add to the set."

"Shouldn't be a problem," Case said. "We've got, what? Fifteen songs?"

"Yeah, but we've really only worked on five of them. We've got seven weeks to get another half a dozen or so in shape. Which ones do you want to start with?"

"'Fused' and 'Everybody's Fault' for sure," Case said.

"Yeah," said Danny. "And 'Circular Firing Squad.'"

"Fuckin' A," Quentin said, surprising everyone. There was laughter all around, and then they got down to business.

They rolled through all the new songs a few times each. There were a few snags—Case had thought it would be a good idea to change the tempo in the bridge section of "Fused," and it still tripped them up a bit—but overall the songs were coming together quickly. The group was starting to operate like a unit, Danny thought. The four of them meshed well, knew how to move with each other's energy. It went so well, in fact, that John wrapped up practice early.

"Who are you, and what have you done with John?" Danny asked, getting another laugh.

"Hey, that reminds me," John said. "Why don't you guys just call me Johnny? It'll be less confusing, and to be honest, the name is growing on me."

"Cool," Case said, without looking up from winding her cable. Quentin shrugged, which seemed to be assent.

Danny frowned. He had a sudden bad feeling about that, about John taking his stage name full-time. It seemed creepy, like the precursor to a drifting away from reality. Alice Cooper could get away with that, but this was just . . . John.

He didn't know what to say about it, though—he'd saddled John with the damn name to begin with. He let Case's affirmative speak for all of them and tried to squelch the unease that came with it.

For Danny, packing up was as easy as getting out of his chair. He and John—Johnny, he reminded himself, and boy, that was going to take some getting used to—went out to the car.

"I'll be home early," Danny said. "You're slipping."

"Nah," Johnny said. "We're really coming together, and we've played hard for the past few weeks. Knocking off a little early won't end the world. We've earned it."

"Yeah. I think so, too." Danny pulled out of the parking space and turned onto the access road. "I hope Gina's not working too late tonight," he said absently.

"Hey! Speaking of Gina . . ." Johnny said. His voice was too casual—Danny had known him for twenty-two years, and this was unmistakably the "Don't mind me—I'm not up to anything here!" voice.

"Yeesss?" Danny dragged the word out. He was nervous already.

"I think you should invite her to the next show." The phony innocence was even thicker this time.

It was too much. "Okay, John—Johnny. What the hell are you up to?"

Johnny looked hurt. "I'm not up to anything." *I don't know* how *that chocolate got all over my face.* "We need a good turnout for the show is all, and I think we're finally good enough that Gina might enjoy it."

"She's got a standing invitation to all our shows—she knows that. And anyway, she's not going to enjoy it. We go on late, for one thing, and for another she doesn't like rock music. You know that. What are you really up to?"

"I'm not up to anything. I just think it would be good if she came, that's all."

That was so much bullshit Danny didn't even know where to start. So he didn't. Like so many other times, he just let it go. "I'll remind her," he said.

***

The weeks rolled away. They got tighter and tighter in practice, but Danny started to have more and more misgivings about John's new persona. There were only little things, he told himself—nothing extreme, nothing crazy. John had found himself a pair of boots that he wore everywhere now along with Case's jacket, and he'd started slicking his black hair back with some kind of greasy glop he'd found God-knew-where. Danny wanted to tell him that his new hairstyle made his already-oversized forehead look big enough to land aircraft on, but he didn't have the heart. It was cosmetic, no big deal. Of larger concern, particularly in public, everything was now a motherfucker. At practice, John never asked to play a song one more time—he always said "Let's hit that motherfucker again." Similarly, Case's guitar and Quentin's bass had both been declared motherfuckers, as in "Are you gonna tune that motherfucker or what?" John was never in the mood to get some chow anymore—but he was sometimes hungry as a motherfucker.

Even Case, whose endless stream of profanity would have not only made a sailor blush but rounded out his education besides, was starting to run out of patience with it. "Lots of mothers getting fucked around here lately," she'd grumbled in practice one evening. John had missed the point or chosen to ignore it.

Little things, Danny kept reminding himself. Just little things. Even if John was taking up permanent residence in his stage persona, it wasn't as though he was checking out from the real world. He still paid his bills—as much as he ever did. At any rate, he still asked Danny for occasional loans to, say, get his water turned back on. He hadn't started studying auto repair or invested in a set of

Craftsman wrenches or, God forbid, a switchblade. *Yet*, Danny couldn't help adding. John had picked up the irritating habit of expounding on what Danny was starting to think of as The Legend of Johnny Tango ("Johnny got in a street fight over there once," John would say as they drove by some abandoned lot. "Got two broken ribs out of the deal, but he put two motherfuckers in the hospital. One for each rib." Or, "Johnny used to drag race down here, before there were so many cops."). On balance, Danny couldn't decide if The Legend was a good thing or a bad thing. It was obnoxious as all hell, but it was reassuring to hear John talking about Johnny in the third person. He hadn't come unraveled—he was taking a fantasy a bit too seriously, that was all.

Thanks to Erin's pushing and his steady paycheck, Danny became the de facto business manager for the band. The band needed a website, she insisted. How could she promote them if they didn't have a website? Danny cobbled together a MySpace page and got it looking halfway decent over the course of a long weekend, only to be told that it was tacky, and they needed a *real* website. She was probably right, so Danny loaned the band a few hundred bucks and took care of hiring a web designer, setting up hosting, and all the other details. It looked all right when it was done. Next she wanted some mp3s to put up on the site, but they didn't have anything worth a damn to give her. There would be a recording session in the not-too-distant future, Danny figured, and that wasn't going to be cheap. He wouldn't be fronting the cash for that exercise. Not all of it, anyway.

"And promo photos," she said. "For your press kit."

They were just the last item on a whole list of promotional items she had laid out. She had a whole plan put together—what they needed, when, in what order, who it was for. Danny shook his head as he read the list, amazed. "Have you done this before?" he asked.

"Nope."

"How did you learn all this?"

"Research!" she'd said proudly.

"Plus you know three out of every five people in the entire damn Metroplex."

"That's what I said. Research."

He thought she was jumping the gun; they hadn't even played their first weekend show yet, and she was mapping out what looked like a ten-year promotional plan. Then again, what did he know? It was thanks to her efforts that they'd gotten the slot at all.

The actual show was almost anticlimactic after the effort that led up to it. No—that wasn't quite true. It was a blast, and Danny thought they played well. Johnny came out in his full Johnny Tango regalia—white T-shirt, black leather jacket, boots, and jeans—and for the first time Danny wondered whether he was trying to be James Dean or the Fonz. Either way, the size of the crowd intimidated him at first, just like the last show, but he warmed up fast.

"Is it hot enough for you, motherfuckers?" he shouted in the quiet part of "Burn," just like the last show, and Danny prayed that that wasn't going to become some kind of catchphrase or motto. It was already old. But the crowd yelled.

And what a crowd! Erin had put her promotional machine in overdrive, and between the people that came to see Ragman and the people who had come for the other bands, there had to have been over two hundred people in the place. Danny found out later that forty-seven of them had been marked down for Ragman—at six bucks a head (the band's share of the eight-dollar cover charge), they hauled in two hundred and eighty-two dollars.

Danny's wife was not among the forty-seven. Johnny had asked after her a couple of times in the days before the show, and Danny had gotten a little pissed. "She'll come if she wants to come, for Christ's sake," he'd snapped. "What's it to you?" After that, Johnny had backed off.

In the final analysis, the band had played well, the crowd had been supportive, and Johnny had held his own—but Case had unquestionably been the star of the show. It was almost scary how much better she was at each show than she had been at the one before, and she'd been pretty good to start with. But as she got more comfortable with the material and got more confidence in the band (they had leaped a major hurdle once she felt like she didn't need to lead Quentin through all the changes anymore), she loosened up onstage. Danny had briefly wondered if the size of the crowd would affect her as it had Johnny, but he needn't have worried. She sucked in energy from the crowd, turned it into searing, soaring music, and threw it back at them. She strutted, preened, and dragged notes screaming from her guitar. Sweat soaked the white fabric of her tank top, and Danny found himself thanking God (and, to a tiny extent, cursing Him) that she was wearing a bra under it. There was a line of guys waiting to get her number afterward, all of whom went away disappointed. Erin circulated among the crowd, though, and the band got thirty-five new signups on the email list, probably half of whom were guys who wanted to catch Case at the next performance and try their chances again, or, failing that, hoped she'd skip the bra next time.

It was just after the show that Danny caught himself thinking, *Man, I'm glad Gina wasn't here. I'm not sure what she'd have made of all that.*

CHAPTER 11

From the Dallas Observer, *September 22, 2009:*

. . . Opening the night were newcomers to the local scene, Ragman, thrashing out a set of greasy rock and roll in the vein of Appetite-*era* Guns N' Roses. *Derivative, sure, but they played it like they meant it, and guitarist Case (she sports a one-word name, naturally) pulled out some of the wickedest licks in town. If you're burned out on the shoegazer scene and in the mood for something trashy and mean, they're well worth checking out. . . .*

***

"Woohoo! Your first press clipping!" Erin waved the paper at Case, grinning madly. She read the brief review aloud. "This goes right into the scrapbook."

For once, they had met for lunch rather than serving it or raising bruises on each other's extremities. The day was unseasonably warm, and they had decided to take advantage of the café's patio. Case poked at the remaining half of her sandwich, thinking maybe she'd give it to the birds rather than try to choke it down. Erin had insisted on meeting early—11 a.m.—and Case's stomach hadn't woken up yet.

Erin's comment about her scrapbook struck Case as odd. When she heard the word "scrapbook," she thought of a dusty old photo album where your grandmother put pictures of you from the third-grade spelling bee. "You have a scrapbook?" she asked.

"More or less. I keep all this stuff, anyway—all part of building your unstoppable publicity machine."

Erin moved to put the newspaper in her bag, but Case stopped her. "Let me see that," she said. Case read it twice and then handed it back. "Oh, good. That'll make Johnny real happy." She had been tired before, but reading the review had pulled out the stopper on her internal reservoir of energy, leaving her suddenly weary. She dreaded the next practice already.

"He still driving you nuts?"

Case shrugged and threw one of her chips at the beady-eyed black bird hopping around by the next table. It jumped away, and a tiny brown bird darted in and stole the chip. "Yeah. Still suffering from little-dick syndrome, thinks I get too much attention and he doesn't get enough. He's been trying to gut the solo or the instrumental section out of every song he can, like that's not obvious or anything. Somehow I don't think our very first review is going to help improve the situation."

"Fun. It's just like my house at Thanksgiving. My uncle Bob and my uncle Dave take turns all day trying to impress my grandfather with how much money they made last year or where they traveled, or whatever. Are all bands like dysfunctional families?"

"All bands are like families," Case said, "and all families are dysfunctional, so I'd have to say yes."

"At least it's a family."

"I guess. Plus, Johnny's actually starting to get pretty good, but that just makes him more of a dick. Weirder, too. I think he's started talking to himself. It's a little creepy."

Erin didn't seem to know what to say about that, so there was a long moment of awkward silence—a rarity around Erin, who usually filled that sort of dead air without effort. Across the patio, a couple left their table. It was immediately swarmed by hungry, fat birds. Case watched two of the birds fight over a scrap of bread with a pile of uneaten chips a few inches away.

"Are you up for training tonight?" Case asked.

"One second." Erin finished doing something with her phone—probably sending a text message; she seemed to send about a thousand a day—and put it away. "I'm sorry, what?"

"Training. Tonight. Are you up for it?"

Erin made an overly dramatic sad noise. "Awww, I can't. I have plans."

"Oh, well," Case said. She tried to hide a disappointment that was greater than it ought to have been.

"Hmmm." Erin stared at Case long enough to make her uncomfortable, then rummaged in her bag, coming up with her phone a moment later. She got busy tapping out another message. When it was done, she smiled at Case. "Oh, look! Tonight seems to be wide open."

"Hey, you didn't have to—"

"How often do you actually ask to hang out with somebody? It's like a lunar eclipse or something. I'm so there." She brushed a stray lock of windblown hair out of her face and fixed Case with a look of concern. "Are you okay?"

"I'm not dying or anything."

"Ooh, you're so tough. Seriously, though. Anything you want to talk about?"

Case looked away. "No," she said. "It's nothing a little exertion won't fix."

"And a beating at the lightning hands of Mistress Erin." Erin held her hands up in what Case presumed was supposed to be a kung-fu pose.

"Mistress Erin? Are you a kung-fu master or a dominatrix for hire?"

"What, I can't be both?"

***

Erin left to go to her next appointment, but Case stayed at the table, drinking water and watching the birds hassle the customers. She had no doubt that Erin would be happy to listen to her outpouring of misery and woe, no doubt at all that Erin would be sympathetic and supportive and listen without judging or laughing—and no doubt whatsoever that she herself would feel completely pathetic by the end of her little ad hoc therapy session.

The show had been great, and afterward there had been the usual flood of interested male parties anxious to get acquainted. That was old news. She'd started thinking of them, probably owing to her own sporadic and flagging job hunt, as applicants, short for Applicants for the Position. ("What position?" "All of them." Erin had laughed herself silly when Case had explained the term.) Most times the applicants aggravated her, trying her patience with dim pickup lines and effusive, ignorant praise. Some nights, though, the attention really *was* flattering; to be perfectly, nauseatingly honest about it, it made her feel sexy. Some of that was a feeling of sexual power, as if she could simply point at any man she wanted and say, "You. Over here," and he would comply, willingly and enthusiastically. The control was intoxicating. Some of it, though—a tiny sliver, she assured herself—was a simple feeling of being desired. Just feeling sexy.

Chains hooked to a whole fleet of tractors couldn't have dragged that admission out of her, though she thought that if she talked to Erin long enough, Erin would somehow summon it forth in that insidious, chipper way she had. Erin would probably understand, too, and she'd likely be smart enough to know that this was not an area where even gentle mockery would be welcome.

Case threw a chip at one of the birds. The wind caught it and spun it past the bird. She threw another, harder. It, too, missed.

The line of applicants had looked especially promising after the show, and it had been one of those nights where she'd felt desirable, felt like she wanted to be desired. She'd gotten off the stage, flushed, sweaty, and overcharged, practically humming with energy, and a small crowd had already been waiting for her. It had been all she could do to plow a path through them and get her gear stowed. She had even felt talkative, and she'd culled a couple of the most promising applicants for further evaluation.

And then, in the middle of conversation (Emerson was the smart, funny one, but Greg claimed to be a personal trainer and certainly looked the part—oh, decisions, decisions), she saw Danny, clear across the room, darting glances her way despite himself. He looked miserable, and it seemed he was trying to self-medicate with copious amounts of alcohol. He downed two shots between furtive glances in her direction. The luster of a post-show hookup and sweaty, frantic, no-strings-attached sex until the small hours of the morning dimmed, faded, and was gone in the time it took to turn her head back to the conversation. Just like that, Emerson became the lame one who was trying too hard, and Greg turned into the King of the Narcissists. The light was suddenly flat and harsh, her mouth tasted like she'd swallowed something dead, and everything was too loud.

She left them without even excusing herself (Erin, she noted, swooped in behind her and attacked the two rejected applicants with the mailing list), threw her shit in the car, and went home straightaway.

That had been two nights ago, and she'd been frustrated and pissed off ever since.

Maybe I really should try to talk about it with Erin, she thought as she threw another chip. But, really, what was Erin going to tell her? Danny—Danny the drummer, Danny the peacemaker, Danny the big oaf who had somehow, through the music experience, pheromones, or some kind of clandestine voodoo he practiced in the dead of night, wrapped up her head so thoroughly that she was actively turning away attractive, available men in favor of going home and doing something that looked suspiciously like *pining* for God's sake, *fucking married* Danny—was, well, *fucking married.*

She had told Erin that, a year ago, it wouldn't have mattered. She'd have done what she wanted to do anyway. She thought that was true. But now there was the band, which she really did care about, no matter what Johnny might think, and which was delicately balanced enough. And there was Danny, who—again, Erin had seen this in her uncanny way—she also cared about.

And, maybe most important, maybe she didn't want to be—as Erin had so aptly put it—a *stone-cold bitch* anymore.

So, she *could* talk about all this with Erin, but it would be humiliating, and what would Erin say? What could she say? Case wasn't looking for permission to do whatever she wanted, and she doubted Erin would give it to her. She was stuck.

No, that wasn't strictly true, she realized. She could see Erin grinning and laughing. *You want to get over this thing with Danny,* Erin was saying in her mind, *then you need to accept an applicant.*

Alone at the table, Case nodded. Of course. A smile came to her lips.

Thanks, Erin!

***

Johnny threw the *Observer* in the trash with disgust. Then he dug it out again, leafed through until he found the snippet of a review, and read it again.

There were no customers in the Starbucks, so he decided he'd stretch his break just a few more minutes. He got out his phone and dialed his brother's cell number.

"Danny?"

"Everything okay?"

"No. Did you see the review of our show in the *Observer*?"

"What? No, I've been working."

"Well then, listen to this bullshit."

"Later. I've got a meeting in five minutes."

"It's short," Johnny said, making no attempt to hide the bitterness in his voice.

"Yeah, okay." Danny's sigh sounded like static over the phone. "Go."

Johnny read the short review. By the end of it, his voice was clipped, almost strangled-sounding. "How do you like that?" he said.

He could hear the shrug in Danny's voice. "Sounds okay. They said to come check us out."

"Sounds *okay*? Motherfuckers called us trashy and derivative!" Johnny was standing now, pacing the floor outside the bathroom in quick, jerky steps.

"Come on, man. You know what they say—any publicity is good publicity. And they *did* say to come check us out."

"They said *Case* is worth checking out."

"They did not."

"Well, we got three fucking sentences, and one of them is all about her. The rest of us might as well have been spectators, as far as they're concerned."

"It's not that bad," Danny insisted in that infuriatingly calm voice.

"Do you have *no* fucking pride? Or maybe you'd take this more personally if you hadn't spent the whole night looking morose and making cow-eyes at her."

"Cool it," Danny said. He was still calm, though. Probably thinking something like, *Oh, there goes Johnny again. I'll have to have a little talk with him later and make him feel better, and then everything will be fine.*

"I don't know if I *can* cool it," Johnny said. "I got half a mind to call up that numbnuts over at the *Observer* office and—"

"And what? Tell him his opinion sucks? Grow up, Johnny."

"Fuck you." Johnny mashed the button to end the call. The phone started ringing almost immediately. Danny, probably wanting to talk him off the ledge or maybe even apologize. Too bad. Sure, Danny hadn't felt bad about the review. It wasn't like he'd actually written any of the "trashy" and "derivative" songs. And of course he didn't care that Case got all the coverage—he was thinking with his dick, just like the motherfucking reviewer. Johnny didn't know what to do about Case, but he was starting to get an idea what to do about Danny. A pretty good idea.

"Hey," Drew said from behind the counter. "We got customers."

"They can wait," Johnny said, and he dialed the phone. It rang a few times, and he tapped his foot impatiently. After the third ring, somebody picked up.

"Hello, this is Gina."

"Hey Gina, it's John."

"Oh. Hi. What's up?" Her voice was too bright, almost brittle. Johnny thought she probably expected an emergency, or maybe she thought he needed money—he wasn't in the habit of calling her, after all.

"Nothing much," he said. He was talking too fast, he realized. He continued, making an effort to sound calm. "I was wondering if Danny had told you about our next show."

"Yes, John." She sounded irritated now. "He tells me about all of your shows."

"Did he tell you how excited he is?"

"Not really. He's always pretty happy to play."

"I think he's really charged up about this one, though. We're getting pretty good now, and there's supposed to be a big turnout. We're opening for Lost Soul Orchestra." That was true, though Johnny had never heard of Lost Soul Orchestra before seeing them on the bill, and he doubted Danny had either. It sounded important, and that was what counted.

"That's very nice. Look, John, I have to go."

"Wait! I'll be quick. It's just that Danny, well—he's really looking forward to this show. I think he'd really like it if you came."

A pause. "He said that?"

"He didn't come out and directly say anything, but you know how he is. He did tell me you probably wouldn't make this show, and he seemed really bummed. He doesn't usually bring that sort of thing up, so I guess it's been on his mind a lot. I think he's worried that if he says anything to you, you'll feel obligated to come, and you know how Danny is."

"Yeah," Gina said. Her tone had softened considerably. "He wouldn't want to inconvenience anyone, even if he had to saw off his own leg."

Johnny chuckled. "That's it. Anyway, I know you're pretty busy. I don't want you to feel obligated either, but I thought you ought to know."

"Thanks, John. I appreciate that. Maybe I'll come see you guys after all. When's the show?"

"It's the fourth of October at the Cavern. We start early. Ten o'clock."

"All right. I really have to go now."

"Take it easy. And thanks."

"You're welcome. Bye." She hung up.

Johnny closed his phone and slipped it into his pocket. *That was uncalled-for*, a small voice said. He shook his head. *No. I'm just looking out for my brother, that's all. That's all.*

"Hey!" Drew said from behind the counter. "If you're done calling your broker, I could use some help back here."

CHAPTER 12

"Would you stop that?" Johnny asked. He folded the corner of his journal back and forth, back and forth. "You're making me nervous."

Danny pulled his gaze away from the door one more time. It was early yet, and the small club was nearly empty, but people were starting to trickle in. Every time the door opened, Danny checked to see if his wife had arrived. Every time somebody else came in, he felt a mixture of relief and guilt.

"I can't help it. Gina's coming. I'm nervous," Danny said. "Because I want us to play well," he added quickly.

"Gina's coming? Cool. The more the merrier."

Johnny's phony tone of surprise told Danny everything. What was it Johnny had said? *I think you should invite her to the next show.* Yeah, that was it. And he'd hassled Danny about it for weeks.

"What did you tell her?" Danny asked.

"Nothing," Johnny said. His tone of innocence was even more phony than his tone of surprise.

"Try again, or I'm going home right now," Danny said. He wasn't sure that he meant it, but he was sorely, sorely tempted.

"You can't do that!" Johnny said, and his shock was genuine, at least. "Look, that's—"

The door opened, and this time Johnny craned his neck to look over his shoulder even as Danny looked up.

Gina stood framed in the doorway, an expression of mild distaste on her face.

"Gina!" Johnny shouted, waving frantically. "Over here!" He turned back to Danny and lowered his voice. "I told her it would mean a lot to you if she came. Don't make a big deal out of this, okay?"

Danny opened his mouth, but he didn't have any words to supply. Gina was already at the table. What would he say? *Gee, honey, I know Johnny said it would mean a lot to me if you came to the show, but really I'd rather you went far away. That way, I don't have to feel guilty about the affair I'm not having with our guitarist.* The guitarist who was, by the by, sitting two tables down with Erin and a few of Erin's entourage. Danny made an effort not to look in that direction—not even remotely in that direction.

"You made it!" he said to Gina. He got up from his chair to hug her, and he swore he felt Case's eyes on him the whole time. He glanced over at the other table, but Case was engrossed in conversation.

Gina sat. Quentin, sitting with one of his buddies at the next table, gave her a small smile, and she waved.

"Where's the guitar player?" Gina asked.

Johnny pointed over his shoulder with his thumb. "She's over there. She's the surly one."

Gina looked over with interest. *Please don't ask for an introduction*, Danny thought. *I don't think I'd survive that.* But that would have been unlike Gina, and thankfully she didn't ask.

Danny got Gina a glass of water, and they waited. He checked his watch. It was twenty minutes to nine, which meant an hour and twenty minutes until they went on—if they started on time, which never ever happened. He held Gina's hand and resolutely avoided looking down the row of tables for any reason. Johnny chattered for a while, but he petered out when nobody seemed interested in taking any of his conversational gambits.

One hour, fourteen minutes.

After another half hour of stilted conversation and awkward silence, the club started to fill up. It didn't take much. The Cavern was crammed in between a couple of other buildings, and it was much longer than it was wide. There was seating for maybe thirty people, Danny guessed, and a hundred might fit standing up, if they all got real friendly with each other. The stage was small and cramped, and, at about eight inches off the ground, hardly worthy of the name. Danny thought that was just fine with him. If there was enough of a crowd, it would be tough to see much of anything onstage from most places in the bar, and the less Gina saw of him and Case in close proximity to each other, the happier he'd be.

Thirty-six minutes.

A clot of people—young men, mostly—started to form around Case's table. Danny tried not to look over there, but Johnny kept turning around. He looked tired, Danny noticed. Alert, but physically drained. *My idiot brother,* Danny thought. What had he been trying to accomplish by getting Gina to come here? Maybe it was his dumbass way of trying to look out for Danny, but more likely it was his equally dumbass way of trying to keep Danny and Case from tearing up the band—in short, looking out for Johnny's interests, as usual. Danny sighed.

At five after ten, the sound guy came over to get them to do their sound check.

Danny gave Gina a pair of earplugs and went to the stage. The drum kit was backed up as close to the wall as he could get it, and he had to squeeze in around the floor tom to get behind it. Case's and Quentin's amps were also crammed in back, right next to him. Case and Quentin themselves had to stand close, with little room to move, and Johnny had only a little more. If Johnny moved too much to the right, Case would end up hitting him with the headstock of her guitar.

Cozy.

Danny did his part of the sound check (three thumps of the bass drum, three whacks on the snare, and five seconds of playing the whole kit), and when he looked up, Case was onstage, four feet away. He could have stood up, leaned over, and touched her hand.

Danny busied himself adjusting the tension on his snare so he wouldn't have to look at her. He could see her move in his peripheral vision. The sound guy had just asked her to turn her stage volume down, and she was twiddling knobs on her amp. She finished, and Danny got the sense she was looking quizzically at him.

He looked back at her and felt that headrush, that uneasy vertigo that had become so familiar.

She raised her eyebrows. *Ready?*

He nodded, and she went straight in to the opening riff of "Rust."

Here we go!

***

The band came in hot, a little too fast but steady and tight. Johnny smiled. The energy was good, and he was ready.

The near constant muttering in his head swelled into that question he'd come to love: *Now?*

Fuck yeah.

There was that rushing sense of power, and his voice poured out, *roared* out, the words filling the room and bursting among the crowd like bombs. *Gonna be hoarse tonight,* he thought, and he grinned crazily. *This* was how it was supposed to feel. The eyes on him didn't bother him now. Let 'em look, by God!

Nothing was going to ruin his night. He had arrived.

***

Quentin had to hand it to Johnny—he was really putting his back into it tonight, really going all out. The skinny, unsure kid Quentin had been playing with for over a year had been replaced by a confident frontman, and tonight he was *killing* it. He howled and screamed and sang—sang like a motherfucker, to use his own word. With the jacket, the slicked-back hair, and most of all the brash confidence, Quentin doubted Johnny's own mother would have recognized him if she'd been there. She would have sat in the crowd, patiently waiting for her son to come on— which would hopefully be right after this loud, nasty band got off the stage.

Case caught Quentin's eye and grinned, nodding at Johnny's back like, *Do you believe this guy?* Quentin grinned right back—he couldn't help it. It wasn't just Johnny who was killing it tonight. They all were. *The band* was. Whatever his misgivings about Johnny's newly discovered vocal prowess, this was rock and fucking roll the way it was meant to be played.

Johnny leaned out over the people at the front of the stage, reaching for their hands, dripping sweat on them, screaming at them. They screamed right back.

He was exultant, and fire flashed in his eyes. After the third song, when a few loudmouths in the crowd yelled "Burn!," he turned to Case, flushed and grinning maniacally.

"Let's do 'Burn,'" he said, off the mic. Quentin could see her gaping at him in surprise. "Burn" was their most popular song, the one everybody seemed to want to hear, and he hated it. The last couple of times people had shouted for it, he'd just scowled. It wasn't even on the set list this time.

"Looks like somebody ate their Wheaties this morning," she joked.

"Fuck yeah, I did. Let's hit it!"

She hit it, and Danny and Quentin followed her in, Danny with a nice little flourish he'd never played before. Case shot Danny one of those electric smiles, and Quentin grinned at the two of them. They plowed through most of the rest of the set, unstoppable.

Quentin was tuning his bass right before their second-to-last song, their one down-tempo number, when he saw the old rocker in the crowd. Once again, the guy's dark, hooded eyes scanned the room, and Quentin saw that his mouth was open slightly, as if he held his breath in anticipation of something.

Then Danny was counting off the song, one of Johnny's tunes called "Watching the World End." Case had worked it into an odd, almost jazzy progression, strange for the band's usual repertoire, but it worked. Quentin usually liked playing it, but something about the man's appearance in the crowd had unsettled him, had rendered the song eerie.

"The sun slides from his sky
Like a drunk man slides from his chair
But he ain't gettin' up this time
He ain't goin' nowhere.
And when the bar closes, baby
And the paramedics come through
The doc shrugs his shoulders
As he looks down,
Says 'There's nothing I can do.'"

A song about a dead man, about a dying day and a sun that would never rise again. Quentin hadn't paid a lot of attention to the lyrics in practice, but now they gave him the creeps. Or maybe it was Johnny's voice. There was a dark note in it, a sort of perverse glee that he hadn't heard before, and it clashed with the grim subject of the song in a way that was deeply unsettling, like clown makeup on a corpse.

It wasn't just him, either, he noticed. Most of the movement and conversation in the crowd had stopped. A few people swayed eerily back and forth, but most of the spectators stood still and silent, casting nervous glances at each other. The creepy guy stood stock-still, finally staring at the stage, at Johnny, and the expression on his face looked like some unholy species of religious ecstasy.

Nausea churned Quentin's gut, and it seemed that the stage had gotten brighter. Fresh sweat popped on his brow. Had the sound guy turned up the lights? What the hell? It had gotten much darker in the club, too. The back of the room near the bar was completely gone in the darkness, though there must have been some tiny trace of light since Quentin thought he could see even darker shapes twisting and writhing back there, midnight on black. He felt sick—

really sick, like he was going to chuck his lunch right onstage.

Even Johnny didn't look so hot all of a sudden. He twisted around in the middle of the song, and though he met Danny's eyes and nodded, Quentin got the impression that hadn't been why he'd turned. For one instant, there had been naked fear on his face, and Quentin was sure that Johnny had turned because he thought there was *somebody else* back there. Behind him. He looked so convinced that Quentin himself looked to the back of the stage. There was only Danny.

Then the song ended, and Johnny stopped singing. The bar faded into view, the lights dimmed to normal. Quentin's nausea was gone as suddenly as it had gripped him, like a cramp that had eased.

There was silence, then a tidal wave of applause, thunderous but solemn.

***

The set came to an end, and Case flipped off her amp even before the last chord finished ringing out. The sound died abruptly. She knew it was better for the amp if she let it cool down for a minute before turning it off, but just then she didn't give a damn. She yanked the plugs out of their sockets, threw the cables in the black duffel bag she used for miscellaneous gear, and started to get her shit off the stage. "Watching the World End" had turned into a nasty surprise, like finding cockroaches in her breakfast cereal, and though that weird unpleasantness was already fading, she just wanted to be gone. Johnny looked her way with a grin on his face, but he looked elsewhere when he got a good look at her expression.

She hauled her amp off the stage and shoved it to the side. There was nowhere to put it here, other than to try to get it out of the way.

"Hey, good show!" somebody yelled.

"Right," she said without even looking up. She slid her guitar case in next to the amp and walked away.

Erin gave her a tentative smile and a questioning look as she approached the table. Case sat down. The question would wait—she really didn't feel like talking.

"Hey! I said 'good show'!"

That guy again. Case turned. Slim guy, tall. Nice eyes. Nobody she recognized. He wore a ridiculous flower print and paisley shirt, unbuttoned halfway down his chest.

"You go out like that in public?" she asked.

He hesitated. It looked like he was trying to decide whether she was actively hostile or just giving him a hard time. "I was only telling you that you played well," he said finally. "Not looking for fashion advice."

Behind him, a small mob of people were lining up. They were already waving at her.

"Be nice," Erin whispered. "I don't know what's wrong—we can talk about that later—but these people are your fans. Don't make my job any harder than it already is."

Case frowned. Erin was probably right. She looked back at the "good show" guy. "Thanks," she said, without much enthusiasm. Erin elbowed her. "I mean, thank you!" She tried on a smile, but it felt like a sneer.

"I'm Brad," the guy said. "You play a mean guitar."

"It's easy. I'm a mean person."

He laughed, though again there was some uncertainty. "How mean are we talking here? Kicking puppies mean, or just cutting off old ladies in the passing lane mean?"

Now she did smile, a little. "*Eating* puppies mean," she said.

Brad nodded. "Now that's mean." He looked so serious that she had to laugh.

"Better watch your ass," she said, still laughing.

Brad wasn't so bad, once you got past the wardrobe. He talked to Case passionately about his band and his music—some kind of funk punk he described as a cross between Prince and Rancid that she couldn't imagine but now had to hear once, just to know what that would sound like. In fact, his band was going into the studio soon, and he wanted to get her to record guitar tracks on two songs where he thought a nasty guitar solo would be just the thing. His guitarist was an awesome rhythm player, he said, and he took care of everything they usually needed, but once Brad had heard Case playing, he'd immediately thought of a couple of places on the recording that could use her talents.

From there, conversation roamed—Brad's last band, Case's opinion of Dallas, dumb stories from shows they'd each played.

"Oh, I *hate* playing there," Case said after he finished one of his own horror stories. "One time we were waiting around after load-in and the fucking sound guy came in and told me to get the hell out. 'Band members only. No girlfriends.'"

"Ouch."

"I told him we could go out in the parking lot, and he could find out which one of us was somebody's girlfriend."

"You didn't."

"The hell I didn't." She gave him a wry grin. "Of course, he fucked our sound up that night. Turned me *waaaaay* down."

Brad laughed. He had a warm, easy laugh that Case liked, and he was fun. The only thing wrong with him that she could see was that godawful shirt, and she thought she might be able to get rid of *that* problem. She was starting to feel pretty good, no matter what weird turn the show had taken.

***

After Quentin put his bass away, he found a table near Erin and the others. There was laughter and shouting all around, but he tuned it out, watching the old rocker between moving bodies. That bad feeling from the stage lingered like the aftertaste of something foul, and, rational or not, he associated it with John's friend, or dealer, or whatever the hell he was.

The guy slipped through the crowd, seeming to touch nobody, looking into one face after another and moving on. Clubgoers turned away from him as he approached and looked elsewhere as he passed by. He said nothing, exchanged no words with anyone, but kept moving, sharklike.

What the hell is he looking for? Quentin wondered. If he were a dealer, Quentin would have expected him to mutter a few words, whisper in an ear or two, negotiate a deal or slip away from a polite rejection—but he never stopped, never slowed his even movement through the crowd.

Around Quentin, conversation twisted and flowed. He ignored it all, intent on the old guy's progress through the room.

***

Brad was talking, and Case really wanted to hear what he had to say—but a jarring, jerky motion in the crowd beyond him teased her vision, and she found herself looking over his shoulder rather than paying attention.

It was just an out-of-place goth kid, hair dyed black, dressed all in black, heavy chain hanging from his pocket and looping up to his belt—in short, stamped from the same mold as a zillion other affected, disaffected kids. Only the way he moved drew Case's eye. He stumbled and shambled through the room, clearing a space around him as others edged away, and at first Case thought he had some kind of physical ailment or handicap.

Then she got a good look at his face. A sense of déjà vu so sudden it was like careening vertigo smothered her, and her heart clenched tight like a fist. The spittle smeared on his chin, the sly grin, and the half-crazed eyes were horribly familiar, so much so that for one second she thought this was the same person she'd accosted at a different club all those weeks ago. But, no—this was clearly somebody else, and that chilled her as much as anything.

Brad trailed off and turned around, putting his elbow up on the back of his chair.

"Am I boring you?" he started, but he trailed off. "What the fuck?"

***

The old guy stopped close to the door and cocked his head, for all the world like a dog hearing a whistle in the distance. Quentin watched him turn, watched his eyes light on something across the room, watched the slow smile of satisfaction spread across his face.

Quentin followed the man's eyes, saw nothing particular in the knot of people at the center of the floor. There were people crowded thickly everywhere he looked, and he craned his neck, looking for whatever had attracted the man's attention.

The crowd moved aside, finally, and Quentin got a good look at the goth kid, who had a little clearing of his own.

Quentin had seen the kid during the show, near the front in fact, and he'd looked like was having a good time. That wasn't the case anymore. Even from here, he looked seven kinds of fucked up, and Quentin thought he was actually drooling on himself.

Quentin glanced around the crowd and quickly spotted the old guy moving toward the kid, eyes afire and mouth twisted in a grin. Indecision seized him, and he looked from the old guy to the kid and back. *This is none of my business,* he thought.

Then he got up. His mouth had gone dry, his pulse pounded behind his eyes, and his hands shook, but he got up. Somebody needed to have a talk with that creepy fuck, and it didn't look like anybody else was on the job. Quentin bulled through the crowd, muttering apologies as he shoved people aside and stepped on feet.

***

Case watched the kid stagger in one direction, then another. Whatever Brad had been about to say was gone, and he stared as well.

"He looks like he might need some help," Brad said uncertainly.

"I'm not sure," Case began.

The kid stopped his slow, weird turning. Case saw his shifty eyes narrow, saw his muscles tighten and his knees bend.

"Fuck!" she said, and she was on her feet, moving across the room. *What are you doing? Surely he's not going to—*

The kid sprang forward in an ungainly motion, half shuffle, half leap, and his arms reached out just as he stumbled. He lurched forward, grabbing a woman by the shoulders. She screamed. A bottle fell and shattered. The two of them, locked together, tottered, but stayed standing.

Case pushed two people roughly aside just as the kid opened his mouth and lunged. She heard his teeth snap shut on air even from ten feet away, even over the music.

The woman screamed again, and the kid pulled back, face contorted with savage joy, mouth open wide—

Case didn't try anything fancy—just rushed forward, buried both hands in the kid's hair, and pulled. The kid was a bundle of sticks, probably no heavier than she was, and the motion threw him to the ground, hard.

The kid bounced, arched his back in pain, and moaned. *He'd better stay down,* Case thought. He pushed himself partway up, then slumped back to the sticky club floor.

The kid looked up at her, wiping his mouth, confusion in his eyes. He looked at the saliva on his hand with complete bafflement.

"Hey, what's going on?" he asked.

Nearby, somebody else yelled, and a ripple of motion in the crowd caught Case's eye.

It was Quentin.

***

"What did you do, you son of a bitch?" Quentin yelled. The last few people between him and the old guy got out of the way. "What did you do?"

The old guy pressed his back to the wall and crossed his arms. "I've got no problem with you, Quentin," he said, his hoarse baritone barely audible over the crowd. "And you've got no problem with me."

"The hell I don't!" Quentin lunged forward and grabbed the guy's shirtfront with both hands, crushing him against the wall. The guy actually laughed, and a ghastly odor spilled from his face and washed over Quentin. Quentin gagged, but he didn't let go. "What did you do to that kid? What did you do to Johnny?"

The old guy put his forearms on Quentin's chest and shoved. Quentin stumbled backward a few steps, flailed his arms, and fell on his ass. He was up again a second later, both hands reaching toward the old bastard—

And somebody stopped him, putting two strong hands on his shoulders from behind. Suddenly, Case and Johnny were both there, Case standing directly between Quentin and the old guy, and Johnny off to the side, looking mortified. Quentin looked behind himself, where some guy he didn't know was holding his shoulders. He wore a terrifyingly ugly paisley shirt and a sickly, embarrassed grin.

"Jesus, that's enough," Case said. "Quentin, why don't you have a seat?" She turned to the old guy. "And you, I keep seeing your ugly goddamn face everywhere. How about you make it disappear tonight?"

The old guy stepped back toward the door and gave an insolent wave. "See you around," he said, and he left.

Johnny scowled at Quentin. "What the fuck was that all about?" Quentin started to reply, but Johnny cut him off. "You know what? I don't care. We'll hash it out later. We had a good show tonight, and I want to enjoy it. Why don't you relax?" He shook his head with weary contempt and walked away, headed toward the bar.

"Case, I—"

"It's cool, Quentin," Case said. "Johnny's right—we can talk about it later. And we *will* talk about it later."

Quentin slunk back to his table, not meeting the curious gazes of his friends there.

***

"Sorry about that," Case said after Quentin and Johnny left. "I'd have put money on me picking ten fights before Quentin got up the nerve to say something mean to somebody, but I guess you never can tell."

"Yeah," Brad said. He scratched his head. "That was . . . unexpected. Your bass player is lucky that old guy didn't beat his ass."

Case gave Brad a searching look. He was barely rattled by the whole thing, and she liked the way he'd followed her to the crazy goth kid, liked the way he'd gone straight for Quentin, trying to pull him out of the fight. Her blood was pumping from the adrenaline, and she could feel her heart beat. The night had been strange and a little ugly, but she was revved up now. The evening didn't have to be a total waste.

"Come on," she said. "Let's get out of here."

Brad raised his eyebrows. "Where are we going?"

"First, you're going to help me carry my shit out to the car. After that . . . we'll see."

That hesitant, unsure laugh again. God, he had a good laugh. "Point me at the aforementioned shit," he said.

With Brad's help, it took only two trips to get Case's stuff loaded. Once that was done, Case tracked down Erin—she wasn't about to make the mistake of disappearing without a goodbye again. Erin gave Brad an appraising look and Case a nod of approval. "See you at the office," Erin said.

"The office. Right."

It was just as Case left that a perverse impulse grabbed her. She pushed the door open and couldn't seem to stop herself from glancing back over the row of tables to where Danny sat with his wife. Danny's eyes met hers and he looked down, a miserable expression contorting his face for one fleeting second before it was gone.

Case smiled at Brad and rushed out.

CHAPTER 13

Johnny danced up the sidewalk toward his house. God, what a buzz! What a night! He had *owned* that room. He remembered the room, rapt and enthralled, during "Watching the World End," and he laughed.

"Could have heard a pin drop during that motherfucker," he said, punching the air.

He put his key in the lock of his front door, and suddenly the feeling that somebody was watching him returned so strongly it felt almost like a hand touching his neck. He spun around, dropping the keys on the ground. There was no one. Even across the street, the lights were out and the curtains closed. That did little to dispel his sudden fear; if anything, it worsened, tightening a cold hand around his heart.

"Anyone there?" he asked, and immediately wished he hadn't. His voice sounded pitiful and frightened, and if somebody was there, it wouldn't do much to deter them.

He looked around again, across the flat expanse of lawn. There wasn't so much as a thin sapling sticking up out of the ground, nowhere for anyone to hide at all. He tried to convince himself that he was reassured, but he didn't really feel better.

He picked up his keys, sure that *now*, when his back was turned and he was in an awkward position, something would leap out of—somewhere—and grab him with sharp claws, either tearing him to bloody bits on his own doorstep or dragging him off to a place he tried not to think of these days—but nothing happened.

Johnny unlocked the door and let himself in.

The stench was thick, almost unbearable, and it came rolling out of the house like a dockside fog bank, conjuring images of gutted fish and heaps of rotting chum. Johnny gagged. His eyes watered and his stomach roiled. This was the worst it had been, ever. He couldn't go in there. Oh, hell no. He turned, leaning back against the outside of the house. The door hung open, gaping idiotically.

"God, what the fuck *is* that?" Johnny asked, covering his mouth and nose. And how had it gotten so bad? There was no way he was going to believe that anything could stink like that unless something dead had gotten into the house. *Right. Like a twelve-foot catfish rotting under the floorboards. Who do you think you're kidding, Johnny?* But again, that line of thought went somewhere he wouldn't want to go even in broad daylight standing in the middle of I-35, let alone here at night, lost in the shadows between the two looming houses on the neighboring lots.

He uncovered his mouth and inhaled tentatively. It was bad out here now, and he thought that if it got much worse the neighbors might finally complain. Hopefully the house was airing out some, though. There weren't a hell of a lot of other places he could spend the night. He took another breath. It was definitely clearing some, at least outside. If he opened a few windows, maybe it would clear out inside, too.

Johnny got up and went in. The smell had thinned out, dropping from inducing instant nausea to merely causing mild dizziness. *The prescription drug from Hell.* That struck him as less funny than it should have been.

Leaving the door open, he stepped into the living room and flicked the light switch. Faces of dead rock stars—and a few living—stared at him from the wall. He imagined he could see approval in some of their faces, though others were more reserved in their approval. Björk, a holdover from the previous tenants that he'd somehow never managed to take down, looked downright baleful. The stare on her pale face gave him the shivers.

Losing your cool here, buddy. Even so, she had to go. He tore the poster off the wall, crumpled it into a ball, and let it fall on the floor where he stood. *Serve that bitch right*, he thought.

He turned and—*and Sweet Jesus Christ, there was somebody looking in the back window!* A leering face was pressed to the kitchen window, tongue outstretched and waggling at him, eyes bulging and rolling. The laughter in his throat turned to one long, wretched scream, and he fell backward, hitting his ass on the slab hard enough to slam his mouth shut. His teeth clacked together and he scrambled back, anything to get away from that horrible face in the window.

The face was gone suddenly, and Johnny heard leaves scratch against the house and a branch break as something heavy ran through the growth. It was coming around the side of the house—*and the door was wide open.* The thought jolted Johnny to his feet, and he launched himself at the door—

Too late. He hit the wood a fraction of a second too late, and the creature on the other side slammed into the door with all its weight, sending the door swinging back, smashing Johnny's face and knocking him to the floor.

He pushed himself backward again, scrabbling for purchase on the slab or the carpet or anything, scooting back toward the hall, back away from the creature, the thing. It walked like a man, and it was dressed like a man—a man who had been out for a few drinks tonight, Johnny noticed even in his terror—but that face belonged to nothing human. It bulged and leered and grimaced and twitched, lips peeling back and tongue flopping and eyes wide enough to show bloodshot white on all sides. A small gold cross on a chain around its neck glinted in the light, adding the final perverse touch that seemed to push Johnny to the brink of madness.

"Johnny!" it said, cackling, and there was wicked delight in its rolling eyes. "Oh, Johnny, Johnny, Johnny!"

Johnny sprang to his feet faster, it seemed, than he'd done anything in his life, and leaped for the door, hoping to get around it somehow.

Not fast enough. It stumbled toward him before he got past—not a pretty or graceful maneuver, but with enough energy to bounce Johnny off the wall. The cheap wall shuddered, and Johnny fell again. The thing hunched over him.

Johnny drew breath to scream, scream loud enough to piss off the neighbors, draw the cops, wake up babies a block away, and then—

A voice. A ragged whisper, right in his mind, calm and forceful, commanding this time instead of questioning.

Wait.

He froze. He could no longer tell if he even wanted to move—he knew only that he wasn't moving.

The creature bent down, seized him by his shoulders with its face twitching and gabbling inches from his own, and pulled him up.

It set him on his feet and then embraced him.

Johnny could hear the weird smacking sounds its mouth made as it jerked and slobbered, and he shuddered, trying to move his head as far away as possible.

Then it started talking, a babbling whisper right in his ear with drops and blobs of spit flying onto Johnny's neck, his ear, in his hair.

"Oh, Johnny Johnny, oh, my brother, oh yes, you called and I heard you, you were far but my ears, yes, my ears are keen, you called and I came, I came, I will come again soon, we will *all* come again soon, all of us all of us for you, Johnny."

The babbling, crazed creature pulled back, holding Johnny's shoulders again for all the world like an aunt about to tell him how big he'd gotten. It had bitten its tongue in its contortions, and now blood as well as spit spattered Johnny's face as it gibbered.

It grinned impossibly wide, showing an unholy number of even, white teeth, and then its eyes rolled up in its head and it collapsed.

Johnny stepped back as it hit the floor. With its face relaxed by unconsciousness, Johnny could see now that it really *was* just a man. Just a man with gelled hair and a couple of days' worth of stubble . . . and small ragged tears at the corners of his mouth with smears of fresh blood around them, from opening his mouth wider than it was ever meant to go.

The man moaned and rubbed his eyes. He seemed perfectly human now, and it occurred to Johnny that he had a strange man, certainly hurt and possibly hurt badly, on his living-room floor. He stared, unsure of what to do. Should he call the cops? An ambulance?

No, the voice whispered. *All will be fine. Simply wait.*

Again, the voice was calm and reassuring, and Johnny felt that it knew the right way to proceed. But what was going on? Had he finally snapped? Why was he getting private messages in his head?

"What are you?" he asked.

He felt rather than heard some vast, dark merriment, and then the voice:

Why don't you call me Johnny?

***

Case walked up the stairs to her second-floor apartment with Brad following closely behind.

Action, she thought. *No thinking.*

She stopped outside her door, put her guitar case down, and got out her keys. She turned the key in the lock.

No thinking. Just doing. There had been a time in her life—most of it, really—when that was all she did. She had just acted. She'd gotten in a lot of trouble and fucked a lot of people over, but she had never felt any remorse over it. People made their choices, and if they didn't always deserve what they got, they usually came close enough. She'd moved on to the next thing, and so had they.

That sort of thing piles up after a while, though. Yeah. You couldn't live like that forever. Eventually you had to stop, stay put, and live with your mistakes, or at least you did if you were serious about being a musician. It was tough to get gigs when you changed towns every eight or ten months.

She pushed the door open. She could feel Brad's presence, a faint warmth just behind her.

No thinking, she reminded herself. *Not now.* All that thinking, all that *consideration* wasn't doing her any favors lately. Or maybe it was, but the favors were the slow kind—goodwill built up over months rather than wiped out with careless words and anger before it could get started, friendship that required more patience than she'd ever demanded of herself outside practice. If there was gratification to be had from all this effort and patience, it sure as hell wasn't the instant kind.

No. And there's a time for instant gratification. That would be right now*, in case you weren't paying attention.* She could feel—or imagined she could feel—Brad's breath tickling her neck, and she wondered how his hands would feel on her skin.

Case picked up her guitar case and went in.

The place was a mess, but she didn't care, and she doubted he would either. She passed the light switch in the kitchen—too bright, too glaring—and turned on a lamp instead. Then she slid the guitar case behind her beat-up secondhand sofa and turned around to face Brad, bringing her eyes up to meet his directly. He might have been hesitant before, but he didn't flinch now. He stared right back, hungry. His lips—full, almost swollen-looking—were parted ever so slightly, and his breath came rapidly. Case felt suddenly warm.

No thinking.

She shrugged off her jacket—an old jean jacket, since Johnny had taken custody of her leather one—and let it drop to the floor. She raised her eyebrows in a silent question or maybe a challenge, and then she slouched back against the wall and waited.

He needed no further invitation. A moment later, he stood in front of her, leaning down as she tilted her head up—and he stopped. He hesitated, but this wasn't his earlier uncertainty. This was deliberate. He stopped, close enough that now she could feel his breath, those swollen, exquisite lips just waiting . . . waiting . . .

She let him wait. His breathing grew louder, and his shoulders trembled when he let a breath out. Two breaths. Three. He put his hands on her waist, and now she stopped breathing. She had expected soft, office-boy hands, but his fingers were hard and callused and rough against her skin, deliciously, intoxicatingly so, and she gasped as he slid them up just under the hem of her shirt.

She leaned in, brushed her lips against his so lightly that it was more of a faint electricity than a touch at all. *Now* he moved toward her, but she pulled back from the kiss even as she pushed her hips against his body. A low moan, warm and musical, escaped his throat. She bit her lip.

Then his hands were moving again, pushing her shirt up below her breasts, tracing lines on her body that set fire to her nerve endings and raised goose bumps all the way down to her feet.

She grabbed his shirt in both fists (and had it been an ugly shirt? could she even remember?) and pulled him to her, and now, finally, at last, he brought his mouth down to hers. He was teasing, then insistent, then teasing again, and now it was her turn to make a noise.

She tore his shirt open. Buttons went flying, bouncing off the carpet, skittering across the kitchen linoleum. He laughed and helped her pull her own shirt off, then pivoted neatly, sitting on the arm of the couch and pulling her after him. She stood in front of him as he nuzzled and gently bit the skin of her neck. A mischievous impulse seized her, and she put her hands on his shoulders to shove him backward onto the couch—

And then, for no good reason she could see, an image occurred to her. Danny, meeting her eyes as she left the bar, then downcast and miserable as she turned away.

It was as though somebody had switched her off. All the electricity drained away, faded just like it did when she turned off her amplifier, with a little sound that died away so quickly you weren't sure you'd really heard it. Her body stiffened. She saw Brad in front of her, half dressed and somehow ridiculous now, his eyes half lidded, his lips pursed and mouth open.

"What?" he asked, and the ridiculous expression was gone, replaced by one of confusion and anxiety. "What did I do?"

NO THINKING! part of her screeched. *Push him down on the couch and LET'S GET ON WITH THIS!* But it was no good. Sex had lost all its appeal all of a sudden, and it wasn't coming back.

Case snatched her shirt up off the floor. "You didn't do anything," she said, busying herself with her shirt so as not to look at him. "You were great."

His brow furrowed, eyebrows pressed together. "I'm always happy to hear that, but usually it comes later in the evening." He tried on a grin. "If at all."

"It's not you, it's me. Really. This may be the only time you'll ever hear that from somebody who really means it."

He sighed. It was a lost sound, and maybe a little resentful. She could hardly blame him. "How reassuring," he said. "So I should probably go, huh?"

"Yeah."

He stood up.

"Look, I'm sorry," Case said. "This is . . . It's just been a fucked-up night, you know?"

He shrugged. "It happens." He put his hands in his pockets and stood awkwardly for a moment. "So I'm going to leave a card," he said. "If you feel like it, call me."

"You still want me for the session?" she asked, surprised.

"Yeah." He took a couple of steps toward the door. "And, you know—I'd like to see you again. Maybe we'll go a little slower next time."

"That would be good," she said. The words sounded harsh. She softened her tone. "I mean, I'd like that."

"All right. See you later."

"Later."

He left.

Case lay down on the couch and stared at the ceiling. *No thinking? Ha.* She had a feeling she was going to be doing a lot of thinking that night. A whole lot.

***

Danny came back to the table after a brief conversation with the manager, the evening's take in his pocket. Amazingly, the manager seemed willing to talk about future booking—must have been a good headcount, Danny thought, because three-quarters of the band had nearly been involved in some kind of brawl that Danny had half-observed from across the room.

"You ready to go?" he asked Gina. She nodded vigorously. He took her hand and navigated her through the sea of people to get to the door.

Once outside, Danny tried to get a read on Gina's emotions. Her face was strained and tired, the way it had been the last couple of times she'd come to a show.

"Headache?" he asked.

She shrugged. "Not bad. The earplugs helped."

"Oh. Good." They walked past a couple of other clubs. Dance music thumped in one of them, making the windows vibrate and the reflections shiver. He led Gina around a puddle of yellow vomit on the sidewalk, still studying her face for some reaction. He saw nothing besides slight disgust at the puke on the ground, but then even that was gone.

It took only a few minutes to get to her car, but it felt much longer. Finally, Danny had to ask, if only to get something from her, some indication of how she felt about . . . anything.

"So. What did you think?"

Now she looked at him. She looked calm in the darkness, but then the headlights of a passing car swept across her face, and Danny's heart clenched like a fist. Her face wasn't calm—it was frozen. Deliberately still. Who knew what currents pushed and pulled beneath that surface?

Glass smashed somewhere, and a man started shouting.

"Do I need to be worried?" she asked him, face still unreadable. Danny knew she wasn't talking about the noise, or about the fight that had nearly gone down earlier.

"About what?" he said. He tried for casual, but his voice was higher than normal and reedy.

She only looked at him, face still impassive. Frozen or maybe chipped out of stone.

"No," Danny said. "You don't have to worry. There's nothing to worry about."

"See you at home," she said, and she got in the car.

Danny stood in the dark lot and watched her drive away.

CHAPTER 14

Johnny pounded the stapler with his fist and got a nice, satisfying *chunk!* out of it. It was two days since the last show, more than three weeks before the next, and he knew it was mostly a waste of time to put up flyers this soon, but it gave him something to do while he wandered up and down Commerce Street, searching. Waiting.

Whatcha waiting for, John? the voice in his head asked.

"Please be quiet, Johnny," he told it. "I don't feel well." It insisted that he call it Johnny, for whatever reason. He'd messed with it a couple of times since it had announced itself, addressing it first as Tony and then later as Captain Howdy, and each time it had sulked for hours. If sulking had simply meant that it shut up and left him in peace, that would have been okay, but instead it had felt like there was a pressurized thundercloud in his head, threatening to storm and rage. He tried to avoid pissing it off now.

Negotiating a truce with the voice in his head. *I'm cracking up,* he thought. It didn't *feel* like he was cracking up, though. *Maybe that's how it is for everyone who cracks up, did you ever think of that?* Who the hell knew? And, anyway, he couldn't do anything about it.

Come on, John, it said. *What are we doing here?*

Johnny sighed. Best to just humor the damn thing. "We're looking for Douglas." He reached another bulletin post, covered in the tattered remains of half a hundred posters, and came around it, out of the shadow to where the streetlight shone. He tacked another flyer up.

In his head, "Johnny" chuckled. *Douglas. Is that what he's calling himself now? Cute. What do you need him for?*

Johnny looked down the street. This part of town was dead on a Monday night, and it was a good thing, too. The last thing he wanted was for random strangers to see the deranged man running around downtown with a stapler, talking to himself. It was a good thing, but not a comforting one. Johnny didn't like this area on an off-night. It was partly that he felt like a target for a mugging or a festive, unmotivated drive-by shooting, but that wasn't all. Seeing this place without the crowds and the noise, the neon in the windows and the thump of bass from every third building, was like seeing the back of a stage set. No, it was worse than that, more of a . . . a transgression. It was like seeing your mother naked—you knew it had to exist in this state sometimes, but witnessing it crossed some boundary that shouldn't be crossed.

He slammed home another couple of staples. "I'm hoping he can tell me about *you.* Maybe he can tell me if I'm losing my mind."

He's a has-been. A miserable old failure, trying to make his amends before the end. Talk to him if you want, but he's got nothing for you.

"Great."

Anything I can help you with?

"You can tell me what the fuck you are." Johnny crossed the street, heading through an alley over to Elm. Even the graffiti looked bored tonight.

I told you. Think of me as your guardian angel.

"Right." They'd covered this ground a few times, and so far "Johnny" had claimed to be his guardian angel, the Ghost of Christmas Past, the voice of God, and even his conscience. That last was sort of bleakly funny, considering, but Johnny didn't laugh. He didn't want to give the voice the satisfaction, particularly considering that its sense of humor worked in only one direction.

Another corner, another couple of flyers tacked up at haphazard angles. He heard the footsteps as he stapled the last corner in place, and he turned.

Douglas stood there in his faded jeans and a white shirt unbuttoned at the throat. He squinted in the streetlight.

"Hey, Johnny," he whispered. "Sounded good the other night."

"Thanks," Johnny said. His questions had gone from his head, and he stood stupidly, staring at the old man.

Ask him about the whore, the voice said. *Ask him about the heroin—see how he likes that one!*

"Shut up," Johnny said. "Jesus."

Douglas gave him a half-grin, but the swagger had gone out of his face, replaced by something like melancholy. "You hear him, huh?"

"Loud and clear." Johnny stuck his finger in his ear as if to clear it. "You knew about this."

A nod.

Johnny wasn't sure whether to be relieved or not. At least he wasn't losing his mind. "What—what the fuck is it?"

Transmissions from Jupiter! the goddamn thing yelled inside his head, loud enough that he flinched.

"Does it matter, Johnny?"

"Huh?"

Douglas walked around Johnny, putting his back to the light. Dark hair fell over half his face. "It's your voice, Johnny. The one that does the singing."

"I didn't sign up for this," Johnny protested.

"No?" Douglas's voice was the sound of bricks sliding together. "Did you check the fine print? How about we get out a copy of the contract and have a look?"

"There is no contract. You know that." *You get what you pay for doesn't mean a damn thing,* Johnny thought, the words of the song dragged up from wherever he'd shut them away. He shivered.

"Ah. Well, near as I can tell, you got everything you wanted out of the deal, so I don't know what you're bitching about."

The voice in Johnny's head laughed. *I guess he told you, huh John? Not bad for an old fucking FAILURE!*

"I didn't get everything I wanted. Do I look famous to you?"

Douglas's eyes, black and depthless in the shadows, never wavered from Johnny's. "Not yet," he said, and there was that faint melancholy again, "but give it time. You will be."

You think he might cry? the voice asked. *I think he might cry.*

"Yeah, sure. Okay. But what about the crazy fucker that followed me home the other night?"

"Get used to crazy," Douglas said. "It's all part of the fame trip. That'll just keep getting worse." He stepped forward and, to Johnny's surprise, put his hands on Johnny's shoulders. He leaned in close. "They'll love you, Johnny, and they'll do anything for you—as long as you keep giving them what they want. Don't ever forget that."

He pulled his hands away with jerk, holding his palms open, and then he walked away.

"Hey!" Johnny said. "What about this goddamn thing in my head? What *is* it? Some kind of—of demon? What?"

"Does it matter, Johnny?" Douglas said without turning around, and the words were so faint they barely reached Johnny's ears. "Does it even matter, as long as you get what you want?"

Johnny stopped in midstep, ready to follow Douglas and harangue the answers out of him if necessary, but the question drew him up short. Did it matter? Really?

He wasn't sure.

He stood on Elm Street at the mouth of some wretched, trash-strewn alley and watched Douglas walk away.

That was terrifically productive, "Johnny" said. *Shall we put up some more flyers?*

***

The next evening, Case walked into the practice room and slammed the door behind her. She knew she wore a mean scowl on her face, but she didn't have the energy to pretend to be in even a neutral mood, let alone cheery. Sleep had been long in coming the past couple of nights, thanks to Danny and that stupidity with Brad. *It's not Danny's fault you're a fucking idiot,* she reminded herself. *He went home with his wife, and do you suppose he declined to put it to her because he was mooning over you?* Of course not. That would be stupid.

It didn't matter, though. It wasn't Danny's fault, no, but he wasn't exactly blameless, either. As long as she was pissed at herself, Danny was going to get the overflow.

Getting her head straight, though, seemed to be taking an inordinate number of sleepless hours.

Danny and Johnny hadn't arrived yet, which was just as well. Quentin was there, though, sitting on his amplifier, bass laid flat across his lap. His eyes were pointed at the floor, and his hands were draped over his instrument as if he had no real intention of playing.

"You okay?" Case asked, stifling a yawn.

He chewed his bottom lip. "I guess."

She dredged up half a smile from somewhere. "I gotta admit, you surprised the hell out of me when you went after that guy the other night. I didn't think you had it in you."

Quentin shrugged.

"That guy was older than dirt, but he looked tough. You're lucky you didn't get your head kicked in."

"Yeah." He scratched at a smudge on his fretboard, then finally looked up at Case. "That guy is bad news. I don't like the way he hangs around Johnny, and I don't like the way Johnny's been acting since he started hanging around."

"It's a free country."

"What about that kid, the one who was wasted out of his mind that night, staggering all over the place?"

Case took her time answering. She plugged in her amp and switched it on to warm up, then got out her guitar. The truth was, she remembered that guy a little too well. That eerie gaze, the crafty grin, and most of all the way he'd tried to bite that woman, had stuck with her. That last image in particular had been popping up from her subconscious for the last couple of days like an evil jack-in-the-box. "I don't know anything about him."

"Well, the old guy was looking for him before things got weird. He spent half the night searching the crowd, and you should have seen him smile when he saw that poor kid. He was going over to meet him when you came over."

"You think he's a dealer?" That seemed possible. Hadn't she wondered if the kid was wasted on something at the time?

"Yeah. Or something." Quentin made a fist, then relaxed his hand. "All I know is, Johnny's my friend. Yeah, he's a dick sometimes—more lately—but I've been playing with him for over a year. One of my uncles got hooked on meth, and I don't want Johnny to get caught up in anything like that."

"How'd you get your uncle clean?"

Quentin stared at her, his eyes glassy. "He's fucking dead."

Case plugged in her guitar. "I'll keep an eye out. This is a good band, and the last thing I want is for Johnny to do a Sid Vicious on us."

"You're all heart," Quentin mumbled, just as the door swung open and Danny and Johnny walked in.

***

Gina was on the couch when Danny got home, absorbed as usual in a legal brief. She didn't look up when he came in. Danny wasn't surprised. Ever since the show, she had barely spoken to him. She hadn't seemed angry, exactly, only distant. *Very* distant. Danny felt guilty just being in the same room with her.

For what? I didn't do *anything.* Except he sort of had. Wasn't there a Bible verse about that? *He who looks at a woman with lust in his heart has already committed adultery,* or something equally uplifting and forgiving of human frailty.

"Good night," he said, walking toward the hall. It was late, he was tired, and waiting around for Gina to pay attention to him—happy, sad, angry, or otherwise—was stupid, and it would only make him feel worse.

"Danny, can you come sit with me for a minute?"

He stopped. He hadn't expected a reply at all, and now she was looking up at him, eyes inscrutable behind her glasses, beckoning him over. Perhaps more amazing than that, the folder and stack of paper she'd been holding was lying on the floor, almost out of arm's reach.

Danny was seized with same feeling he got whenever the phone rang in the middle of the night. *Something is bad here. This is not normal. Whatever comes next, I don't want to hear it.*

He walked over with small, hesitant steps and sat down on the opposite end of the couch. A memory sparked in his mind of the interminable afternoon they'd spent shopping for this damn thing, combing every furniture store in Dallas. Gina wasn't particular about much, but she had taken to furniture shopping like a holy calling. He remembered when she had, at long last, finally decreed that this couch—yea, verily, this very couch!—was the one that would grace their home. He had wrapped his arms around her and collapsed onto it with her right in the middle of the store while the sales guy had stood there with a dry smile and impatience reflecting from his darting eyes.

"How was practice?" Gina asked.

"It was okay," he answered warily.

Gina sucked in her lips and looked at her hands. Silence settled in between them like it had packed a lunch and was planning to stay awhile. The ice maker in the kitchen spat out another cube with a clunking noise. *Am I supposed to say something?* Danny wondered. If so, he had no idea what. This was the apotheosis of minefield conversations, and he didn't dare put a foot in it.

"This is hard for me," Gina said, and Danny's heart rate doubled instantly. "Did you have a good time?" she asked, sincerely, and the words and tone were so out of place that Danny actually heard her say *I want a divorce* before his mind rewound and played her statement back.

"Wha—?"

She moved to the middle of the couch to be closer to him. "I know your music is important to you. I don't understand it, and I know I haven't been all that supportive. But if it's that important to you, I want to try to understand better."

"Gina, I . . . Where is this coming from?"

"You leave two or three nights a week and go hang out in a little room with an attractive woman—"

"And two other guys."

"And two other guys," she conceded. "But please don't tell me you're not attracted to her."

Danny picked at the seam on his jeans.

She touched his face, tilting his head up until his eyes met hers. "I trust you, Daniel. I don't think you're going to do anything to hurt me."

He didn't trust himself to speak. Already, his eyes were filling with wetness, and his throat felt as if an iron bar were lodged in it.

Gina brushed his cheek with the backs of her fingers and smiled sadly. "But I don't feel that good about this. I don't want to turn into the nag who won't let you leave the house without being suspicious, and I don't want to put you in a spot where you have to choose your brother and your music or me." Her voice trembled, and now Danny saw moisture in her eyes as well. "So, please. Help me feel better about this. Tell me what it is about playing music that you love so much. Tell me why you keep going back, why you spend so much time on this. Tell me anything that makes me feel like you're there for music, and not for *her*."

For once, a thousand replies leaped to Danny's mind, but as the first tear slipped free from behind Gina's glasses, he silenced them all and reached for her.

"I love you," he said, holding her tight against him. She cried silently, with no sobbing, no sound at all, and the wetness where her skin touched his neck started him crying, too. He held her tighter. After a few minutes, when his own tears slowed, he pulled away just far enough to kiss her.

***

Afterward, in bed, he talked. It seemed to him he had nothing earthshaking to say, or even particularly interesting, but as he warmed to the conversation, it struck him as odd that they'd never talked about this before. Had he just assumed for all this time that she didn't care? He thought that was part of it, maybe, but as he spoke he realized that mostly he'd been afraid. Afraid she wouldn't understand at all, afraid she'd question his motives or think him childish.

"This isn't about some kind of rock-star fantasy for me," he said, hoping she'd believe him. "I think that's part of Johnny's thing, but I've been a grown-up for too long. For me it's that moment when everything clicks—when you're making something amazing with a group of people that you couldn't have made by yourself." He pushed back the covers and propped himself up on one elbow. "Even if we never played another show, I'd still want to make noise in that ridiculous little practice room with a bunch of talented musicians. Music means that much to me."

Gina listened quietly and watched him with wide, curious eyes. Had he thought this would be boring for her? Why? He realized that he wasn't bored when she was talking about her cases or the latest aggravating court decision, even though that wasn't his world any more than music was hers.

Danny talked for a long time.

CHAPTER 15

The stage again, the first song of the night, two bars in and Case already had that performance high going full blast. God, nothing was better than this. Erin had outdone herself, and word-of-mouth was starting to pick up, and the result was that there were a *lot* of people in this little club. Some of them were people Case was starting to recognize from past shows, pushing to the front, getting close to the stage—always crowding more thickly stage right. Not all of them were there to hear Ragman, though Case thought most of them were.

Johnny came in, and he sounded *good*. Case was again amazed at how far he'd come in such a short time, and she grinned. Danny was thrashing away with a similar smile on his face, right in the pocket, nailing it. Only Quentin seemed immune to the energy onstage—he was playing his parts okay, but he scanned the crowd, searching for something the way he always did lately. Looking for that old dude, probably; maybe he was spoiling for another fight.

They played through the set to ever-greater cheers from the audience, but as the set neared its close, a formless dread built up around Case, like a static charge. There was something about this part of the set she didn't like, though she couldn't really remember why. Sure, they always did one of the slower numbers about now, and those weren't her favorites because they brought down the energy so much, but that wasn't enough to explain the prickles of gooseflesh that had broken out on the back of her neck, her arms, her thighs, or the slow beads of cold sweat that trickled into her eyes.

She caught a glimpse of Quentin, and he'd gone pale. She followed his eyes—and there was that old fucker in the audience, circulating, whispering in ears, pausing to look in one person's eyes for an unseemly long time.

They moved on to the next song, the slow number Johnny liked so much. Half a dozen people—regulars, Case thought—leaned in at the front of the stage, gazing raptly up at Johnny. One reached out toward him, hand scrabbling on the stage inches from Johnny's foot.

The sound guy dimmed the lights and brought a spotlight up on Johnny as the intro figure closed. Johnny moved up to the mic.

"The sun slides from his sky . . ."

One of the stage lights flared briefly and burned out, and Case jumped. It was really dark now, except where Johnny burned white in the spotlight. Even the bar lights had dimmed, and Case could see nothing of the crowd other than a few glimmering eyes and reflections off glasses. The hand that clawed and scrabbled for Johnny onstage looked almost disembodied, as if it had been severed by the darkness.

Where's that old guy? Case thought, suddenly unnerved by the fact that she couldn't see him anymore. *Where did he go?*

She missed the fingering for the next chord, eliciting a wooden thud from her guitar, and scowled. *Just fucking play the song, okay?*

The song went on and on, and even though it wasn't a loud song, Case couldn't hear anything from the crowd. Not the usual murmuring of a large group of people, not a single shout. It felt like the world had disappeared outside the stage. She edged farther away from Johnny's spotlight, trying to get her eyes to adjust so she could see *something* out there.

There was a movement in the crowd, a ripple as somebody pushed through the bodies. Even that didn't get a response that Case could hear. The vague shape—she thought it was a man, though she couldn't be sure—pushed forward, approaching the stage.

The song reached the final verse, and Johnny's voice rose in an eerie, wavering crescendo that made Case's skin creep.

"Hey, fuck this!" the guy in the crowd shouted, his voice cracking with hysteria. There was a swift motion, a blur through the darkness, and then a beer bottle appeared in the spotlight, spinning end-over-end toward Johnny's head.

Johnny's mouth was open wide as he belted out the last chorus, and in her mind's eye Case could already see the bottle hit, smashing through his teeth, exploding, and sending shards of glass into his tongue, his palate, his throat. She had no time to scream a warning, barely time to inhale—

And the bottle was spinning past, missing Johnny's head by a hairsbreadth before sailing over Danny and shattering against the back wall.

Johnny didn't even blink.

The song ended and the lights came up, and the usual solemn ovation that followed that particular song broke over them. Four people in the front, including the one who'd been reaching for Johnny, turned, watching avidly as the bouncer grabbed the bottle thrower by the arm and dragged him out. One of them pointed at the man and smiled a crooked, awful smile that seemed horribly out of place on her pretty face.

Johnny was staring at Case.

"You all right?" she asked him.

"Huh? Yeah, fine. Start the song already, will you?"

She checked the set list, tuned up her E string, and began the last song of the evening.

***

"Wow!" Erin shouted. "You were amazing!" She gave Johnny a giant hug as Case stood by and watched, conflicted. This was Johnny's moment, and she ought to be happy for him . . . but the room still didn't feel right.

A hand touched her shoulder. "Looks like your boy really turned it up a notch since last time I saw him."

"Brad! You came!" Case found a smile now, and it even felt genuine. She'd done the session work for his band just the week before, and he had been so professional about it that she'd nearly given up on any personal interest. To be sure, though, his professionalism had helped. She hadn't had any experience in a real studio before, and it had turned out to be surprisingly nerve-racking. The sense that every note was under intense scrutiny had been pervasive and distracting, and the environment, despite its funky decor, oddly sterile. She had supposed that came from playing with recorded tracks instead of the push-pull action and reaction of a live band, but whatever the cause, it had been tough at first. Once she'd gotten the hang of it, though, she had laid down some tracks that got an appreciative nod from the engineer and made the band happy besides. She'd thought there was a good chance that would be the last she'd see of Brad, but now here he was.

"Come on," she said. "I'll buy you a drink."

"Lady, are you tryin' to get me all liquored up? Ain't gonna happen. Besides, you're working tonight—it's on me."

"Sold."

They made their way to the bar. Case did her best to be polite to the fans that wanted a word, and she even talked shop briefly with a couple of admiring guitarists ("How did you get your guitar to sound like bagpipes in that one song?" one of them asked. Baffled and laughing, she answered, "I don't know, but if you figure it out, tell me so I can make sure I never do it again!"). She wasn't entirely comfortable with the attention offstage yet, but it was becoming tolerable.

It would be a great night if she could just shake that ugly feeling from the stage. Already, the specifics were hard to recall, and all she could remember was a feeling of dread, and then the bottle thrower.

Case and Brad edged in next to the bar and ordered a couple of drinks.

"Hey," Brad said, shouting over the crowd, "where the hell did Johnny learn to sing like that?"

"Just like getting to Carnegie Hall," Case said uncomfortably. "Practice, man, practice."

"I gotta talk to his voice teacher. That slow tune was amazing. Up until that jackass threw something at him, I think everybody in the crowd was holding their breath. It was *intense*."

Case took a drink.

"Seriously," Brad continued. "He puts this weird excitement into this song about the end of the world, but it's kind of sad, too, and it's creepy as—"

"You want to get something to eat?" Case asked. The room was too loud already, and from the pointy guitars of the band that was setting up now, it looked like there was going to be some awful metal blasting real soon.

"Yeah, all right," Brad said. "Let's get outta here."

CHAPTER 16

Alan kicked angrily at a newspaper on the sidewalk. "That was some bullshit!" he said to no one in particular. A couple of clubgoers gave him the hairy eyeball and crossed the street. "Fuckers!" he shouted, whether at them or at the muscled-up security meatheads who'd thrown him out of the club he wasn't sure.

What the hell had happened in there? He'd heard of Ragman around town—it was impossible to miss the flyers, if you spent any time down here—but never seen them before. He and his buddies had come down to catch the Judas One Thirteen show and walked in on the last half of the Ragman set. It was kinda cool, up until the end—not as heavy as his usual thing, but they rocked all right, and the chick playing guitar was hot.

Then—then what? He pressed his palms to his temples as if he could squeeze the memory out of his head. Things got bad. Everybody was all "oooh, aahh," but that was some sick shit even by his standards, and he was a guy who liked his album covers with exploding heads and eyeballs and shit. The singer's voice had done—something. It had gone weird, and dark somehow, or something. It was bad, that was all Alan could remember, like the guy was fucking with his head on purpose. That he couldn't remember exactly what had happened was all the proof he needed.

By his reckoning, it had taken him way too long to decide to put a stop to it.

"Too bad I fuckin' missed," he said. The only thing that sucked was that his friends had pretty much just waved goodbye to him as he was dragged out. "See you later, Alan," Deke had said. "We're gonna stay and watch the show." Asshole.

Alan walked to the end of the street, past the lights and the occasional line of people. He heard the thump and buzz of a car with an oversized stereo a street down, and over that, a woman's laughter. More laughter after that, from behind him, and there was an eerie, familiar quality to it.

Alan turned around.

There were four of them, skinny rocker kids from the club. The laughing woman was, he was pretty sure, the woman who'd pointed at him on his way out, like she was marking him. She wasn't much more than a girl, really, and an underfed one at that, and the three bony punks she was with didn't look like much, either.

"What the fuck do you want?" Alan asked.

She giggled, and the other three stood smirking to either side. Two of them started to come closer, flanking him.

"Oh, is that it?" Alan asked. "I didn't like your favorite band, so now you think you're gonna fuck me up? Give me a break." They were nuts if they thought that would fly. He was off the main strip, sure, but lights blazed and people shouted only a block or so away. Even if they got a few lucky shots in, somebody would call the cops or something.

And, really, Alan was bigger than any two of them put together. Who were they kidding?

Unless one of them has a knife or something, he thought uneasily. If they did, though, they weren't going for it. Both of 'em had their hands in full view down at their sides, gangling around. They stumbled, too—probably drunk.

The kid on his left moved into the light, and Alan took an involuntary step away from him. The kid's cheeks twitched, and his eyes blinked in a strange, erratic pattern.

Is he fucked up on something? Alan didn't care anymore—it was time to go. He turned to run and stumbled himself, and before he could take one more step, they were on him. One grabbed his belt and hauled on it, dragging Alan to the side, and another lunged for his T-shirt, fingers catching the neck and tearing it open.

Alan reeled, then shoved the kid pulling on his shirt. The kid staggered back, stepped off the curb, and fell flat on his back. Alan thought he heard something crack, but he didn't have time to think about it. A third guy jumped on him. Alan pushed the guy away, but he sprang back like some kind of hyperactive monkey, small but determined. Alan pulled back his fist—and, goddammit! The kid who'd been hanging on his belt let go and grabbed Alan's arm with both hands. He wasn't strong, but he was heavy enough, and Alan's blow never came.

"What the—"

The girl lunged at him then. He tried to swat her away, but suddenly that other fucker was there, and Alan's left arm was all tangled up, too.

"I'm hungry," the girl said, and the words had barely registered in Alan's brain when he felt a searing pain in his right biceps.

She was biting him, and not a little. Her mouth was open wide, teeth buried deep in his flesh, and she was still pushing, still biting.

WHAT THE FUCK??

Now she was *burrowing*, digging and tearing, and finally, Alan had the presence of mind to scream.

"Help! Help!" He pushed and screamed and flailed around with his left arm, pulling it loose from the psycho cannibal maniac who'd been clinging to it at last, and using it to smash a fist into the other psycho cannibal maniac who was eating his goddamn arm. He hit her in the head, and she pulled away, taking a huge chunk of Alan's flesh with her.

Blood poured down Alan's arm, down his side, soaking the remains of his shirt, and he lurched, just trying to get somewhere, anywhere away.

"HELP!" he yelled.

***

Case stepped out of the bar with Brad close behind, and the sound of screams coming from down the block hit her like a slap. A jolt of adrenaline hit her bloodstream.

"Call the cops," she said, and she started running without waiting for Brad's reply.

A crowd was already drifting in the direction of the screams, but not in any particular hurry—more like a clot of idle rubberneckers approaching a car accident. Case pushed through, shoving and shouting, and that seemed to galvanize a few of them into motion.

She slowed down as she reached the end of the block. There was nobody in the street ahead of her, though the last building cast a long, black shadow. Anything could have hidden in there.

Half a dozen of the braver souls from the crowd trailed her. "Anybody hear shots?" she asked. "Anything?"

She got a chorus of muttered "no"s in response, which at least lowered the chance that she was about to walk around the corner and get her head blown off. It was reassuring to have a handful of people with her. The only time she'd ever heard screams like that had been when somebody got knifed in a bar she shouldn't have been in, and this had all the hallmarks of the same kind of bad scene.

A strange snuffling, shuffling sound from the darkness ahead reached her ears, and she slowed. "Hello?" she said. "Anybody there?" No answer, but the sound got louder as she approached. She checked to her right and left and saw fear on the faces there—but nobody was backing away. Counting herself, there were eight people, which seemed like good odds.

"Do you need help?" she asked, and she turned the corner.

It took precious seconds for her eyes to adjust, but she got a sense of bodies, three or four, huddled and squirming on the ground around a limp mass.

"What the hell is going on here?" she asked.

Two of them turned. She saw eyes, and mouths ringed with a dark substance, and just as she began to understand that it was blood, blood smeared over their faces and dripping off their chins, one of them—a young woman, Case thought—bolted.

Case didn't think—she took off after the woman. The race wasn't even close. The woman tripped over her own feet and fell, and Case caught up a second later as she tried to get to her feet.

Case wasn't taking any chances. She hauled off and kicked the woman in the gut before she could stand. There was a grunt and a wheeze, and the woman fell gasping back to the pavement.

Behind her, the crowd she'd brought over had subdued another three blood-streaked crazies. She was just about to congratulate herself when the cops rolled up, illuminating the back side of the building with a spotlight.

The bloody mess of flesh lying in the corner was barely recognizable as a human being, but Case saw a pair of jeans, dark with wetness, and the sole of a black boot sticking out of the gore.

She looked away. Nearby, a couple of people fainted.

***

"Are you all right?" Danny asked. It was maybe the fortieth time somebody had asked her that in the last couple of hours, and maybe the tenth time Danny himself had done so.

"Yeah," Case said, pushing her coffee away. The six of them—Brad, Erin, and the four members of Ragman—sat crowded around a small table at an all-night diner. The coffee was terrible and Case felt like she might never be hungry again, but the glare of cheap fluorescent lightbulbs had never seemed so inviting, and she was in no hurry to leave.

"I'm not," Brad said, raising his hand. That got a few weak smiles. The police had quickly cordoned off the area and tried to disperse the crowd, but Brad had gotten there in time to see the human wreckage in the corner, and Case didn't figure he'd forget that any time soon. She knew she wouldn't.

She'd never been so glad to see cops. They'd taken the woman she'd been standing on from her, which would have been plenty to earn each of them a gold star right there. The woman freaked Case right out, twitching and babbling, the blood around her mouth a bright red smear in the spotlight, and Case was only too glad to get away from her.

After that, there was a short round of questioning, and Case had been relieved to find she was under no suspicion whatsoever. There had been plenty of witnesses to her actions, the cop said, and he only wanted to know what she'd seen.

"What was wrong with those people?" Case had asked him. "Were they on something?"

The cop tapped his pen against his notebook. "Yeah, probably. We're having blood and urine tests done, but I've never seen anybody act anything like that unless they were flying high on something."

"Like what? What could make a person do *that?*"

"PCP, maybe, or a bad trip on some kind of hallucinogen. Any number of things." He didn't sound very convincing, though, and he looked down at his notebook while he said it.

The others had undergone only cursory questioning, since most of them weren't there when Case found the body. Afterward, nobody had wanted to go home yet, and they'd found their way here.

"It's that fucking guy," Quentin said, interrupting Case's thoughts. "Johnny's friend, the old dude."

"He's not my friend," Johnny said. "But I don't think he had anything to do with that shit."

"I saw him talking to those kids during the show," Quentin said. He wiped sweat from his forehead.

"So? Fuck, I think I talked to them before we started playing. Does that mean I had something to do with it, too?"

"I think you might have gotten really lucky tonight, Johnny," Case said.

Johnny looked at her, eyes even wider than normal. "What do you mean?"

"I saw those kids, too—right up front. One of them was trying to touch you during the set. It's a good thing they didn't come after you."

Brad cut in before Johnny could reply. "I don't think they would have," he said softly.

"Why not?" Case asked. "They were crazy—there's no telling what they would do."

Brad put his elbows on the table and leaned in toward her. He looked from Johnny to Case and back. "I heard some of the guys in the club talking. The guy who got killed—he was the one who threw the bottle."

"So you're saying what?" Johnny asked, his voice rising in pitch. "Those four psychos did this on my account? This is somehow my fault?"

"What? Jesus, no. I was just saying you probably weren't in any danger."

Johnny sat back in his chair. "Oh," he said, mollified, but his glance darted around the table, and he didn't look at Brad. "Well, they got the killers in custody now. We won't have to worry about that shit anymore."

"Unless it *is* the old guy," Quentin said.

Johnny fixed a cold glare on him. "Quentin. Shut the fuck up."

CHAPTER 17

Johnny woke the next morning sweaty and shaking. It was bad dreams nonstop lately, and last night's insanity hadn't helped that any. He wondered if he'd ever get a good night's sleep again after that.

There was a noise from the other side of the room, and Johnny started as his guests sat up. Another show, another unwelcome visitor afterward—and this time there had been two of them waiting by his front door when he got home.

"Where the hell am I?" the woman asked. She looked around the room, taking in with mounting disgust the stained carpet and the plant tendrils forcing their way in around the air conditioner.

"Johnny's place," the man said. "Johnny, Johnny, Big Johnny T. Everything's gonna be fine, sweetheart."

Johnny looked at the guy with genuine alarm. The tone in the man's voice was unmistakable—that strange dark excitement that seemed to inhabit all the creeps who followed him home, who had been taken in by . . .

By the spell. Or whatever.

The voice in his head made a kind of snorting sound. He ignored it.

The last couple of times, the *spell* (for lack of a better word) had broken after only a few minutes. This time, when his two visitors had shown up, it had been decidedly different. They had babbled, as always—cryptic, unsettling statements about being lost in the darkness punctuated with promises of undying loyalty and gratitude—but it had been a lot more controlled than before, the crazy contortions damped to moderate tics. They could have passed for normal, if they'd have just shut the fuck up.

What had worried him last night was that the spell didn't pass. They'd eventually curled up on his floor and gone to sleep—and this morning, the man didn't seem to be better yet.

"Are you okay, man?" Johnny asked.

The guy cocked his head and grinned. "Right as rain, darlin', but hungry, so hungry, we'll have to eat soon, oh yes!"

"Randy, what the hell is wrong with you?" The woman slapped his shoulder.

These people need to get out of my house.

These are your friends. Let 'em stay. What will it hurt?

Are you fucking kidding me? You're out of your mind. He stifled a laugh. Out of someone's mind, anyway. And when, exactly, had he started talking to "Johnny" without actually talking? He had the feeling it had been going on for a few days now, but how had he missed it?

Regardless, this was nuts. He had weirdos following him around constantly, and if he needed an object lesson in the dangers of that, he only had to think back to last night. He hadn't seen the body, but the descriptions had been plenty colorful.

"Look, you people need to get out of my house."

The man rolled his eyes and leered. "No way. We're with you, Big Johnny."

"Like hell we are," the woman protested. She stood, steadying herself with one hand on the air conditioner. "You can stay here as long as you want, but I'm gone." She pulled her hand off the window unit. A film of oily dust was streaked across her palm. She made a face, then wiped her hand on the wall.

"God, this place stinks," she said.

Johnny watched as she walked to the hall. She hesitated, looking back expectantly at Randy, but he only bobbed his head from side to side. She shuddered, folded her bare arms, and left. Johnny heard the front door open and close.

"What am I supposed to do with *you*?" Johnny asked.

Be nice, John. This is one of your adoring fans.

Randy giggled.

This was not going to work. Bad enough this creepy bastard had shown up here at all, but the thought of him hanging out here all day was wholly unacceptable.

Douglas, Johnny thought. *He'll know what to do.*

Johnny stood. He was still dressed in last night's clothes, and the smell was pretty ripe, but just then he didn't give a fuck. He slipped on his shoes.

"Come on, Randy. I'm leaving, and you can't stay here by yourself."

Randy got awkwardly to his feet and lurched after Johnny. His gait smoothed out somewhat after a few steps, but he still walked like he wasn't familiar with the equipment.

Oh, good. Night of the Living Dead following me around all day. Fucking fabulous.

Johnny went outside, and Randy followed. Johnny squinted at the bright sunlight. Randy's face contorted into an exaggerated expression of shock and disgust, his tongue extended and his eyes almost closed. "Augh," he said. He held both hands up to shelter his eyes. "Bright. Bright."

"Hangovers are a bitch," Johnny said. *Sure. He's just hungover. Right.* "I'll get you a hat." He went back in and returned with a Rangers cap and a pair of sunglasses. He had to help Randy a bit with the hat—it was too small for him, and he hadn't got the hang of the adjustment in back—but after that, Randy seemed much happier.

There was no car parked out front; in fact, Johnny's nighttime visitors never drove. Johnny's house wasn't that far from downtown, and given the odd coordination problems his visitors had, Johnny suspected that driving would be a disaster for them.

"Looks like we're walking," he said. Randy nodded eagerly.

Johnny walked quickly through the neighborhood. Most of the neighbors were probably at church, but it would be awkward if he ran into any of them. He didn't know them well, and Randy didn't seem like a great conversationalist. Plus—dammit!—Randy insisted on walking behind him. Johnny slowed down a couple of times and even tried to guide Randy into step next to him, but Randy wasn't having any of it. No, he had to walk two paces behind Johnny, close enough that Johnny could hear his joyous, insane mutterings, close enough that when Johnny slowed, Randy ran into him.

What is wrong with this guy? he asked "Johnny."

He seems fine to me. Perfectly happy, in fact.

Bullshit.

Laughter. *Ah. Well, since you're so smart on it, maybe you can figure it out and explain it all to me.*

No help there. "Johnny" was a complete pain in the ass when he wanted to be.

They walked down Fitzhugh and onto Columbia, past the convenience stores and pawnshops squatting behind their iron bars. Only a few people were on the streets at this time on a Sunday, and the few he saw walked with their heads down, so preoccupied with their own thoughts that they paid no heed to Johnny and the shuffling weirdo behind him.

Johnny was coated in sticky sweat by the time they reached Main Street. The tattoo parlors and junk shops were closed and locked, the glare off the empty street a bland white like fossilized bone. If Johnny thought it was desolate down here on a Monday night, it was infinitely worse in the daylight, a marauded skeleton, picked clean and left as a warning.

Douglas wouldn't be here, Johnny was suddenly sure. The kind of business Douglas did wasn't daylight business.

Stupid. What the hell am I doing here?

For once, "Johnny" had no comment, or at least chose to make none.

"I'm gonna get some water," he said. "You want some?"

Randy made no answer.

Irritated, Johnny turned. Douglas was there, staring at Randy, who was looking back with great interest. In the sunlight, Douglas looked even older than usual, pale skin folded into deep creases around his eyes, his hair more grey than black. He looked familiar somehow, too, though Johnny didn't know from where.

Douglas broke off his staring match with Randy. "What do you need, Johnny?" he asked. His whisper barely carried to Johnny's ears.

Johnny rubbed the back of his neck. "I, ah—look, I don't know what to do with this guy." He pointed at Randy. "I don't know where the hell he came from, and I don't want him around."

"All right. That it?"

"Now that you mention it, no." Johnny took a breath, then plunged ahead, avoiding the black holes of Douglas's eyes. "These crazy fuckers that keep following me around—what is the deal with them? Are you—you're not, I mean . . ." He looked away, across the street, to where a woman in a black tank top unlocked the door to one of the shops. "Are they, uh, dangerous?"

"Depends," Douglas said. Across the street, the woman went inside. To Johnny, it looked like she locked the door behind her.

When it became obvious that Douglas wasn't going to say more, Johnny pressed on. "Depends on what?"

"On what you mean by dangerous. They're not gonna hurt you, Johnny. You already know that."

With an effort of will, Johnny forced himself to meet Douglas's gaze. The older man's eyes watered from the glare, but he didn't blink. "They killed somebody last night, man. Motherfuckers tried to *eat* him right on Commerce Street."

Douglas arched one eyebrow. "You know this for sure?"

"It was four kids from the show last night, and they were acting all crazy when it all went down. I don't need a jury to give me a verdict on this one. Christ, the other guys in the band think you're selling some kind of psycho drug to people that come to our shows."

"I told you," Douglas said, and there was a knife edge buried in the whisper. "Crazy people are part of it. Bitch and moan all you want, but deal with it."

"They *killed* somebody."

"I'm sure it won't happen again. It's not your fault. Get over it."

"And they're staying crazy now. Randy here has been out of his goddamn head for over twelve hours," Johnny said, his eyes flicking to the man next to him. "What is going on?"

Douglas put his hands in his pockets, and the line of his mouth drew tight. "Don't ask questions you don't want answers to, Johnny."

Once again, Johnny broke eye contact. The voice in his head snarled. *Are you gonna let this fucker push you around every time you see him? Do you mind if I . . .?*

Johnny felt that push again, the one that came before he sang. *Go for it.*

"Douglas, you miserable prick, you're fucking this up. Again."

The words came out of his mouth, but, unlike when he sang, they were dissociated from his thoughts—he was every bit as surprised by them as he would have been if somebody else was speaking.

The older man's eyes widened, and he leaned in toward Johnny. He bared his yellowed teeth in a smile. "Is that you? Is it really you?"

"Don't ask questions you don't want the answers to," Johnny heard himself say in a mocking voice. Douglas smiled wider.

"I won't screw up this time," Douglas whispered.

"Goddamn right you won't. Now, take *this* sad sack of shit away, and I don't want to see another one." Johnny was so wrapped up watching the reactions on Douglas's face that he didn't notice his own arm move to point at Randy without any apparent instruction from him.

"Sure thing," Douglas said.

Ha! Johnny thought. *Take that!*

Douglas turned to go, guiding Randy with a hand on his back. "See you later," he said.

"Yeah. See you," Johnny said, and his voice was his own this time. He watched Douglas walk away with Randy, and then he started home.

***

Douglas left Johnny behind, pushing the dumb babbling bastard that Johnny was so worried about in front of him. The guy—Randy was as good a name as any—muttered and mumbled, but he went where he was told. Probably he'd recover his wits in another day or so, and if not—well, so much the better.

A dark excitement filled Douglas's body, tingling like electricity to the ends of his fingers and toes. The voice, the boss, had spoken to him—harsh words, sure, but he had failed too many times not to understand the impatience.

Randy tripped over a tiny crack in the sidewalk, and Douglas watched him fall, making no move to help. He got up after a short struggle.

This was the most dangerous part, Douglas knew from bitter experience. The disciples, as he thought of them, were stupid at this stage, and too weak to completely control either their bodies or their hungers. Some vague vestige of intellect usually kept them from doing anything too stupid in public, but last night they must have been hungry indeed.

That should never have happened, and he would have to heed the boss's warning—it couldn't happen again. Not where Johnny might find out. Soon the disciples would be strong enough, but until then Douglas would have to be even more vigilant. Johnny could still stop everything, if he really wanted to. Others had, Douglas recalled with a bitter pang. One had even managed to commit suicide, long after Douglas had thought success was assured.

And there was his own failure, too, the one that hurt most of all.

Not this time. He thought of the boss's words, and that dark thrill ran through his body again.

"Johnnyyyyyy," Randy said, dragging it out in a wavering, exultant wail.

Douglas grinned. "You said it, man."

CHAPTER 18

Case took one look at the booth and eased in next to Quentin, across from Danny.

"Where's Johnny?" she asked.

Quentin pushed his menu away. Danny, she noted, hadn't even opened his.

"He's not coming," Danny said.

"Tough to have a band meeting without Johnny."

Danny inclined his head toward Quentin. "This is Quentin's show."

Quentin half-turned in his seat to be able to see Case better. There was a second's pause while his eyes moved from Danny to Case and back, and then—

"I think we need to take a break from the band for a while," he blurted.

Case made no response, watching as red blotches bloomed on Quentin's face, like ink clouds spreading through water. Quentin folded his hands, unfolded them, and then put them in his lap.

"A break," Case said at last.

"Yeah. Maybe a few months. Maybe—I don't know. Longer. I mean, not too much longer. Just until, you know. Things calm down."

"Until things calm down. Which things? Our fan base? I'm sure they'll get good and calm after we just go away indefinitely. Or do you mean the clubs that are actually asking us to play now? I bet they'll calm down plenty."

"Case—"

"Or how about my fucking landlord? No, wait—he's not going to calm down at all, because three hundred bucks a month is going to vanish from my income, which cuts pretty close to the goddamn bone. Are you insane? We've worked our asses off to get here, and, what? It looks too much like success for you?"

Case knew she was shouting, and she could see people at neighboring tables gawking, but she didn't much care. This was absurd.

Quentin fiddled with his water glass. "I'm not afraid of success. But that stuff that happened the other night—that freaks me out."

"No shit?" Case said. "You think *you're* freaked out? I was right fucking there, and I've had nightmares about the body ever since. What the hell does that have to do with the price of eggs?"

"I don't know," Quentin said, holding up his hands. "It's just—you know. They were at the show, just like some of the other weirdos we've seen. And Johnny keeps getting weirder. Did you see the way he flew off the handle the other night? I don't think any of this is good for him. He's losing it."

"You didn't think maybe you'd get his opinion on whether or not he's losing it? We're going to decide without him and let him know the verdict?"

Danny finally spoke. "I think Quentin's right about Johnny," he said. "He's taking that stage persona of his way too seriously. I've never seen him like this."

"So talk to him," Case said. "Or something. I'm not going to sit here and decide what's best for him." She breathed out, trying to calm down, and addressed Quentin. "I'm not ready to 'take a break.' Not on Johnny's account, and not on yours. If you want some time off, do what you gotta do." She lowered her voice further and forced herself not to look away. "We'll—*I'll* miss you."

Astonishment wrote itself all over Quentin's face. "My God," he said, "I think that's the nicest thing I've ever heard you say to anyone."

"Yeah, well, don't get all choked up over it," she shot back, but she smiled.

"I want this as much as you guys do, you know. I don't want to swing a hammer the rest of my life, and playing music with you guys is—well, it's the best thing I do. But this is getting weird, and I don't like it."

"Give it another couple of shows," Case said. "If you can't take it after that, we'll figure something out. But I'm telling you, what happened after the last show was a fluke. It *can't* get worse than that."

"Yeah," Quentin said. "You're probably right."

***

To Quentin's relief, the next show went well, as did the one after that. Johnny's creepy friend didn't come around, and the strange behavior of the audience had all but stopped. Quentin doubted the two were unrelated. Johnny still worried Quentin, and some of the songs still gave him a bad feeling, but overall, Quentin was optimistic and even starting to have fun again.

Erin continued to deliver one record crowd after another, and soon they were moving to bigger venues. Christmas came and went, and the old year sloughed away like so much dead skin, revealing the shiny pink new year beneath it. They ended the year on a high note, playing New Year's Eve to a sold-out crowd, and the band had a blast and got good and drunk afterward. It was like the old days, almost, only better.

"Only good things from here on out," Quentin said, raising his glass.

They all drank to that.

CHAPTER 19

From the Dallas Observer, *February 12, 2010:*

Ragman Draws Crowds

When you ask Ragman frontman Johnny Tango who his biggest influence is, he gives you a look designed to make you think you're the dumbest son of a bitch he's ever set eyes on.

"Dylan, man." He shakes his head. "You need to do your motherfucking homework."

And that's how the interview starts.

We sat down with Ragman's lead singer Johnny Tango and guitarist Case, representatives of the band that took home our Readers' Choice Award for Best New Act for last year. The pair of them are Dallas's up-and-coming current answer to the dynamic duo of Keith Richards and Mick Jagger, or the Toxic Twins Steven Tyler and Joe Perry—comparisons Case, at least, seems to relish.

Johnny, it turns out, is more of a Dylan fan.

The two of them are a study in weird contrasts and unexpected similarities. Case won't sit on the couch—she pulls out a wooden chair from the table nearby and perches on that, coiled as though ready to strike at any moment. Johnny affects a more languorous attitude and stretches out on the couch with his arms spread wide across the back—but if you look closely, you can see that he, too, is vibrating with barely controlled tension. He grins and sneers and sulks and swears like a sailor. She keeps her face deadpan during the whole interview and also swears like a sailor. He's got the leather jacket, and she wears the leather pants. They both wear white T-shirts. He slips back and forth from coarse vulgarity, a caricature of pool-hall machismo, to academic English-speak without being aware of it. She looks at you like she just might decide to break your nose, and never wavers. They seem as likely as any pair to be the latest bastion of rock and roll in Dallas.

We asserted that we had not, in fact, done our motherfucking homework, and picked up the interview from there.

Observer: Bob Dylan?

Johnny: Yeah.

O: That's a strange influence for a band as heavy as yours.

Johnny: It ain't that fuckin' strange. Dylan was as heavy as they come. Loud, too. Pissed a lot of motherfuckers off when he went electric, but he didn't care. Doesn't get heavier than that. Had a nice bike, too.

O (laughs): Still, you have to admit it's not typical.

Johnny: Only because people don't listen to what the man said. Apocalyptic visions, impassioned rants against the establishment, drug addiction, cryptic messages from wherever-the-fuck. He was fearless. He tackled everything, head-on. Nobody was as rock-and-roll as Bob fucking Dylan, not before or since.

Case: Except maybe Johnny Thunders.

O (to Case): Johnny Thunders—now there's a name you don't hear much these days. Is he one of your major influences?

Case: Yeah.

O (after a pause): Who else?

Case: Anybody who ever hung a heavy fucking piece of mahogany around their neck and played no-bullshit guitar.

O: Such as?

Case: Jimmy Page. Joe Perry. Slash. Neil Young—he gets some of the ugliest sounds out of a Les Paul you ever heard. It's fucking great. Martin Barre. Clapton, before his balls fell off. Kerry Buchanan, from Crashyard. He doesn't get enough credit.

O: Your band has had a fair amount of success locally in a very short time frame. What do you attribute that to?

Case: Good PR.

Johnny (glares at Case): Good fucking music.

O (to Johnny): Anything specific?

Johnny: Yeah. We rock the fuck out without treating our audience like eighth graders. (He pauses, thinking for a moment.) Plus we put on a hell of a show.

***

"It's time," Erin said, putting the paper away. "Thou shalt go to Austin."

Later, Case would trace a bitter wealth of misery back to that statement. For now, she just raised her eyebrows. "Oh?"

"Sure. The band's doing pretty well in Dallas, but you guys are never going to make any money playing to the same hundred people every month. Time to start spreading the love. Austin's a good place to start making regular visits."

Case sighed. "A new town. Empty rooms. It'll be just like starting over again."

"No guts, no glory. Besides," Erin said, adding a wink, "I know a few people."

Case laughed—it was hard not to. "All right. Let's set something up."

***

"Austin." Gina's voice betrayed no emotion.

"Yeah," Danny said. "We talked about it, and it makes sense. Good music scene, lots of college kids. If we're going to be serious, we can't sit in Dallas and hope the world comes to us." He smiled nervously. She didn't smile back. "You wanna come?"

"No."

"It's just an overnight trip. We'll be back before you know it."

She gave him a brittle smile. "I really don't feel like driving three hours to go sit in a smoky bar. Especially not on a weeknight."

"Take the next day off. It'll be fun."

"No thanks. I can only imagine what your boss would say if he knew why you were taking that Friday off."

Danny laughed, showing more than a little strain. "My boss is older than God, and he thinks Lawrence Welk was the pinnacle of Western musical achievement. He'd want to know why I'd waste even a minute of my precious vacation on that goddamn noise."

Gina just looked at him. He didn't need her to make her point any plainer than that.

"Don't have too much fun," she said, and Danny cringed. Ever since that fucking show, there had been an ugly tension under the surface of their relationship, like a saw blade draped under a silk sheet. It threatened to tear through only when he talked about things related to the band, but it seemed like it was always there, just waiting for him to push against it too hard.

"I won't," he said.

She turned back to the contract she was reading.

CHAPTER 20

Another Dallas show, another packed house. The band's momentum had picked up like Johnny never would have believed after they won the Best New Act award, and it wouldn't be long before they'd have to move to even larger venues. Room for a couple hundred was no longer enough, amazingly.

Johnny woke the morning after the show, sweaty and shaking. Another Dallas show, another bad dream. Another bad dream that seemed a little too real. At least nobody was following him home anymore. Douglas had taken care of that problem, or it had gone away of its own accord—he didn't care which.

He was rolling over in bed, trying to fall asleep again, when somebody pounded on his front door. Johnny got a sudden, very bad feeling, like ice water poured down his spine.

Let it go, the voice suggested. Johnny thought that sounded just fine. Ignore it and it will go away.

"Mr. Tsiboukas, this is the Dallas Police Department. We'd like to have a few words with you." More pounding.

Oh, fuck. Johnny got up. Ignoring this would do nothing but make it worse. "Just a second!" he yelled, and he scrambled for some pants.

Johnny went out to the living room and opened the door. A heavyset guy in a cheap coat waved a badge at him.

"Detective Ortiz," he said. "Dallas Police Department. Sorry if this is a little early." He didn't look sorry.

"'Sall right. What can I do for you?"

"Can I come in?"

Johnny flung the door wide so the detective could see past him into the living room, but he didn't get out of the doorway. "Actually, I don't have any chairs. I live in squalor, as you can see."

The detective wrinkled his nose.

"Uh, yeah," Johnny said. "Carpet gets wet every time it rains. Stinks to high heaven." Johnny stepped outside and pulled the door shut. "Probably better just to talk out here. What's going on?"

"Do you know Kevin Stevens?"

"No," Johnny said, puzzled. "Who is he?"

"The young man who was killed behind the Curtain Club last night."

Johnny's eyes widened in real shock—and, he fervently hoped, nothing more than shock.

Relax, the voice told him. *Dallas is a violent place. Like most big cities. Something bad happens every night.*

The detective watched his face with interest.

"Uh, sorry," Johnny said. "That's . . . kind of shocking. My band played the Curtain Club last night. I was right there."

"Yeah. I know. We're talking to everybody we can track down who was there. Did you see anything unusual last night, either in the club or outside when you left?"

"Not really. Just a bunch of drunk people, you know?" *Had* he seen anything unusual? He didn't think so, no. In fact, he was sure of it. Douglas hadn't been there, and even the crazies were nowhere in evidence these days. He was really in the clear—of course he was. So why did he feel so guilty?

The detective nodded. "Can you give me the names of anyone else who was there?"

"Sure." He gave the detective the names of the guys in the band, the names of the other bands, and any other names he could remember. The detective wrote them all down dutifully. A short interview followed. The questions were all pretty basic. What time did you get there? What time did you leave? Did you leave by yourself or with someone?—and Johnny relaxed as it went on. There really was nothing to worry about.

"All right," the detective said after about five minutes. "Thank you."

That was it? "Anything else I can do?"

The detective smiled without humor. "We'll let you know. Probably not." He turned to go, then stopped. "You ought to have your roof fixed. That carpet is something else."

Johnny managed a sickly grin. "Tell me about it."

***

They went down to Austin just as they had gone to their long-ago college show in Wichita Falls, with the addition of Erin. She sat in the front seat of Case's car and jammed Johnny in back with the gear. Johnny didn't seem to mind—he stared out the window and fiddled with his notebook and generally kept quiet. That suited Case just fine. He'd been so edgy lately that it was starting to rub off.

At least in the backseat she couldn't see him bouncing his legs and folding his notebook.

The venue was about as Case expected—a dozen or so people hangin' out in a badly lit little club.

"It'll fill up," Erin said, giving her a reassuring smile. "Maybe not a lot, but I've got some friends around here."

Case shrugged. It wasn't like she hadn't played empty rooms before. The five of them waited around, each buried in their own thoughts except Erin. She had gone over to chat up one of the other bands that was scheduled to play that night, a bunch of bearded guys that looked like a bunch of scrawny lumberjacks.

Fucking jam band, Case guessed, but she smiled a little. *I must be getting spoiled already—I'd forgotten all about the joys of new band night.*

The joys were just beginning, it turned out. The jam band dragged their stuff onstage, and ten o'clock rolled around with no sound guy in evidence. There were now maybe two dozen people hanging out in the club, and no sound guy. The lumberjacks stood around staring at each other. One of them scratched his head while the rest bore the slack expressions of the terminally stoned.

A quick look around the place, and all Case was able to find in the way of responsible parties was the bartender, so over to the bar she went.

"Hey!" she said. "Who's running this show?"

The bartender himself looked like a scrawny lumberjack. An unlit cigarette hung off his lower lip, hovering over his beard.

"Tom, I guess," he said.

"Where the hell is he?"

The bartender scanned the room. "Fuck, I dunno. He's usually on time. Maybe he's in jail or something."

"What are we supposed to do?"

"His shit's all in a box under the stage. Go ahead and use what you can find."

Case went over to the stage and lifted one of the panels, and sure enough there were two cardboard boxes full of tangled cables next to a disorderly heap of mic stands.

"What's goin' on?" the head lumberjack asked her, peering over the edge of the stage.

"Sound guy's a no-show. You wanna play, get down here and help me get this stuff set up."

"Who's gonna run sound?"

Case slid one of the boxes out. "*I'm* going to run sound for you guys. Then you're going to run sound for my band when we go on. Sound fair?"

"Cool."

Danny came over while she was pulling cables from one of the boxes.

"What's going on?" he asked, unknowingly echoing the head lumberjack.

"No sound guy, so we're doing it ourselves."

Danny laughed. "That brings back some memories. Just like the old days."

She smiled despite herself. "Not all that old. But, yeah. You wanna set up some mic stands?"

He pitched in, and with the help of the lumberjacks (they moved veeerrrry slowly, but there were five of them), they got set up quickly. It also helped, Case thought wryly, that there were only four microphones. She'd heard or read somewhere that, if you only had a few mics, you should always mic the kick drum and the snare, so she had them do that. The other two mics were left for vocals, and the band would have to turn up their amps to do the rest. She would be "running sound" mostly by pointing at various band members and using her thumbs to tell them to turn their amps up or down. That had a kind of absurdity to it that she thought would have righteously pissed her off a year ago, but it made her laugh out loud tonight.

Danny handed her the cable from the kick drum mic. He was grinning, too. "This is ridiculous," he said.

She grinned back, and she felt a sudden warmth in her belly as she met his eyes. "Yep." She laughed again and went over to the mixer to plug in the cable.

***

The lumberjacks played the set Case expected—three songs, each about ten minutes long, consisting of endless noodling over the same two chords. She was a good sport about it, though, and took her job as impromptu sound guy seriously. She hoped they weren't too stoned to do the same for her. They wrapped up late, partly because they'd gotten started late, and partly because Case didn't feel like cutting them off when they'd gone on too long. The bar was filling up, a little, and she thought she'd let that happen for a bit longer. Anyway, the jam band guys were harmless. They'd be done soon enough.

"Thanks," the head lumberjack told her after he got offstage. "That was a cool thing to do."

"Lead vocal is channel one, kick and snare are three and four. Good luck."

There was a bunch of fucking around to get everything onstage and get the volumes right, and some more fucking around when the lead vocal wouldn't turn up—somehow the stands had gotten moved around, so the mic Johnny ended up in front of was actually on channel two—but Case didn't care. She flashed Quentin and Danny a grin just before they started. "No pressure tonight," she said. "Let's have some fun." Johnny scowled at her as though fun was strictly verboten. She ignored him and started the first song.

She had a blast. There was nobody to impress here, nothing to prove—just loud fucking rock and roll, and the equipment situation made the whole thing too silly to take seriously. She ended up sharing a mic with Quentin on some of the backup vocals, leaning in suddenly and surprising the hell out of him the first time it happened. The look on his face was priceless, like he thought she was going to bite him or tweak his nose or something. She'd had to turn up her amp to ungodly levels to get it loud enough for the whole room, and it sounded *amazing*. It also fed back like crazy, but she used that to extract some hellish noise out of her guitar that she thought was actually pretty cool. *I think I'm made to play dive bars,* she thought, and that made her laugh some more.

Even better, the vague weirdness that had haunted so many shows lately was gone. Johnny just sang, just rocked out, and he sounded good. Case lost herself in the deafening noise, the crash and thunder and squeal, even forgetting to be cautious long enough to go back and jam with Danny for half a song. The old electricity was still there, like a switch that had been waiting for someone to flip it, and the look he gave her was so hungry, so intense, that she bit her lip to keep from moaning. Then she laid into the bridge of the song, almost running back over to Quentin's mic to get on the backing vocals before she missed the line.

She was leaning out over the monitors, holding the guitar in front of her in an overly theatrical pose while blowing through the solo in "Walkin'," when a face in the crowd snagged her attention. There was an older guy, maybe forty, nodding his head along with the music and smiling, and something about him was terribly familiar.

It clicked a fraction of a second later. *Holy fuck. That's Kerry Buchanan.*

An awful squawk came from her guitar as she flubbed the end of the solo. She shook her head, trying to focus, but she couldn't help stealing a second glance. It was Kerry Buchanan all right, and she recognized a couple of the other members of Crashyard, too.

Case turned her back to the small audience and concentrated on finishing the song without fucking up. As the song ended, she went back to Danny and leaned toward him.

"Kerry Buchanan is here!" she yelled, but he was already starting the next song, and he just gave her a puzzled look.

Fuck it. He'll play better if I don't tell him. With that thought, she tried to push Crashyard's presence out of her own mind and just play the way she always played. That didn't work spectacularly well—every third thought seemed to be *Kerry Buchanan is here!* and if she'd ever imagined she was immune to being starstruck, she was being sharply corrected now. Her fingers felt thick and clumsy, as if they were cold, and her playing sounded wooden to her. Luckily, the set was almost over.

The band wrapped up the last song a few minutes later, and Case started to unplug her stuff in the time-honored tradition of getting the hell off the stage so the next band could set up.

"What else you got?" somebody yelled. "Play some more!"

Case wasn't looking at the audience, but she knew the voice. *Holy fuck,* she thought again. Johnny was looking, though, and she saw his mouth drop open with the surprise of recognition. Danny and Quentin were only a second behind.

"Man, I really appreciate that," Johnny said into the mic. His swagger had all but vanished for the moment. "But we gotta make way for the next band."

"Ain't nobody else!"

"Who's playing next?" Johnny asked, looking across the crowd. Nobody said anything.

"Ain't nobody else!" the bartender shouted, echoing Buchanan.

Johnny, Quentin, and Case huddled together around Danny, pulled automatically as if by chains.

"What do you think we should do?" Quentin asked.

"I'll tell you what we're gonna do," Johnny said, his face alight with fevered excitement. "We've got another hour or so of good shit we know backward and forward, and we're gonna play until that motherfucker says stop."

Case nodded appreciatively. "That's what I'd say."

"Let's do it," Danny said. "Go ahead and call the tune."

"'Burn,'" Johnny said. When Case gave him a surprised look, he shrugged. "It's a tight fucking song, and everybody loves it."

"No complaints here," she said, and she started the song.

***

They played another dozen songs before they had to admit they were tapped out. By the second or third song, thanks in large part to shouts of encouragement from the crowd, Case loosened up and felt—and played—more like herself. A kind of euphoria set in, and despite the shitty sound setup and the comical mic sharing, they played a pretty good set. Danny *really* threw himself into it, pounding the skins with a manic energy Case hadn't heard from him in a while, and she found herself back there jamming with him over and over again, sharing that intensity, staring a challenge into his eyes and receiving the same until she thought she might explode.

They got off the stage at almost one, ears ringing and bodies dripping sweat, all four of them grinning widely—

And the guys from Crashyard were waiting for them.

"Good fucking set," Kerry Buchanan said, and Case almost squealed with glee. *Kerry Buchanan just told me I played a good set!* "What are you guys drinking?"

There was a shocked pause, and then they all answered at once. "Screwdriver." "Shiner." "Jack and Coke." "Beer."

Buchanan grinned. "All right, then. Let's get 'em lined up."

They ended up sitting around a couple of pushed-together tables—three of the guys from Crashyard (the rhythm guitarist, it turned out, was dealing with a family emergency elsewhere); the four members of Ragman; and Erin—the fifth Beatle, as Case had taken to calling her. Outside the circle of the table, a few crowd members and the entire cast of the lumberjack jam band hung out, hoping for some kind of acknowledgment they never got.

"Good band," Buchanan said, and the four of them glowed. "You guys remind me of us when we were younger."

Case thought she might pass out, and she caught a dazed grin from Danny next to her.

"Can I give you some advice?" Buchanan asked. Nods all around. "Whatever else happens, no matter what deal somebody offers you, keep your publishing rights."

Case blinked. She'd expected something along the lines of "turn down the gain on your amp a little," or "make more eye contact with the audience," not a piece of contract wisdom. "Huh?" she said.

Buchanan took a sip of his drink—beer, Case noticed, and barely touched. "You guys are *not* major label material."

Johnny bristled immediately. "Why not?" It was a challenge, not really a question.

Buchanan shrugged. "I don't mean you're not good enough—you got rough edges, but any idiot can see you guys have your shit down. But the market . . . Well, timing is everything. Believe me, I know." Case knew what he meant—Crashyard had started playing their brand of rude, mean rock just about the time Nirvana killed off the hair bands and the entire music world rotated to focus on mopey "alternative" rock from Seattle. Crashyard was a great fucking band, but the kind of huge market that would have propelled them to superstardom had vanished right when they hit their stride. Buchanan didn't seem to care, though. He smiled, a kind of cocked half-smile that wouldn't have looked out of place on a younger Harrison Ford, if Ford had been hit in the face a lot more often. "Crashyard started out with a major label, but the label dumped us after we didn't recoup our advance for the first album. There was a nasty little clause in the contract that we'd been too drunk to care about when we signed—and it gave them the publishing rights for every song on that album. The label sold some of the songs to fuck-knows-where—car commercials, movie soundtracks, and shit like that. I still hear 'em cropping up in weird places. The label gets paid for all of it, and I don't get a dime."

"No shit?" Johnny said.

"No shit. Don't get me wrong—I got nothin' to complain about. We're on a little indie label now that likes us, and pop radio can go fuck itself. We're not playing arenas or anything, but we've got loyal fans, and we've been making a good living doing what we love for fifteen years. Point is, if you're gonna be in this for the long haul, nail down your publishing and you'll be collecting checks for years. Without major-label marketing support and a huge fucking audience, those royalty checks will be a larger part of your income than you'd believe."

Case filed that away for future reference, and the conversation (thankfully) lightened up after that. Buchanan told a bunch of tour horror stories—with color commentary from the other guys—that had them cracking up. Alcohol flowed liberally, and Case started feeling a pleasant buzz.

"I don't mean to be rude," Quentin asked after the fourth round, "but what the hell are you guys doing here?" There was laughter all around, and he blushed.

"We got started in this shitty bar," Buchanan said. "Me and Jason and Barry—he was the drummer then—played our first show here. Gotta remember your roots, man."

There was much sober nodding at this comment, but by then that was the only thing that was sober. They all got drunker and louder and yelled over each other, and periodically the whole rowdy group was swept with gales of laughter as somebody got off a good one, often at Buchanan's expense. Case could feel the presence of Danny's body next to her, and her skin tingled every time he accidentally—accidentally?—touched her leg or elbow.

At bar time, the bartender chased everybody else out and locked the door, but he left their group alone. "Any friend of Kerry's," he said, and he served up another round.

Case's every nerve was on edge, and she imagined she could sense Danny's body from inches away. She started to make a game of it—how close could she get before she felt him? The conversation went on around her, but she didn't hear much of it. There was only Danny and the occasional brush of her arm on his, setting off crackling charges of electricity up and down her body. He was warm, she realized, and she could feel heat rolling off him. *Am I torturing myself? Am I torturing him?* She didn't know, but she edged ever so slightly closer. Her shoulder touched his, and she felt his whole body go rigid.

She looked away, enjoying his discomfiture and her own delicious tension, so she didn't see him move. Under the table, his hand slid up the inside of her thigh, shocking her so badly she made a little squeaking noise before she could help it. The touch was gone as suddenly as it had come, but she felt her face flush. Surely somebody had heard that noise, she thought, looking around the table. If they had heard anything, it didn't show. The noise and laughter went on, and nobody paid her any special attention.

What are you doing?

She didn't care. She ran her foot up the back of Danny's calf, felt him push his leg against hers, and then reached for him under the table. He was hard and hot, and as she pressed, he made a low sound and then erupted into a coughing fit.

Laughing, she pulled away, folding her hands demurely in front of her on the table. Next to her, she could feel Danny trembling.

Don't do this, she thought again. But why not? She wanted to. He obviously wanted to. Who was she to tell him what he ought to be doing outside his—in his personal life? She slammed another drink.

"All right, guys—I'm done," Buchanan said, standing. "Goin' home." That seemed to be the signal for the party to break up, and everyone stood—Danny with some awkwardness, Case noted with an interior grin.

"Hey," Buchanan said as people started moving toward the door. "You guys should come on tour with us this summer."

The room went quiet.

"I'm serious," Buchanan said.

Erin was the only one with the presence of mind to speak up. "Hell yes!" she said. "Give me your contact info, and we'll work it out!"

"I think this calls for one more round!" Quentin said, and there was more laughter and general agreement.

One more round was served.

***

Danny sat on the edge of his motel-room bed, staring across the dark room at his own shape in the mirror. Quentin was already asleep in the other bed, and Johnny was passed out on the floor, muttering ominous-sounding nonsense syllables.

Case, Danny knew, was two doors down—alone. Erin had stayed out with some of her friends, her energy barely dampened by the late hour and Christ knew how many drinks. "Oh, I couldn't sleep anyway," she'd said happily. "Too fired up!"

Danny wasn't exactly fired up, but he knew all about the couldn't-sleep part. He wasn't exactly *not* fired up, he thought as he sat with his elbows on his knees, dry-washing his hands nervously. He was wound up all right, but his energy had a sour flavor to it.

Touring with Crashyard. Maybe it wouldn't happen—maybe Buchanan had just been drunk and running his mouth, but Danny didn't think so. He hadn't been *that* drunk. It might just happen. God, how cool would that be? Crashyard wasn't playing arenas, like Buchanan had said, but they still had a pretty good draw. Ragman would get to play in front of *thousands* of people. Thousands. It was the chance of a lifetime, and ten years of playing in shitty high-school bands and shitty college bands and shitty local bands had made Danny keenly aware of that fact. He ought to be thrilled. Hell, he *was* thrilled . . . except . . .

The tour would be what? Six weeks? Eight? He *might* be able to arrange for a leave of absence from work. More likely, his boss would tell him he was out of his mind, inform him that he got two weeks of vacation a year and he'd best use them wisely, and that would be that. What then?

Would he be willing to quit his job for this?

Yeah. It wasn't hard to imagine finding another engineering job down the road, driving a CAD station in his cubicle until he was old enough to retire, but it was impossible to imagine that another opportunity like this tour would come along.

But what would Gina say? Try as he might, he couldn't conceive of her being happy for him. Not for this. She would be pissed if he even seemed like he was taking it seriously, most likely skewering him with the same sort of condemnation she reserved for John. Tragic waste of potential. Socially irresponsible. *Immature.* He had no idea how severe her reaction would be if he actually quit his job and went through with it, but he suspected it could be terminal for their relationship.

Danny felt sick. He wanted to call Gina and tell her the good news, share the excitement with her, but he knew that could never happen.

He thought he could find somebody that would be happy to talk about the good news just two doors down, if she was still awake. Talk about the good news, and maybe . . .

And maybe what, Danny? What are you thinking?

The same things he'd been thinking when he'd touched her leg at the bar, the same things he'd thought when she'd touched him in return. Not really thoughts at all, just chaotic, unchanneled desire, desperate for some kind of release. Just remembering that quick, furtive pressure was enough to make him hard right now.

Danny stood up, shaking, his breath rough in his ears. Had he actually made a decision? Gina or Case, cube farm or rock-and-roll stage—they seemed like the same dilemma. Nice, stable, and predictable; or exhilarating and wild, something that might propel him to dizzying heights or explode spectacularly.

He slipped the plastic key card for the room in his pocket and went out into the hall.

He stopped at the door to her room. Light winked out at him through the peephole.

Danny took a long, shuddering breath, and then he knocked softly on the door.

It opened almost immediately, before he could draw another breath.

***

When the knock came, it was as though Case had been waiting for it. She had been pacing, catlike, for what felt like hours, tense and unable to sleep, and she was in fact already walking toward the door when she heard the soft rap.

She opened the door wide, and even though she had known what she was going to see, her stomach flipped over.

It was Danny, of course.

His eyes locked with hers with that same intense look he got onstage, the one that shot heat and lightning through her whole body, and he didn't flinch. He waited just long enough for her to say something. When she didn't, he stepped into the room, put his hands on her waist— feather-light, oddly gentle for such a big man—and kissed her.

Case wasn't so gentle. She pulled him into the room by his shirtfront, slammed the door with one hand, and pushed him against the wall. She kissed him, hard, and ground her hips into his body. Then he was pulling at her shirt, and she at his, and there was nothing in the world but her body and his.

They never even made it to the bed.

CHAPTER 21

Danny sat up in the bright light of late morning and took in the disaster. They'd made love—if you could call it that—twice in the night. The first time, on the floor, had been frenzied but hadn't ranged too far from the door. The second time had been fucking cataclysmic. They'd made it to the bed eventually, but on the way a lamp had gotten knocked over and an end table destroyed, and a stuffed chair had been hauled halfway across the room and tipped on its side. They'd pulled the headboard off the wall, too, and it was lying across the chair at an angle.

The destruction seemed appropriate, he thought soberly. He'd destroyed more than a hotel room last night. The guilt would come crashing down any minute, but for now he was oddly calm.

He studied Case's sleeping form, its curves and planes so different from the ones he was used to.

From your wife's, you mean.

Yeah.

She opened her eyes and stretched. "Oh, God," she said, smiling. "Morning."

"You don't have enough tattoos," he remarked.

"Uh, good morning to you, too," she said, giving him a curious look. "Actually, I don't have *any* tattoos."

"I noticed. It's weird."

"You don't have any, either."

"Well, no, but I'm a good product of my society. You, on the other hand—with the fuck-you attitude, I'd have thought you'd have ink from head to toe. It's almost standard issue for the rebel crowd."

She rolled onto her side, pushing the sheet down to her hips. "Nope. No piercings, either. Not even my ears. One thing to be said for martial arts training is that it teaches you a lot of respect for your body."

"Not much respect for mine, though," he said, looking pointedly at the clusters of red half-moons she'd clawed into his chest.

She started to grin, but it faded fast. "Are you going to be okay with this?"

Danny sighed. He didn't like the way her face had lapsed into its stock expression—an expressionless expression, with a slight hint of wariness. "Are you?"

She shrugged. "I'm fine. I'm always fine."

"Don't do that," he said. "Not unless this was just about fucking for you."

Another searching look. No answer.

"Well, was it? About fucking, I mean."

"What if it was?"

He thought about it. It wouldn't have changed his decision, he realized, though he knew now that he *was* hoping for more—had been all along. He thought she wanted something, too, and it was only that wariness of hers that made her so evasive. "I made my choice. I'm ready to live with it either way," he said, though he wondered if that was really true. "But I'll be honest. This wasn't only about sex for me, and I hope it wasn't for you."

A ghost of a smile flickered across her lips, and then it was gone. "Took a lot of guts to say that," she said.

"And?"

She smiled for real this time, though the cautious look didn't leave her eyes. "We'll see."

There was sharp pounding on the door, followed by Johnny's voice:

"Goddammit, Danny, are you in there?"

***

Johnny had woken up disoriented and confused, tangled in a blanket with Quentin's feet hanging off the bed over his head. The curtains hadn't been closed, and the light stabbed his eyes. He rubbed his temples with one hand to try to ease the pain in his head. What the hell had he done last night?

Then he remembered—Crashyard. The tour.

He sat up, a smile forming on his face despite his headache. This was going to be great! Danny would—

Danny. Where was Danny? The room's second bed was empty. From the look of it, it had not even been slept in. That was enough to piss Johnny off all by itself, since he'd spent a lousy night on the floor, one that had probably tweaked his neck and his back pretty good and would doubtless make for an extra pleasant trip back to Dallas. But worse, *where was Danny?*

You know where Danny is, the voice told him. *Down the hall, dick still wet from fucking our guitarist.*

No. That couldn't be it. He wouldn't, and anyway Erin was with Case . . . wasn't she? Johnny couldn't remember. The last part of the night was hazy, and the only thing that stuck in his head was the tour invitation. He hoped he hadn't made that up.

The two things sat uneasily together in his head—the tour invitation, and Danny fucking Case just down the hall.

He's gonna fuck it all up for us, the voice told him. *Maybe he already has.*

Johnny got up. He staggered and almost fell as a spike of pain split his head, but he put a hand on the dresser and steadied himself. He collected himself and slowly walked to the door.

Moments later, he was beating on the door to Case's room. Each thump hammered nails into his brain, but he kept pounding anyway.

"Goddammit, Danny, are you in there?"

There was no sound. Johnny started to wonder if maybe he'd been mistaken after all.

Then Danny's voice, muffled: "Just a minute."

Johnny's heart sank at the same time the voice in his head went into a spasm of gibbering, inarticulate rage.

Oh, Danny. What did you do?

He fucked *it up, he* fucked *it up, he* fucked *it up!*

The pain in Johnny's head redoubled. He ground his teeth together.

The door opened just wide enough to let Danny out into the hall. He closed it behind him.

"Hi, John."

The name caught Johnny off guard and started the thing in his head howling. "Johnny."

"I've got some things I need to deal with this morning, Johnny. Can we pick this up later?"

"What did you do, Danny? Danny, what did you do?" Johnny seemed incapable of thinking anything else. The hall had contracted to a tight bubble around him and Danny, and he felt off-balance and dizzy.

"I think you can figure that out without my help," Danny said, trailing off toward the end and looking down at the floor.

That small gesture of deference helped Johnny regain his equilibrium. The thing in his head smelled blood and started up its ungodly howling again. "Why? Why did you have to do it *now*? Danny, if you fucked this up for me—if you fucked this up for *us*, I . . . I . . . Jesus *Christ*, Danny!"

"I didn't fuck anything up for *you*, John."

"Yeah? What about the tour?" Johnny knew as soon as he said it that he shouldn't have. Danny gave him a solemn look.

"Oh, you're worried about the tour. I thought you might have been here trying to look out for my well-being."

Johnny squirmed, lost for a reply, but the voice whispered the words. He merely repeated them. "Your marriage is your business, but the band affects me, too. How could you be so selfish?" That sounded like as ripe a load of bullshit as Johnny had ever heard, even to his own ears—but it hit home. He could tell.

"The tour will be fine," Danny said softly. "I want that as much as you do."

I doubt that, Johnny thought, but this time he said nothing. Somewhere, he was wondering whether Danny might not really need him, might need a little support, but his headache and the whispering thing and his own terror at the possibility of losing the opportunity to tour with Crashyard buried it. Danny was the big brother—he'd be fine.

"Promise?" Johnny said, hating himself as the word escaped.

"Yeah."

"Okay," Johnny said. "I'm gonna go, uh, take a shower."

"Okay."

***

It was on the way back to Dallas that the guilt finally caught up with Danny.

CHAPTER 22

Gina's car was in the driveway when Danny pulled in. He'd actually been in Dallas for a few hours, but he hadn't been able to bring himself to go home right away. He'd driven in circles on I-635 until he couldn't stand it anymore.

By the time he got home, he had a pretty good idea of what he needed to say, and he was looking forward to it like a root canal sans anesthetic.

He had a tight feeling in his chest and throat as he opened the front door.

She was on the couch, a stack of paper on her lap as always. That made it a little easier.

Danny walked around to the other end of the couch and sat. "Gina, we need to talk." He had it worked out. He would begin by talking about the tour and the things he wanted out of life—the things she didn't approve of and wouldn't understand. He didn't see any reason to lay this at Case's feet, and Gina deserved a complete explanation. It wasn't nearly as simple as sex. Of course, he'd have to admit sleeping with Case eventually—his body was covered in evidence—but that would come later, after Gina understood the larger framework.

She looked up from her paperwork, an expression of grim knowledge on her face. "You fucked her."

The air rushed out of Danny's lungs. His whole orderly plan went out the window, and he stared stupidly at Gina. "What?"

"That's what you were going to say, right? It's all over your face, Daniel." Her lips were thin, and he could see her jaw working, tears glistening in her eyes.

Tears came to his own eyes in response. *You did this, Danny. Nice fucking work.* "It's not about that, Gina."

"You didn't?"

He made a pained expression. "Would you listen to me?"

One tear slipped free and rolled down her cheek. "Tell me you didn't fuck her."

Danny looked at his hands, then forced himself to look Gina in the eye. He owed her that much. "I can't do that," he said.

She laughed, a bitter, jagged laugh from deep in her throat. More tears slid down her face. "I knew I was being stupid. All that crap about not making you choose between me and your music—just stupid." She laughed again, and the sound cut Danny's heart like a fistful of broken glass. "You're a child, Danny, always thinking you can have everything, always thinking you can make everyone happy. I should have known better than to trust you that far."

"I can explain," Danny said, though even he wasn't sure what possible explanation he could provide.

"Get out."

"Gina, I—"

"I don't care. You don't get to talk this out. I know you, Daniel—you're just looking for some absolution. You're not going to get it here. Just pack your things and get out."

He swallowed, trying to dispel the lump in his throat. Of course it wouldn't go. Gina's face was a heartrending mask of pain and fury, and suddenly he wished he could take it all back, undo everything, make a different set of decisions. *Like what?* a cynical voice asked him. He shook his head, numb and unknowing.

"I love you," he said. Maybe it was a plea, maybe it was what she said—one last attempt to get her to absolve him.

Scorn twisted her features. "You're pathetic, Danny. Just go."

He didn't bother to pack anything. His socks and underwear seemed supremely unimportant just now.

He looked back one time before he closed the door. Gina's face was buried in her hands, and her shoulders shook with heavy sobs.

The image would stay with him for the rest of his life.

CHAPTER 23

"That's it," Case said as she put down her phone. "Erin says the tour's confirmed."

"It's really gonna happen," Danny said, wonder in his voice. He lay, propped up on his elbows, on Case's bed—a mattress on the floor, actually, one of the few things she had in common with Johnny, he thought. It had been a futon until a few days ago, when they'd broken the frame during a particularly energetic session.

"Yeah." She smiled. To Danny, she looked like a kid contemplating summer vacation and all the joys it would entail. It was an odd expression on her usually cynical face. He liked it.

"You ready for it?" he asked.

She took her time replying. "I think so." Another surprise. He'd expected a "fuck yeah" or something of the kind. Something more definite.

"Me, too." Danny turned, looking for his pants. He pulled them on quickly, then searched for his shirt for a futile moment before remembering that it had come off just inside the front door and was still there. "I'm gonna take off," he said. "Dinner tonight?"

She didn't answer for a long time. He finally looked back over his shoulder to see if she'd heard him.

"You don't have to go," she whispered, barely audible. "I mean, you can stay. If you want."

He thought about it. She hadn't made the invitation lightly, he knew—he could hear the strain in her voice. Turning back to her, he took her hand. He tried to choose his words very carefully. "This is not a great time. I mean, I spend a lot of time lately just trying to sort things out in my head—moping, basically—and I'm not going to be very good company much of the time."

Her eyes hardened briefly, but then she nodded. "If you're trying to say you need some time alone, I get that."

"Is your offer still going to be good in a few days?"

"Unless you piss me off, yeah."

He leaned over and kissed her. "Thank you. Dinner tonight?"

"Yeah."

***

Erin's butt had barely hit the chair at lunch when she leaned forward, an inquisitive gleam in her eye. "So," she said. "You and Danny."

Defiance was in Case's eyes as she nodded. "Yeah." *You got a problem with that?*

"Are you okay?"

Case blinked. That was not the kind of question she'd expected. "You mean, like, am I out of my fucking mind?"

"No, I mean, like, are you okay?" Erin said. "Really okay? The kinder, gentler Case—is she all right with this?"

"You mean the one who was trying not to be such a stone-cold bitch."

Erin smiled patiently. One of her more aggravating traits was that it was impossible to get a rise out of her when you were feeling combative, Case thought. Case waited, but it didn't look like Erin was going to give up any time soon. The waiter passed their table on the way to somewhere else, denying her even that brief reprieve.

"I don't know," she finally admitted. "I mean, I'm not flogging myself for it or anything—he had a choice, too, you know? *Has* a choice."

Erin nodded.

"And I think this has been brewing for a while." She was certain of it, in fact. Danny had wanted to explain some of his reasons, and after some initial reluctance, she'd let him. A lot of it seemed to boil down to simply needing someone to share his thoughts with—so much so that she'd felt vaguely ashamed for not knowing her own reasons so well. Sure, there was chemistry, and she felt that she had other, deeper, reasons; but she hadn't looked very hard for them. Introspection was not her strong suit. "So, you know. The situation sucks, but I haven't been wallowing in self-loathing between fucking marathons."

"Charming," Erin said.

"So, yeah. I'm okay."

Erin frowned, raising one eyebrow skeptically. "You don't *seem* okay."

"I'm fine."

"Not worried about being Rebound Girl?"

There it was, dammit. Case winced. She liked Danny—a lot. A lot more than she had anyone in a long, long time, and even though their situation was far from ideal, it was the picture of health compared with the shit she typically got herself into when she liked somebody a lot. The whole thing felt precarious. Inviting Danny to stay with her this morning had taken effort on par with tearing out her own liver, but it was as close as she could come right now to telling him that this—that *he*—mattered to her, and she had still felt horribly exposed.

"You really care about him," Erin said.

"What are you, Dr. Phil? Would you quit that? I mean, seriously?"

"All right," Erin said. "I'll lay off. But I'm here if you need to spill your guts."

"Thanks."

Neither of them said anything for a minute. Around them, the chatter of the restaurant continued unabated.

"So," Erin said in a low voice, "how is it?"

Case laughed. "Unbelievable. My neighbors are so pissed. We'll be lucky if we don't put each other in the hospital."

"Ha. I've sparred with you. He'll be lucky if *you* don't put *him* in the hospital—you've got nothing to worry about."

"Maybe so."

"And now, on to business."

And, God, there was so much business. Case looked at the list of things they had to take care of to get ready for the tour with mounting dismay. They'd been invited on the tour, so the booking and road crew were taken care of, but that was about it. They needed to arrange for their own transportation, their own food, their own lodging. Crashyard's record label would put Ragman's name on a few things, but for the most part they had to do their own promotion, too. Erin had a whole plan for that, as usual, but it involved sending out a ton of promotional material, including copies of their CD, to various radio stations and record stores.

"We don't have a CD," Case pointed out.

"You've got seven weeks to come up with one. It would be ridiculous to go on a tour this size without a CD to sell. And speaking of selling stuff, we're going to need to talk about merchandising."

Case groaned, and Erin jumped back into the list. There was a never-ending tide of details that needed to be attended to, and each one had a price tag attached.

"How much is all this going to cost?" Case asked, after Erin had at least ticked off all the major items.

"Depending on how much the recording costs, if we assume you sell your cars and buy a van, and you sleep in the van so you don't have to pay for rooms most of the time, and we assume cheap food—I'm guessing about eleven thousand dollars."

There suddenly seemed to be no oxygen in the room.

"Congratulations, rock star."

CHAPTER 24

"Sorry, sorry. Sorry, guys." The song stumbled to a halt, and Danny looked down sheepishly. "I got a little preoccupied. Let's hit it one more time. I'll get it this time. Really."

Case took her headphones off. "Give it a rest," she said.

The recording engineer apparently had the same thought. "Hey, how about you guys take five?" he said, his voice small and distant through the headphone speakers.

"Or fifteen," Case said. God, she hated the studio. Not this particular studio—it seemed decent enough, and the engineer was cool—but the general aura of all recording studios. Stuck in a sterile room, the sound coming out of obnoxious and uncomfortable headphones with a cable that always seemed to get in the way, and no *vibe*. The scrutiny was the worst, though. Trying to play rock and roll in a room like this was like getting a pelvic exam in front of an audience.

"I can get it," Danny protested.

Case put her guitar down. "Enough." Before she could see Danny's sad eyes, she walked out.

Johnny and Bill—the engineer—were waiting in the control room when she came in, sitting in front of an enormous mixing console. Bill had a kind smile for her. "There's always one song that just won't come together," he said. "But there's always one you knock out in two takes, too. It'll come around."

She sat down in the nearest chair and massaged her temples.

Danny came out a moment later, looking like a dog who'd just been scolded for pissing in the corner.

"What the fuck, man?" Johnny asked. "You know this motherfucker backwards and forwards. We've probably played it in front of a couple thousand people by now."

"I told you, I'll get it." Danny's embarrassment was changing to irritation with uncharacteristic speed.

The bass thumped, loud through the control-room speakers. Whatever was going on out here, Quentin was still having a good time. Bill turned him down a little.

"Why don't you get it then? Clock's ticking!" Johnny pulled back the sleeve of his motorcycle jacket—*his* jacket, since Case had reclaimed hers a while back—and tapped an imaginary wristwatch.

"Good thing it's my dime, then, isn't it?"

"Oh, it's your dime—that's why we were all waiting on your late ass this morning?"

"Hey! Enough, all right?" Bill's good-natured grin was gone, and now he looked like somebody's pissed-off dad. "Just cool it."

"I'll cool it when—" Johnny started, but Case cut him off.

"Outside," she said, pointing sharply with her thumb. "Now."

He gave her a mean little squint. "Or?"

"Or we'll have to pay for all the stuff I break with your head in here."

He sneered, but he got up.

Although she talked a good game, Case was getting very worried. It wasn't just the studio vibe—*everything* had a bad vibe lately. Somehow, more responsibility kept falling to her. Hell, if she'd become the band's peacekeeper, things had gotten very bad indeed.

The glare off the pavement in the parking lot was intolerably bright. Case stayed back next to the building where there was a sliver of shade, and Johnny followed suit. He crossed his arms and waited.

"What is wrong with you?" Case asked, low anger in her voice.

"What's wrong with me? I don't want to fuck this up, that's what's wrong with me. And my idiot brother can't seem to get his drumsticks out of his ass."

"Lay off. He's stressed out, and you know it."

Johnny curled his lip. "Nice arrangement you've got there. He gets his excuses made for him, and you get your oil changed."

"Don't." Her voice was calm, but the word came out crisply, the "t" sharp and explosive. She felt calm, too—the same calm she felt right before going onstage, right before a tournament fight—or right before some real violence went down. She wanted this tour as badly as anyone, but if Johnny said one more word like those last few, somebody was going to get hurt and fuck the consequences.

He must have read that in her face, because he dropped his gaze. His voice took on a whining tone. "Maybe we should try one of the new tunes."

Case groaned. This again. "Let it drop, Johnny. Now is not the time."

"They're good fucking songs."

"I don't know about that, but I do know that we haven't even learned them yet," she said. "I'm not sure we'll *ever* learn them."

"What's that supposed to mean?"

"I told you, I fucking hate metal. I'm not putting my name anywhere near a song with a name like 'Black Goat with a Thousand Young.'"

"Johnny says—" He stopped abruptly, closing his mouth with a click. "They're good songs," he said.

Great. Now he's talking about himself in the third person. One more thing to reinforce her growing sense that the band was unraveling. Danny had gotten flaky lately, showing up late for practice and recording, flubbing easy parts, and forgetting important pieces of equipment—like his goddamn *snare drum* on one occasion. His preoccupation in the studio was becoming standard. She could understand that, sure, but the timing was spectacularly bad. Johnny, for his part, alternated between being a massive dick and withdrawing into an anxious, inward-directed silence. He gave her the creeps, and while she didn't like to think about that too much, it was getting worse instead of better. She thought he was neglecting his personal hygiene, too—that could be the only explanation for the very faint, rank odor that clung to him all the time these days.

That was not today's problem, but it occurred to her that she'd have to talk to him about it before they all ended up in a cramped van together.

"Case says they're not that good," she said, garnering a look of pure hatred that was gone almost before it registered. Almost. "Anyway, *we don't know them.*" There. That was as much conciliation as she could muster. It would have to count as an attempt to keep this conversation from going off the rails.

It seemed to be enough. "Yeah. Okay."

Case breathed out, and that unearthly sense of calm left her. Seemed there wouldn't be a fight after all. "Now, do you suppose we can go back in there and pretend to like each other long enough to finish this fucking CD?"

Johnny nodded. All at once, he looked oddly lost.

"Good," Case said, and she opened the door. "Great."

***

The weeks leading up to the tour were brutal for Quentin. He needed money, so he'd picked up a bunch of overtime on the construction site. When the recording sessions started, he worked out a deal with his boss to get off early so he could make the sessions. He didn't want to give up the overtime, though, so part of the deal was that he'd come back after the sessions—often after midnight— and clean up the site and cut stock for the next day. He was down to about three hours of sleep a night, and his whole body hurt all the time. By the end of ten days of recording, he couldn't exactly remember a time when his whole body *hadn't* hurt.

That was cool, though—it would pass. The recording was done, and that's what counted. He knew Johnny and Case had some problems with the way it had come out, but he was thrilled. He had never imagined it would sound so good when they got done. The pressed copies wouldn't be ready for a couple of weeks yet, but he'd gotten a burned copy from the studio, and he had it cranked as he drove to the club for load-in.

One last show in Dallas, and then the tour. *The tour.* What a weird thought. Very cool, though. He hoped the turnout for the show was good—they were counting on the cash from the show to pay for the CDs and fund some of the trip.

He turned the CD up to deafening levels as he accelerated up the on-ramp to Central Expressway. It sounded *great*. He supposed he could see why Johnny wasn't too happy about it—Johnny sounded pretty good, but his voice was missing some of the magic it had during the live show. They'd tried a dozen or so microphones in the studio, just about driving the engineer nuts, but none quite nailed it. Maybe it was the space, or Johnny's nerves, but it wasn't quite *right*. Close enough, though—Johnny still sounded pretty good. The rest of the band sounded incredible. Quentin had listened to his own bass coming out of the speakers in the studio and it had sounded so good he was ready to tackle the engineer to get him to divulge the secret of that sound. That hadn't been necessary—Bill had been pretty forthcoming, and, incredibly, the "secret" turned out to be nothing more than a touch of equalization and compression. Just amazing. When Quentin got a few bucks, he was definitely going to have to get a decent compressor for his live rig.

Quentin was singing along with "Changing Gears" and wondering about how much a good compressor cost when he pulled up outside the club.

***

The club filled up, and by the time the third band of the night went on, Quentin realized he shouldn't have worried about the turnout for the night. Ragman was getting a pretty good local following, and Erin had cranked her unstoppable promotional machine into high gear besides. At the current pace, the club would be turning people away at the door before he and the guys took the stage.

He saw Danny and Case sitting at a high table off to the side of the stage, and he thought about going over to say hi. The two of them obviously had something going on these days, but it seemed cool. That was about the only thing about either of them that was cool lately, though. Danny was a roaming ball of stress, and Case looked like she was half an inch from tearing Johnny's head off most of the time. Quentin wished she'd just relax, but he wasn't sure he could really blame her. Since the weirdness of the last few months, even Quentin didn't like to be around Johnny any more than he had to. Still, it was too bad. He thought Case and Johnny would write some even more kickass tunes together if they just learned to get along.

Ah, well. He didn't see Johnny anywhere, so the tension at Case and Danny's table probably wouldn't have attained its usual stratospheric heights yet. He bought a screwdriver and a couple of beers and ambled over.

"Drinks all around," he said. He put them on the table and gestured at the room full of people. "Pretty cool, huh?"

"Yeah," Danny said. He looked more like himself than he had in weeks. "I think it's gonna be a good show."

Even Case flashed him a smile. "Get that compressor yet?"

Quentin grinned back. "Nope. Saving up for the tour."

"Me, too," Case said. "I ought to get some new tubes for my amp, but they're damn expensive. I'm praying the ones in there now last the whole tour. If they don't, I'm fucked."

Quentin was about to reply when Johnny showed up at the table—also with an armful of drinks. He had a big grin on his face, and he looked genuinely happy. It seemed like a long time since he'd been without the expression of frustrated anger that was carved into his face lately, and Quentin was glad to see it gone. Danny smiled, too, and patted him on the shoulder.

"Gonna be a good show tonight, I think," Johnny said.

"I'll drink to that," Quentin said.

The four of them raised their glasses.

***

"Yeah!" Quentin yelled, though nobody heard it over the roar of the band, amplified to deafening levels. Whether it owed to finally being out of the studio or to the reinforcement of having recently played the same parts over and over again in the studio, the band was firing on all cylinders tonight. He especially loved the bass at a live show, the thunder of the cranked subwoofers vibrating his whole body on the low notes, the kick drum pounding his chest. There was nothing like it in the world.

Johnny was hot tonight, as if to make up for his lackluster performance in the studio, and his voice tore ragged, white-hot holes in the air. Enough people knew the songs that they were starting to sing along with the choruses, which Quentin thought was the coolest thing.

They started up one of the newer songs Johnny'd been pushing for, an unsettling tune called "Ashes and Bone." It might have been a creepy tune, but the intro the band had worked up for it just plain rocked. They nailed it, and Quentin looked back at Danny and grinned. *I might get to do this for a job,* he thought, and his grin widened. Danny grinned back—and then Johnny dropped into the first verse of the song. The whole atmosphere of the room changed. The grin melted from Danny's face, and from Quentin's too.

> *"There's footprints under my window*
> *Cigarette ashes in a neat little pile*
> *Cross made out of chicken bones*
> *He's been coming for a long, long time"*

The crowd got quiet, doing that hypnotized thing they sometimes did when Johnny was on a roll. Usually, though, they did it during the slower, mellower songs. This was a more raucous number, but the crowd was swaying and weaving, making barely a noise.

The stage lights seemed too bright, the back of the room shrouded in darkness. Even the lights Quentin could see through the open door to the street looked dimmed. He knew that must be an illusion caused by the stage lights being so bright, but it was unnerving all the same—as if the real world outside this room were fading away.

It got worse when Johnny hit the chorus.

> *"He's waiting for me out there*
> *Coming for to carry me home*
> *Waiting for me somewhere*
> *Out among the ashes and bone*
> *Standing in the ashes and bone"*

Shadowy shapes seemed to flicker in the audience, shifting and writhing. They were never in Quentin's direct view, always at the edges no matter where he looked.

It occurred to him that the last time things had felt this bad during a show, Douglas had been circulating through the audience, whispering in ears. If that prick was here tonight, Quentin was going to be furious.

What if he follows us on the tour?

Oh, hell no. Things had been going reasonably well lately, and Quentin was not about to allow that creepy old bastard to screw them up. If he was here, Quentin was going to have a word with him.

The song came to an end. The crowd seemed to return to itself, applauding wildly, and Johnny held up his hands as though blessing them.

The lights came up, and sure enough, there was Douglas, slouching by the door, looking up at Johnny with shrouded eyes.

Quentin played through the rest of the set with a troubled mind.

***

"Fifteen hundred bucks!" Danny said jubilantly. They were the last band of the night, so the tally had been ready for them when they finished. Already, the place was starting to clear out.

"You're kidding," Case said. "There's no way they could have fit three hundred people in here."

"That's gotta violate fire code," Quentin mumbled. He looked from face to face at the thinning crowd. Douglas had been here, maybe still was, and that worried him. He'd lost track of the guy some time during the last song. Maybe that meant Douglas had gone—and maybe not.

"Ladies and gentlemen," Johnny said, "we have finally fucking arrived."

Quentin didn't know about that—he was finally fucking leaving. For once, he didn't have to work in the morning, and he wanted nothing more than to get the hell out of here and get some sleep. *Maybe that's it,* he thought. *I'm just overtired.*

No, wait—there was Douglas. The older man was slipping out the door right now.

Quentin watched as half a dozen kids in the crowd coalesced into a group and exited behind Douglas. Maybe they were just leaving, like everyone, but there had been something in their faces as they'd watched Douglas leave that he didn't like.

"Guys, I'm exhausted," Quentin said. "I'm gonna head out."

"Good show," Case said.

"See you Tuesday?" Johnny added.

"Yeah. See you Tuesday." He slung the gig bag holding his bass over his shoulder and moved toward the door.

Outside, the small clot of kids had been joined by another two or three, and a handful of others trickled in, swelling their numbers. Quentin could barely see Douglas, a block or so beyond them.

He thought of the group that had killed somebody outside one of their shows before, and he made a decision. He walked quickly to the lot next to the club where his car was parked, popped the trunk, and slid his bass in. He checked the charge on his cell phone. Full. He could dial 911 before those kids even looked at someone cross-eyed.

He started to close the trunk, then paused. Pushing his bass aside, he groped for his tool belt and pulled the heavy framing hammer from its loop.

Just in case.

He ran back to the sidewalk. The little mob hadn't gotten far. He started walking behind them, ignoring the strange looks from the handful of people who bothered to notice him.

***

That's it, Douglas thought. *Almost done.* The disciples were learning, growing in strength, and he'd managed to keep them away from Johnny for the last few months, managed to keep their more unpleasant activities quiet, or at least quiet enough. Now they were ready. He had seen them at the club. They had watched Johnny raptly, but other than that, they seemed normal enough. They moved like normal people, and they spoke like normal people, and they didn't do anything to attract attention to themselves. Only Douglas noticed the strain they were under as they fought to keep from either throwing themselves at Johnny's feet or sating their other hungers on whoever was convenient.

There was precious little left for him to do now but watch and wait.

He heard the footsteps behind him as he neared the end of Commerce Street, where the streets snarled together and the streetlights faded, and he smiled.

Douglas turned to meet the disciples. There were ten or so, walking toward him, murmuring in quiet voices. They walked smoothly, and their voices were low and controlled.

"Evening," Douglas said.

"Your work is done, old man," a hard-faced kid in an old bomber jacket said. "Johnny told us." The others echoed him. "Johnny," they said. "Johnny, Johnny."

Douglas stood straight as he felt his burden fall away. He was close to his god, now, so close he felt he could almost fly to meet him. "Come on, then," he said, gesturing toward a nearby alley. "Let's get out of the road and do this."

Hungry white grins split their faces, and they moved after him.

***

Quentin watched the old man slip into the alley, the clot of kids following close behind him. Whatever business they were doing, they wanted to do it away from the street.

It's nothing good, then.

Quentin walked toward the mouth of the alley, digging his phone from his pocket. He'd take a quick look, see what was going on and, if appropriate, call the cops.

He looked around the corner of the building. Enough light reflected off the white wall of the opposite building that he could make out figures moving in the alley. There was Douglas's thin figure, topped with a cloud of dark hair. Others stood arranged around him in a circle.

What the hell was he doing?

Douglas lifted his arms to either side and looked heavenward. "This is the end," he said, the whisper slithering along the night breeze to Quentin's ears.

The kids sprang toward the center of the circle. Cloth tore, baring Douglas's bone-white chest, and—*what the fuck?*—the kids jumped him. A tall one lunged at his shoulder, burying his teeth in the meat. Blood, black in the dimness, flowed down Douglas's body. Another kid clawed and gouged at his belly. Still another stuffed Douglas's fingers in his mouth and bit down with an awful crunch.

A moan, horribly ecstatic, came from Douglas as he slumped to his knees.

JESUS CHRIST! Quentin backed away from the alley, fumbling at his phone. There was a sudden motion coming from behind him, and somebody slapped the phone to the ground.

"No no no," a woman's voice said, and she leered at him with hunger and insanity in her eyes. "You shouldn't be here."

A second later, the knife punctured his stomach, then struck again, and again.

There was blood, so much blood, and pain, and then the world went black.

CHAPTER 25

The practice room felt like a funeral parlor.

Case sat on the floor in the place where Quentin's amp used to be, her eyes fixed on a random spot on the far wall. Danny sat beside her, hand entwined in hers. She had no clear idea if she was supposed to be receiving comfort or giving it, but she was glad he was there. Erin was on her other side, weeping silently into her hands.

Johnny sat against the door with his legs stretched out in front of him. Grief and confusion twisted his features, interrupted by an occasional flash of rage that seemed to come from nowhere and return just as quickly. He had called her just before the cop showed up on her doorstep that morning, and she thought she would be forever grateful for that. The thought of hearing the news from a stranger made her stomach sick.

Because this is your family, she thought. *It's a stupid, fucked-up, dysfunctional family, but all families are, and this one is yours.*

Johnny had called, and it had seemed like the most natural thing in the world that they should meet here after the police finished with everybody. There would be a real funeral service later in the week, but Case thought the farewells from the four of them would take place right in this shitty practice room—were taking place right now—where they'd all spent so much time together.

She wondered if she'd be able to play in this room again.

Quentin was dead. He had been knifed to death a few blocks down from the club, and Case inferred from the questions the cop had asked ("Did Quentin have any enemies?" "Did he have a drug habit?" "Did he owe anyone money?" "Do you know if anybody would have wanted to make an example of him?") that the killing had been spectacularly brutal. That was impossible to imagine. Quentin with enemies? No way. She thought of all the time she'd spent going over song parts with him, drilling him over and over, getting exasperated and calling him names, rolling her eyes, trembling in frustration. His patience was endless. He'd never so much as snapped at her—and she had to hand it to him, once he'd (finally) learned something, it was there to stay. Had been. He'd play it the same way every time, completely solid, one hundred percent reliable.

Who could hate Quentin? Who could *possibly* hate Quentin?

"I—" Johnny began, but then he stopped, confused. For once, Case knew just how he felt. What could be said that wouldn't cheapen Quentin's death by trying to encapsulate it in some lame, limpdick, meaningless phrase? *"I'm going to miss him"*? *"He was a swell guy"*? *"He was a good bass player"*? Or the perennial favorite, *"It's not fair"*? All of those statements were true, and they were all hopelessly inadequate.

"It's not fair," Danny said. Case had the presence of mind to bite her lip before a bitter laugh escaped. Her chest hitched, and Danny, perhaps mistaking it for a sob, put his arm around her. Rather than getting angry, she moved closer to him. Later, she would be pissed, if not about Danny's lame commentary, then about the whole damn thing in general. She would rage and curse and maybe—probably—break a bunch of things. Not here, though.

***

Later, Case could never remember who said it first. They had been sitting in the practice room for quite some time, silent except for the occasional awkward comment, and then somebody—Danny, maybe?—said out loud what (surely) they'd all been thinking:

"We're going to need to start auditions really soon, if we're going to find another bass player before the tour."

Nods greeted this statement, as though it were a foregone conclusion—to everyone except Erin. Erin lifted her head and looked around as though they'd all gone crazy.

"We have to get a different room," Case said, ignoring Erin. "I can't—I don't want somebody else to stand *there*. That was Quentin's spot." Sentimental, she knew, but she felt strongly about that.

Johnny nodded. "We'll change rooms. I'll talk to the owner."

Danny wiped a tear off the end of his nose. "I'll put an ad for a bass player on Craigslist. Unless you know somebody who might want the job, Erin."

Case looked at Erin automatically. Her face was pale, with livid red spots high on her cheeks and the expression of someone who has just been slapped, hard.

"You can't mean that," Erin said.

Danny's tone was defensive. "I just meant, you know. You know everybody."

"Quentin is *dead*," Erin said. "He's dead, and you all are talking like he just walked off the job one day, and you've got to find someone to fill his shift before the dinner rush. He's *dead*. Don't you get that?"

Case felt her temper stir and stretch its claws. "Do you know how many hours I spent in this goddamn room with Quentin? Do you have any idea? You think I don't notice the ragged fucking hole here? Maybe I just missed it?"

"And you think the best way to respect Quentin's memory is to carry on like nothing happened? Replace him at the earliest opportunity, and move right along?"

Case could hardly believe what she was hearing. "Jesus, no! I'm—*we're*—going to miss Quentin like crazy, but life goes on, you know? We've got *three weeks* before we leave. What do you want us to do?"

"You can't mean to go through with it."

The statement hit like a physical blow, and now Case felt like *she* was the one who'd been slapped. "Are you saying we should cancel the tour?"

Erin lifted her chin. "Yeah. Maybe you should."

"Are we supposed to stay home and mope? Stare at the ceiling for a few weeks? That's how we're supposed to *respect* Quentin?"

Erin stood up. "Quentin is *dead*," she said yet again.

Case couldn't figure out what that was supposed to prove, but she didn't like Erin looking down at her. She stood. "I know he is," she said softly. "We're not."

"Oh, that's—"

"Shut up," Case said. Erin flinched. "You've had your say. Quentin is dead. I know. We all know. But this isn't a hobby, Erin. Not for us. We've poured our lives into this— Johnny, Danny, and me. We've worked our asses off, and you can't even imagine some of the things we've sacrificed." She pointed to Danny, but an uneasy thought of Johnny intruded. "This is what we are meant to do with our lives, and if Quentin were here, he'd come along. But he's not. That sucks, but I'm not ready to hang up my guitar because of it."

Johnny nodded his agreement.

"You, too, Danny?" Erin said, tears standing in her eyes. "Is that how you feel?"

Danny looked at the floor. "Yeah."

Erin looked at each of them in turn. Case met her eyes, unsmiling.

"Then fuck you," Erin said, and she left.

***

Finding a bass player to fill in turned out to be a lot easier than expected. Brad's band was on temporary hiatus while the keyboard player took a couple of months off to focus on his wife and newborn son, and the bass player—a tall, gangly guy named Allen Sorenson—was looking for something to do. The only holdup was that it took Johnny two days to track down the owner of the rehearsal space and negotiate a room change. No matter what the rush, nobody was willing to audition a bass player in the old room. There wasn't even any discussion on that topic—it was understood.

The audition went flawlessly, much to everyone's surprise and relief. They went through "Burn," "Changing Gears," and "Rust," and Allen played them all note-for-note as they had been recorded. Just to make him work for it, the band walked him through "Ashes and Bone," the new, unrecorded tune. He picked it up immediately. Case felt an odd sorrow at that, but she tried not to let it show.

Thirty minutes after the start of the first audition, Ragman got itself a new bass player.

***

"I've been thinking about what Erin said," Danny announced to Case later that night. They were in bed, as usual, but still in their clothes for once. Sex was the farthest thing from either of their minds right then.

"Me, too," Case admitted. She'd done her best to stay angry at Erin, but the anger had eroded away day by day, and now she simply missed her. There was more in that fifth-Beatle joke than just a joke, she was starting to realize. With Quentin and Erin both gone, the band felt like a technically good but soulless facsimile of Ragman. Once she'd admitted that she missed Erin, she had been forced to revisit that day in the practice room, and it had opened up questions she had thought she'd never ask.

"I'm not saying we should have canceled the tour," Danny said. "But maybe we should have waited or something. I just saw the whole thing slipping away from us, and I felt like we had to do *something* right away."

Case rolled onto her side and put her hand on Danny's chest. "I know." She wanted to leave it at that, but she forced herself to continue. "I think music is the only thing I'm really good at. Without it, I'll be asking 'Would you like a to-go box?' and collecting shitty tips the rest of my life." She sighed. "So when Erin said we ought to cancel the tour, I blew up. There were probably a million better ways to handle that."

Danny put his hand on top of hers. "I don't know. Yeah, I suppose." He turned his head and looked her in the eye. "Do you think she'll accept an apology?"

"Maybe." Erin's self-righteousness bugged Case a lot, but probably only because she was right, or at least she was painfully close to being right. It would suck, but Case could talk to her.

"I think we've gotta do the tour, though," Danny said. "I really feel that. Don't you?"

Case nodded.

***

Ten days before the tour.

Erin hadn't been at work in over a week, so it wasn't as easy as running into her at the restaurant and making up. She wasn't answering her phone, either. Case would have to show up at her apartment, and she dreaded that idea. In Case's world, confrontations had largely been short, violent, and final—either outright physical brawls or shouting matches that Case walked away from, making sure to burn the bridge behind her. The scorched-earth model of human interaction, so to speak. Only now was she willing to concede that maybe that model hadn't served her all that well in the past. Trouble was, she wasn't quite sure how to replace it.

She parked in the lot at Erin's apartment complex. Her stomach, she was darkly amused to note, was full of butterflies—and moths, grasshoppers, and a whole insect army besides, from the feel of it. How was she even supposed to start this conversation? And how would she avoid getting pissed off and doing something unreasonable? She had no idea.

Oh, well. "Do something, even if it's wrong" had been one of the few pieces of advice her father had ever given her, and it seemed applicable now.

She got out of the car and walked up the two flights of stairs to Erin's apartment. She raised her fist to knock on the door, and then stopped. No epiphany had occurred to her on the way up the stairs, but the butterflies seemed to be hosting a keg party now. *You could leave,* she thought.

"Fuck that. Do something, even if it's wrong."

She knocked. No sound came from inside the apartment, and she wondered if she'd worked herself up for nothing. Maybe Erin was out somewhere—but, no. Case had seen her car in the lot. She knocked again.

"Just a minute!" Case heard movement, and the bolt slid back.

And there was Erin. She was in her pajamas—ghastly purple and green flannel things—with the phone in one hand. Her brow furrowed as she looked at Case.

"Hi," she said.

That one word was enough. Case had been mortally afraid, she realized, that Erin would stare blankly at her for a short eternity and, when Case couldn't think of anything to say, slam the door in her face. But now it was going to be okay.

"Hi," Case said. She still wasn't sure how to approach this problem, but she knew she wasn't any good with subtlety. "They're gonna revoke my Tough Chick card for saying this, but I miss you."

There was a pause. Case could hear a car horn honking down the street. One floor down, a door opened and then closed. She felt her face getting warm. She'd given Erin an opening big enough to drive a truck through, and a list of potential biting retorts scrolled through her head. Top of the list was *You miss me? Just like you miss Quentin?*

Erin wasn't saying anything, though, and her expression hadn't changed. It was still—what? Expectant? Accusing? Maybe just puzzled? Case didn't know, but she was starting to think this had been a horrible mistake.

"I'm sorry," Case said. "I mean—we're all sorry. But I shouldn't have blown up like that."

Still no answer.

"Look, I didn't mean—didn't mean to bother you. I guess I should get going."

"You wanna come in for a minute?" A ghost of Erin's old grin hovered at the corners of her mouth.

"God, yes."

Erin held the door open for her.

***

"It's good to see you," Erin said. "I didn't think it would be, but . . ." She shrugged.

"Yeah." Case sat on the arm of a living-room chair. "I wasn't kidding. I do miss you. I understand if you want to stay away from the band, but I'd hate for one stupid argument to . . . you know."

"I don't know if I'd call it stupid," Erin said.

"I didn't mean you were stupid," Case said hastily. "I mean, I didn't handle it that well."

Erin put the phone down and sat. "No, you didn't. Neither did I, though." She held her hands open. "It's hard to keep everything in perspective. How do you weigh the opportunity of a lifetime in a situation like this? I don't know."

Case shook her head. "Neither do I."

"Did you find another bass player?"

Case looked down at her hands. "Yeah." She felt the urge to explain, but Erin nodded.

"Good."

"Good?"

"Maybe. I don't know." Erin shrugged. "I do know that mourning can only go on so long before it becomes unhealthy. I have to admit, yesterday I started thinking about who was going to handle the email list and the merch booth during the tour."

"You're kidding."

"No, not really. Work isn't a bad way of coping, they tell me. Also, I think it might be cool to book a homecoming show here in Dallas. Make it your last stop."

Case laughed. "You *have* been thinking about this."

"Nothing definite, but yeah."

"Cool."

Case thought that maybe everything was going to be okay after all.

CHAPTER 26

The tour started in Atlanta on the fourteenth of June. They'd managed to buy a conversion van by selling Danny's car and making a loan on hideously unfavorable terms, and the five of them crammed into it with all their gear.

"This is cozy," Danny remarked.

"See how you like it in another three weeks," was Case's reply. Johnny laughed an eerie laugh that ran up the scale and back down again and gave Case the creeps.

Nonetheless, spirits were high. They arrived at the venue with ample time, and Case was thrilled at the luxury of getting a real, professional sound check.

"Gonna be scary," she said. "I'll actually be able to hear Johnny for once."

Johnny grinned. "That *is* scary."

The guys from Crashyard walked in as the road crew was setting up ("Roadies!" Danny had said, laughing and pointing at the crew. "We get roadies!"), and they offered words of encouragement.

"You'll do fine," Kerry Buchanan said. He smiled wickedly. "Just try to forget that there will be two thousand people watching your every move."

Case looked at Johnny, expecting him to start coming down with a bad case of nerves starting right then, but he looked jazzed. "No problem," he said, showing his teeth, and she thought he meant it.

Sound check went smoothly (one of the mic cables turned out to be dead, but the sound crew identified that and swapped it out in record time), and the five of them laughed and joked backstage.

"A real road crew, a real sound check, *and* a real green room," Danny said wonderingly. "What's the world coming to?" They had a few hours before the show, but nobody suggested going anywhere. Erin asked if anybody was hungry. Nobody was.

"I'm too nervous to eat," Case admitted. "It's a big show." Danny nodded his agreement. Even Johnny's cocksure swagger didn't look so hot on a face that had taken on the color and texture of pale cheese. Allen looked frankly terrified, and he got out his bass a full two hours before the show and started warming up.

"Little early for that, huh?" Case asked him.

He gave her a sheepish grin. "It gives me something to focus on besides sheer terror."

That actually didn't sound half bad. Case got out her own guitar and started practicing scales. Twenty minutes later, Danny produced a practice pad from somewhere and started whacking on it. "You know we're all going to be too tired to actually play by the time we go on, right?" he joked.

An hour passed, then another. Case had expected her anxiety to wane as the show got closer—she hadn't been nervous before a show in years—but it worsened.

"It's a big show," she said to nobody in particular.

Fifteen minutes before the show was supposed to start, Johnny raised his hand. "Quiet," he said. "You hear that?"

Case stopped her restless hands and listened. There was a dull grumbling noise that sounded muted but vast. She felt her face pale.

"Holy shit. That's the crowd."

Danny's eyes opened wider than she would have imagined possible. "Shut the door, for Christ's sake," he said. "I don't need to hear that."

The crowd couldn't have been *that* big, Case thought; she would be surprised if the room was even half full for the opening act. Then she remembered the size of the room. Half full might be more than a thousand people.

Over the next fifteen minutes, the anxiety in the room ratcheted up to levels that nearly shrieked. At five to nine, Case stood up. "Are we going, or what?"

"Gotta wait for the road manager," Danny said. "He'll tell us."

"Is he gonna make us wait until the Second Coming?" she snapped, even though they had five minutes before the show was even scheduled to start—and she knew they'd go on late. It was like the eleventh commandment: Thou shalt go on late.

At ten after, the road manager popped his head into the room.

"Showtime," he said.

The four players looked at each other.

"Give 'em hell!" Erin said cheerfully.

***

They await us, "Johnny" said. It never shut up anymore, offering a seething running commentary on everything, and today gave no exception or reprieve.

These are your people, John. These are our people. They hunger for us, though they do not yet know it. We can raise them above their miserable little lives. Make them better. Make them something more.

Yeah, I know, Johnny told it. He didn't, not really, but he didn't know what "Johnny" was talking about most of the time, only that it wasn't a good idea to piss it off. "Johnny" was the only thing keeping him steady right now, keeping him from running down the back alley in a complete panic.

They took the stage in the dark, but there was no disguising the sound of hundreds of people, and the sharper eyes in the crowd saw the members of Ragman even in the low light and raised a cheer.

They've been standing around bored for hours, Johnny thought. *Of course they're cheering.* Nonetheless, the sound bolstered his courage.

He took his place in front of the microphone, and the lights came up.

Do you see them, John? They will be ours one day soon. Every one of them.

He couldn't *not* see them. Christ, there were so many!

Behind him, the band started. "Burn," of course—always a crowd-pleaser, and with the short set typical of an opening act, they had to make every song count. They started too fast, *way* too fast, but maybe that wouldn't be too bad. The song cooked—maybe it would cook that much hotter faster.

Then it was time to come in, and "Johnny"—the voice, the thing in his head—surged forward. It didn't bother asking anymore, just channeled itself through his vocal cords.

"Johnny" sang.

***

This is it, Danny thought. *This is what it's all about.* Case had started the damn song too fast, but it didn't matter. The energy was good—smoking, in fact—and that's what counted. The band was into it, and so was the crowd from what Danny could tell.

What a rush!

Case and Allen made their way back to the drum riser—it seemed to take forever, the stage was so wide—and jammed with him during the bridge, both of them grinning like happy drunks. The song was barely half over, and already sweat poured off Case's face.

Up front, Johnny milked the crowd. Before the last verse, he whipped out that tired line again, screaming "Is it hot enough for you, motherfuckers?" at ungodly volume, and the audience went nuts.

He's gotten really good at this, Danny thought with a surge of pride for his little brother.

They finished the song, and applause rolled over them, crashing down like thunder. Case shook her head in disbelief and gave him a huge smile. Then it was on to the next song.

Case was hot tonight, there was no doubt about that, but Johnny was incredible. He growled and snarled and soared, drawing the audience in and inciting them to ever-greater frenzy. That ominous, paranoid sensation Danny sometimes felt during shows crept in, that weird sense that something malevolent watched him and laughed, but it was weak and buried beneath the adrenaline rush.

The last song was "Rust," and Danny couldn't believe the set was almost over. Hadn't they just taken the stage?

Johnny held his hands high before the last chorus. "My children!" he said. "Sing with me!" That was weird, Danny thought—next he'd be announcing that he was the Lizard King—but the audience ate it up, and the chorus was simple enough that they could follow along. Amazingly, hundreds of them did. Danny stared in shock, muscle memory and hundreds of hours of rehearsal the only things carrying him through the song as he stared at the crowd.

Then the show was finished. The cheers and shouts of over fifteen hundred people followed them off the stage.

***

"Holy hell, guys," Erin said. "We're going to need to call up the duplication company and see if they can press a lot more CDs and ship them to us. At this rate, we're going to run out before we get to Chicago."

There were cheers all around. It had been a good night, no doubt about that. Kerry Buchanan himself had found the five of them after Crashyard had finished and given his congratulations—and that wasn't all. He'd beckoned to Case, pulling her out of the knot of loudly chattering people.

"Great fucking show," he said. "But you can't gig without a backup axe." He handed her a guitar case, one with a very distinctive shape and the words *Gibson USA* on the top.

"You can't be serious," she said.

"Open it."

She didn't need to be told twice. She put the case on the floor and knelt in front of it. Her hands shook as she flipped the catches. Dimly, she was aware that a small crowd had gathered around her.

She opened the guitar case. Inside was a pristine Les Paul Standard guitar, wine red and utterly, completely gorgeous.

"Oh my God," she said. Looking up, she met Kerry's eyes. "I can't thank you enough for this."

He smiled. "You did good, kid." Once, not long ago, she would have assumed he wanted something—sexual favors, most likely—for such a gift, but today she didn't feel quite so cynical. He seemed genuinely happy for her, and in any case his wife was standing next to him, also smiling.

Case looked at her bandmates, who grinned and clapped her on the back. Except Johnny. The blood had drained from his face, and he had the look of a man about to vomit. He grinned weakly at her. "Cool," he said, and he put a hand to his mouth.

After the revelry, there was a quick conference to determine sleeping arrangements.

"We did pretty well tonight," Erin said. "We could probably afford a motel. But we don't know if every night will be like tonight, and I have a feeling we're *really* going to want beds in a couple of weeks. I'd hate to be short on cash then."

The vote to spend their first night in the van was unanimous.

***

Case couldn't sleep. It wasn't the van, either. She had drawn the luxurious front seat, passenger side, and that didn't even rate on the list of uncomfortable places she'd slept. She thought her insomnia might be an ugly aftereffect of her post-show high, but the others were sleeping just fine. Danny had dropped off almost as soon as he'd put the van in park. She certainly felt exhausted. Her legs were sore from being cooped up all day and then the sudden, spastic exertion of performance, and her whole body felt drained and achy.

She turned on her side. It was awkward, even with the seat all the way back, but at least this way she was pointed away from the light. There were only a couple of lights in the parking lot, and Danny had made an effort to park away from them, both to help everyone sleep and to stay far away from the prying eyes of any of the cheap motel's employees, who might take exception to their freeloading. There probably wouldn't be any problems—with Crashyard's bus in the lot, the staff was undoubtedly more worried about how trashed the rooms would be in the morning.

Having her back to the light was a definite improvement. The light glided over her shoulder, lighting up Danny's arm and hand, but at least it wasn't in her eyes anymore.

She lay still, listening to the night. Semis roared by on the freeway, and crickets and frogs chirped noisily nearby. There was a faint dank scent in the van. Perhaps it came from whatever marshy home the frogs made for themselves, but she thought it was that smell Johnny carried around with him. Nasty. Behind her, Allen breathed loudly. That was kind of obnoxious, but she tried to fall into the rhythm, and soon enough, her eyes fell shut. Images of the day spun in her head, and she sank down toward sleep.

There was a noise, and she sprang to full wakefulness, her body tensed from head to foot.

What was that?

It came again—a scraping noise that Case immediately identified as that of a shoe on pavement. Her heart thumped in her ears.

Calm down. This is a parking lot. People come to places like this to get in their cars. The sarcasm didn't put her mind at ease. She waited, listening. She didn't hear the click of an opening car door, or the clunk of a closing one.

Another scrape, closer this time. There was somebody by the side of the van. She was almost sure of it.

Somebody's fucking with us. She thought of the equipment in back, adding numbers in her head. She guessed there was maybe twelve thousand dollars' worth of gear back there. Had somebody got it in their head to liberate some of it? *If so, they'd goddamn well better be armed.* Anger welled up in her, but it seemed a small, feeble thing next to her fear. Something about this felt very bad, and there was a familiarity to the *badness* of it that she couldn't place.

Another scrape, closer still, and this time a shadow fell across Danny's arm. There was somebody right behind her. Her skin prickled with gooseflesh. Case could feel eyes tracing her body. The door was locked, right? Sure. That was basic Sleeping in the Car 101. They couldn't get in without breaking the window, and when they did, Case would go for the eyes. Or maybe she'd turn around right now, pop the door open, and slam it into the psycho standing back there. Both options sounded bad—sounded terrible, in fact—not least because Case felt paralyzed with fear.

She could wake Danny.

Even as she thought of it, somebody looked in through Danny's open window, appearing suddenly and leering at her.

She screamed.

Danny jolted upright, and there was movement from the back of the van, too. Erin screamed next, piercing and terrifying in the close confines of the van, and even Allen yelled.

Case turned, and—*Jesus Christ!* There was another person pressed to the window behind her, flattening the side of its face to the glass. The mouth was pulled back in a horrifying grimace, and one eye rolled madly. It settled on her, and the grimace stretched.

Case pushed back, almost landing in Danny's lap. Then she remembered the other one on Danny's side, and she froze. The person on her side started clawing at the glass.

"Johnny!" it said. "Johnny Johnny, we love you Johnny!"

And then from the other side: "We missed you Johnny! We missed you where it's so coooold." It opened its mouth, reared back, and tried to *bite* the window. Its top lip split open and one of its front teeth broke off. It didn't seem to notice. It tried again, tearing its lip open wider and leaving a cloudy smear of blood on the window. "Johnnyyyyyy! We love you!" Erin screamed again.

"For fuck's sake, Danny, get us the hell out of here!" Johnny said. "Drive, goddammit!"

Danny seemed to remember where he was, and he cranked the starter. Not bothering to check behind him, he backed up as fast as the van could go. The side mirror knocked one of the people down, and Case heard it laughing as it slammed into the pavement.

Once they'd backed up, Case could see all of the people who had crowded around the van while the others slept. There were five of them, staring stupidly after the departing van.

"Fucking *go*!" she told Danny. He didn't need telling by that point—he peeled out of the parking lot without looking back.

In the backseat, Erin burst into tears.

CHAPTER 27

"What the hell was that all about?" Case asked once they got on the road. Her voice shook slightly, and Johnny could see her checking the mirrors every few seconds, though it was impossible that anyone would be able to keep up with them. At least not on foot, he thought.

Perils of fame and glory, John my boy, "Johnny" said.

"Perils of fame and glory," Johnny said without much conviction. Case turned in her seat to look at him, and he suddenly got very interested in the view out the window.

"Bullshit," she said. "Let's ask the guys in Crashyard how often this happens to them—I bet the answer is never, and you know it."

We don't know that, "Johnny" said. Johnny was too freaked out to argue. He just repeated the words as they came into his head.

"We don't know that," he said. Pause. "Besides, they have a tour bus and rented rooms. They probably haven't slept in the van for ten years."

"That's crap, Johnny." Everyone was looking at him now. Even Danny kept glancing in the rearview mirror. Case's face was serious as death. "What did you do?"

He tried on an expression of surprise. It felt natural enough. "What do you mean, what did *I* do?"

"Johnny Johnny Johnny," Case said in an ugly, high-pitched voice. "Those creepy bastards were all looking for you."

Johnny was silent. *It's not my fault*, the voice prompted. "It's not my fault the local mental hospital went on a field trip today. And you know I didn't arrange this—I was with you guys all night!"

Some of the fire seemed to go out of Case, but suspicion hung in the air like a particularly noxious perfume. She turned around and curled up in her seat, staring forward.

"I don't know what any of that was about," Allen said, "but it was some creepy shit."

On that, everyone could agree.

***

They found another parking lot—a *much* more well-lit parking lot, which seemed both prudent and unfortunate as far as Case was concerned. She supposed it didn't matter. The odds of her getting any sleep before dawn were vanishingly small by now. Sure enough, sleep didn't come. It didn't come for Danny, either, though incredibly the three in back didn't seem to have any trouble. Even Erin had dropped off.

Danny talked about the show in a low voice. They'd talked about it at length earlier that evening, but he was still thinking about their thirty minutes of fame, rehashing the high points and talking about the things he needed to clean up at the next show. It was reassuring talk of mundane things, and it helped bury the events of the last hour.

The sun came up, and Danny started driving. It was six or seven hours to their next stop, Raleigh, so they had plenty of time, but since neither of them could sleep, it seemed reasonable to get a head start. Maybe they'd sleep when they got there. Johnny woke up when they started moving and asked if they could stop and get breakfast before leaving Atlanta. They got greasy breakfast sandwiches at a rest stop, and Johnny picked up a newspaper.

"Maybe we got a review," he said defensively when Case eyed the paper. To her practiced ear, he sounded like he was full of shit, but she was too tired to argue about it. If Johnny wanted to keep up on current events, that was his business.

By 7 a.m., Atlanta was a smudge in the rearview mirror.

***

The show in Raleigh went much as the show in Atlanta had, except the band was less terrified. They all agreed afterward that they played much better than the previous night, though the rush of performing didn't seem to have diminished any.

"I could get used to this," Allen joked.

The only worry they had afterward—unvoiced, but clear in the nervous eyes of all five of them—was that they'd get another nocturnal visit from the nutjob patrol. Danny drove them to a spot that was well clear of the venue and equally far from Crashyard's hotel, and though nobody slept well, they weren't bothered.

After that, they fell into a routine. Arrive early, get a couple hours of rest. Then sound check and a few hours of waiting. The thirty minutes they got onstage seemed terribly short for all the effort, but it was anything but anticlimactic.

Each night, the crowd seemed more fired up than it had before.

"Some of the same people keep coming back," Erin said after one show.

"Are you sure?" Case asked. "These venues are hundreds of miles apart."

"Yeah, I'm sure. The tall girl with the blue mohawk is hard to miss. There are others, too, but she's the most obvious."

"Friend of the band? Die-hard Crashyard fan?"

"Maybe," Erin said skeptically. "I don't see them up front during Crashyard's set, though."

"Huh. Diehard Ragman fans. Who'd have thought?"

"Yeah," Erin said. She didn't sound like she thought that was a good thing.

After each show, they'd party with the guys from Crashyard and then go find a place to park for the night—always somewhere with lots of lights, always far away from both the venue and Crashyard's motel. There were no further nocturnal visitations.

The shows were getting creepier, though. After Erin's comment about the girl with the blue mohawk, Case started paying more attention to the crowd. That very night, she saw a tall girl with a blue mohawk over on Johnny's far side, staring raptly up at him and licking her teeth in a decidedly hungry-looking manner.

By the seventh stop—Boston—Case had identified no fewer than half a dozen recurring showgoers. The girl with the blue mohawk was keeping some very strange company. There was a middle-aged guy in a tie, with his white shirtsleeves rolled up to his elbows. A biker, complete with enormous beer belly, bushy black beard, and Harley Davidson T-shirt. A heavyset woman covered in tattoos. Two college guys who typically showed up in polo shirts with their hair combed up in idiotic-looking fauxhawks. Case wanted to deck the both of them, and she was baffled by the fact that the girl with the blue mohawk hadn't already done so. The group seemed to travel together, though, and each night when Case spotted one of them, the other five were nearby. The lot of them seemed to have eyes only for Johnny.

"Is it normal for groups of people to follow you from show to show?" Case asked Kerry one night.

He shrugged. "It happens sometimes. I haven't had to get a restraining order yet. If you're worried, just give their descriptions to security. They'll keep an eye out for anything weird."

Case did just that, but she wasn't reassured. It didn't help that the whole vibe surrounding Johnny was getting weirder and weirder. He talked to himself constantly, and she didn't think he was aware of it at all. His voice was getting deeper, too—not lower, exactly, but *deeper*. He sang the same songs night after night at the same pitch as always, but his voice sounded larger than it used to somehow. It worked, she couldn't deny that, and the audiences loved him, but it unnerved her. His voice got better and stronger every night—it was unnatural.

It would be easy to dismiss it as paranoia, but paranoia was itself part of the weirdness around him. Ever since the episode in the parking lot in Atlanta, Case felt like she was being watched. Each night that Johnny sang, casting his eerie spell on the crowd, the paranoia intensified. She didn't smoke much pot anymore, but she had spent most of the year after she graduated high school stoned out of her mind, and this paranoia felt worse than a bad high—far worse, and much longer-lasting.

In Philadelphia—the twelfth show, maybe? maybe the thirteenth?—Johnny substituted a whole line of ominous-sounding gibberish for one of the lines in "Changing Gears." Those strange, crackling syllables made Case shudder, and when she looked at Allen, his eyes were wide with alarm. He'd heard it, too, then—it wasn't just paranoia.

She accosted Johnny moments after they got off the stage.

"What the hell was that?" she asked.

Johnny was grinning, still bopping his head to the music. "That was a good motherfucking show, that's what that was. What's your problem?"

"In 'Changing Gears'—what were you singing?"

Confusion flickered across his face, replaced a moment later by an uneasy grin. "Just singing the song," he said.

"My ass. Those weren't words. That wasn't English. What the hell were you singing out there?"

His grin got steadier. "Oh, I just forgot some of the lyrics. Brain freeze. I faked it, but I don't think too many people noticed. Looked like they were having fun, anyway."

She glared at him but she let it drop. Living in a van with five people, you learned to pick your battles.

She wasn't the only one who had noticed, though—and not everybody was willing to let it go.

***

Erin got the new shipment of CDs in Chicago as planned, and it was a good thing, too—they were down to only a dozen CDs. The good news was that they were making way more money than expected. A quick review of band funds told them they were far enough ahead that a night in real beds would fit comfortably in the budget. They got a couple of rooms in a Motel 6 off I-90, and Erin gave them a complete update on the state of their finances while they lounged in beds and chairs in the guys' room.

"At the current rate, you'll be able to make Danny whole on the recording costs and even make some money by the end of the tour," she said. She looked edgy, and Case didn't miss the pronoun—*you'll* instead of *we'll*. That wasn't like Erin.

"So that brings me to the last item of business," Erin said. Her voice wavered on the last word, and Case could see tears shining in her eyes.

Oh shit.

"This has been wonderful, guys, and I'm so glad you brought me with you. But this was my last stop." She let out a long breath. "I'm going home."

There was an outcry from everybody in the room—except, Case noted, Johnny. He merely sat up and looked at her with narrowed, suspicious eyes.

"Why?" Danny asked.

"Yeah, what's up with that?" Allen chimed in.

Erin's eyes darted to Johnny and then away. "This is just too intense for me," she said. "I wasn't made for sleeping in a van, waking up in a new city every day, eating french fries nonstop. All this chaos. It was fun for a while, but I'm completely fried, guys."

"Come on," Allen said. "You know we can't run this traveling circus without you!"

"I'm sorry. I just can't do it anymore."

A somber silence greeted this pronouncement.

"We're gonna miss you," Danny said finally. "Like you can't imagine."

At that, the first tears fell from Erin's eyes. "I'll see you when you get back to Dallas. The show's been confirmed, by the way—I'll make sure everybody's waiting for you when you get back."

There were hugs all around, then, and a proposal was put forward to get sloppy drunk. Erin begged off.

"I get an actual bed tonight. I think I'll enjoy it." She smiled thinly. "I'll see you guys at breakfast. My bus leaves at ten."

She left, still wiping tears from her cheeks.

Case followed.

Once the door to their room was closed, Case went over and sat on the chair by the window.

"I can't say that was the best surprise I've gotten lately," Case said.

Erin sat on the edge of the bed. "Yeah. Sorry." She brushed hair out of her face and wiped her eyes again. "I was gonna talk to you first, but then I thought if I did, I'd lose my nerve. I thought you'd talk me out of it."

Case nodded. It stung, but she understood. She probably *would* have tried to talk Erin out of it. "So what's the real reason?" she asked. "That line of crap about this being too intense for you might go over with the guys, but you're not fooling me."

Another weak smile. Case noticed for the first time how tired Erin looked—she had dark smudges under her eyes, and there were lines on her face that Case didn't think were there when they'd left Dallas.

"Don't laugh," Erin said.

"I'm not even smiling."

Erin took a deep breath. "This tour is scaring the hell out of me."

Case watched her face carefully. "That night in the parking lot?"

"That night in the parking lot was plenty bad, but there's more. Did you watch the crowd? Have you seen the people I told you about?"

"The girl with the blue mohawk," Case said.

"Yeah."

"There are others, too. Five or six more, I think."

Erin shook her head. "Guess again."

"Huh?"

"I think there are about fifteen now."

All at once, that lurking paranoia intensified. They were on the third floor, but Case got up and closed the curtains. When she sat back down, Erin was drinking from a cup of water. "Fifteen?" Case asked.

"Yeah. Something like that. There are a lot of them, anyway."

"Kerry told me that was kind of normal."

"Do you believe that?"

Case shifted her shoulders. "I didn't give him all the details, exactly. I'm not sure it's normal. Not at all."

"That's not all, either." Erin lowered her voice to a whisper. "Johnny's starting to really give me the creeps."

"Me, too," Case admitted.

"Yeah?" Erin said without much surprise. "Did you hear that weird—I don't know—*chant* or whatever it was he slipped into one of the songs the other night?"

"Yeah. I didn't like the sound of it. Neither did Allen."

"You should have seen the crowd. Most of them got real nervous about then, but Johnny's special followers looked like they had a collective orgasm." A dark, cryptic expression spread across Erin's face. "I almost left after that show. I should have."

A sudden insight bloomed in Case's mind. She leaned forward, studying her friend's face. "Erin, what happened tonight?"

Erin smiled sadly. "It's that obvious?"

"*What happened?*"

"You've never been in the audience, so maybe you don't feel it. Johnny—he's got a gift. The real deal. Sometimes when he sings, it's like he pulls you into this trance, and all you can see is the spotlight on him, and all you can hear is his voice. You catch yourself thinking strange thoughts, and sometimes you feel that everyone around you has *changed*, but you don't even care. There's Johnny, and there's the music crashing down like waves. Sometimes it makes you feel bad, but mostly it's intoxicating—and you don't always remember the bad parts very well later."

"I get paranoid," Case admitted, fascinated. "I feel like there's something watching us—something besides the audience."

"I get that sometimes, too."

"What happened tonight?" Case asked, though she was no longer sure she wanted an answer.

"Johnny was singing, and the light got brighter around him—it was so bright that Johnny was all I could see from the back of the room. As the light got brighter around him, it got darker in the rest of the room. Scary dark. I was half in that trance, but I tried to move away.

"There wasn't far to move, though—I was already at the wall, back behind the table with the merch. I pushed against the wall, but I could still feel something watching me, something *behind* me, even though I knew that was impossible. You ever do too much coke? It was like that, only worse.

"Then something touched me.

"It brushed against me. *It touched my face.* It was cold. Cold and awful. It was like, I don't know—it was like it was *pressing* on me. Somehow I broke free of the trance enough to push back at it. I couldn't see anything, but I could feel it move away.

"A moment later, it was gone. But a guy standing in the back row turned around and looked at me. I remember the light glinting off the rings in his ear—so many rings it looked like he'd wound the wire from a spiral notebook into the outer part of his ear.

"He winked at me, Case. He turned around, looked directly at me, and winked. Then he went back to watching the show."

"Jesus," Case said.

"You know what the worst part was? The worst part was that part of me wanted that *thing* to touch me—wanted it so bad I almost reached out for it." Erin rolled the plastic cup between her hands. "I don't know if I'll be able to stop myself next time."

"Are you okay?" Case asked.

"Do you mean, am I nuts?"

"No. I believe you." She did, mostly. She wanted to chalk all this up to Erin freaking out from stress, but too much of it matched her own experience. Too much of it lined up with things she was already worrying about. "I mean, are you okay?"

"I don't know. I do know that I need to get away from this. Either I'm cracking up, or something bad is happening."

"I don't think you're cracking up," Case said softly.

"Either way, I'm getting out of here." Erin paused. "You might think about doing the same."

"I can't do that. It's not like they can just replace me."

"I don't know if that matters anymore."

Case shook her head. "It matters."

Erin raised a skeptical eyebrow to show what she thought of that. "Watch the crowd," Erin said. "Look for a thin man with a spiral notebook wound into his ear.

"I bet he'll be right up front at the next show."

CHAPTER 28

She knows, Johnny thought. It was an effort just to think those words clearly. His head seemed so cluttered lately, crowded with thoughts that were not his own.

Knows what? the voice in his head said scornfully. Johnny winced. The voice didn't whisper anymore—it spoke so strongly that sometimes he caught himself looking around to see if anybody else had heard it. *She wasn't cut out for life on the road? Few are. Relax, John. Go back to sleep.*

That sounded like a good idea. Sleep. "Johnny" probably had the right idea—it usually did. *Look what it's done for me so far,* Johnny thought with genuine gratitude.

That's right. We're going places together, you and me. Now go back to sleep. "Johnny" sounded irritated with him.

Well, we're all tired in here, Johnny thought, and he laughed. It sounded desperate and hysterical, even to him. In the other bed, Allen stirred.

Despite his leaden limbs and sluggish mind, Johnny forced himself to sit up. It was five-forty, which meant the newspapers would be out. He got out of bed and grabbed his backpack.

This is foolish, John, the voice said, like a stern parent. *There's nothing to prove, and you're only making yourself upset.*

Nonetheless, Johnny walked to the door. He reached for the handle, and for one dreamlike moment, his body stopped moving. His hand stopped in midmotion and wouldn't go forward, and his legs were stuck in place. Then the moment was gone, and he moved forward just as smoothly as if he'd never stopped.

Did that really happen? Am I losing my mind?

No, the voice said, though it didn't seem especially sincere. *You're tired. You need rest.*

He ignored it as best he was able and left the room.

Downstairs, the motel staff was starting to set breakfast out. Johnny had no interest in that. He found a copy of the *Tribune* and settled in to one of the chairs in the lobby.

He found what he was looking for in the local section. A young man had been brutally killed late last night—beaten to death, apparently, though the article hinted that an animal had been at him after he was killed. The article also gave an address where the body was found, and though Johnny didn't know anything about Chicago geography, he didn't guess he needed to. It would have happened near last night's venue.

It always did.

You're being stupid, the voice told him. *This obsessive fantasy of yours isn't doing anyone any good.*

He took his journal and a pair of scissors from his backpack. His vision blurred, but he shook his head and it cleared. A woman in a business suit walked by, giving him a wary look.

He flipped to the middle of the journal. Once, the journal had been a log of daily thoughts, events, fragments of lyrics, but lately it had become a grisly sort of scrapbook. At the top of each of the last thirteen pages was a city and a date. Below most of the dates, Johnny had taped an article from the local newspaper.

Atlanta. June 17, 2010. Two Concertgoers Killed in Apparent Parking Lot Brawl.

Raleigh. June 18, 2010. Woman's Body Found Mutilated in Alley. No suspect in custody.

Richmond. June 20, 2010. Man Mauled to Death Downtown. Police suspect feral dogs.

It went on for thirteen pages, one page for each stop they'd made on the tour so far. Charlotte. Baltimore. There was no article on the page for New York—Johnny had combed the papers and found nothing. Perhaps nothing had happened that night, or perhaps New York suffered an embarrassment of riches in the violence department, rendering the nightly crop of bodies found in Dumpsters and alleys less than newsworthy. Boston. Columbus. Indianapolis. Detroit. No article for Cleveland, for whatever reason. Philadelphia. Milwaukee.

He cut the article for Chicago out with trembling hands.

Put it away, John, "Johnny" told him, disgusted.

What are we doing, Johnny? he asked it. *What are we doing?*

We're not doing anything. These are big cities, Johnny, and the human race is teeming with barely suppressed violence. That the cup should run over sometimes is hardly a surprise. It runs over nightly, everywhere. You're looking for patterns in chaos, John. Save your energy for something worthwhile.

Numbness filled Johnny, but while he felt no pain, no guilt, there was a slight pressure reminding him that he *should* feel something.

Erin knows, he thought. *Maybe not anything specific, but she knows something has gone wrong here.*

Nothing has gone wrong here, "Johnny" told him. *Put this foolishness away and go to sleep.*

Through the fog in his thoughts, Johnny made a decision. The thing in his head wouldn't like it—but fuck him. This was going to end tonight.

John, what are you thinking? I can't hear you, John. The voice sounded faintly alarmed, Johnny noted with satisfaction.

He taped the article in under Chicago.

***

Erin said her goodbyes at breakfast, and there were no tears this time. She gave Johnny a searching look before giving him a hug. He didn't miss her hesitation, or the way she wiped her hands on her jeans afterward, but he tried to smile even as the voice in his head cursed and called her foul names.

They dropped her off at the bus station, and then it was on to St. Louis.

What are you thinking? the voice asked him. He stared out the window at the cornfields and tried to tune it out. *Don't hide from me, John. We're in this together, you and me. All the way to the end.*

Johnny didn't like the sound of that, but he didn't answer. That thing wasn't going to get anything from him. Not again.

It called to him as they passed the St. Louis arch. *Talk to me, John.* Again as they got off the interstate. *John, it's awful quiet in here. Let's talk.* Again as they got to the venue. *Please, John? Don't shut me out. We have so much left to do.* It was whining now, and Johnny took a grim joy in that. Maybe it couldn't read his thoughts exactly, but it picked up on his emotions. *Why would you want to hurt me, John? We're good together. We've done so much. Together.*

"You okay?" Danny asked him as they got out of the van.

"I'm good," Johnny said, though he could feel the strain in his face, his neck, and his back. The constant wheedling and the endless stream of entreaties were wearing him down, and "Johnny" kept getting louder and louder.

Sound check was awful. Singing was a tremendous amount of work with all that racket in his head. The band started running through "Burn" and the voice started up again, more insistent than ever.

Please, John? Don't leave me alone in here.

"Goddammit, will you *shut up*?" Johnny snapped into the mic, right in the middle of the song. Everybody stopped playing, and he could feel the others looking at him.

"Pardon?" the sound guy said through the monitors.

"Sorry. Sorry. Can we take it from the beginning?"

He made it through with nothing more than raw, bloody-minded effort, but wasn't pretty.

"You okay?" Danny asked him again after they wrapped up sound check. "You don't sound too good."

"I know how I sound, okay?" Johnny said. "I'll get it together."

"I didn't mean *that*," Danny said, though it was obvious that that was exactly what he'd meant. "I mean, you seem like you might be getting sick or something."

He's right, the thing said. *You don't sound too good. It will be all right, though. I can help. Let me help you.*

Johnny gritted his teeth and ignored it.

He had to clench his fists to keep from shaking by the time they took the stage.

"You okay?" Danny asked him for the third time. Johnny was ready to hit him. "We can call this off if you're too sick to go on."

"Fuck that," Johnny said, a trace of fire in his voice. "We came here to make some noise, so let's rock this motherfucker." That sounded good—he wished he felt it.

The thing in his head had left him alone for an hour, but he could feel its excitement as he stepped in front of the mic. Case played the opening riff to "Burn" and suddenly all eyes were on him. There were a dozen or so people in front that he'd come to recognize staring excitedly up at him. He thought of them as Johnny's Fan Club, and he drew confidence from their cheers. *This might be okay,* he thought.

Then it was time to sing, and he felt the thing in his head push forward to work its magic.

NO, he thought.

It stopped as abruptly as if it had hit a wall. He felt it slam forward again, and again he thought *NO.* Frustration and panic welled up inside the thing, and it let out an unearthly howl that rang the inside of his head like a bell.

Johnny missed the first line of the song, but he caught up at the second, and he—he, alone, John Tsiboukas—sang it with everything he had.

His pitch wavered, and the sound was anemic. It was as though eight months of practice and performing had peeled away in a moment, leaving him with the same lousy voice he'd always had.

A look of shock spread across the faces of Johnny's Fan Club, eerily synchronized. Moments later, shock was replaced by a nasty look he didn't like at all. They leered and sneered and booed him. The rest of the crowd didn't follow their lead, thank Christ, but the rest of the crowd didn't seem particularly impressed, either. Some people watched with interest, but others milled about in little clots, spread out across the floor, talking to each other over the music. Many of them, Johnny noticed, gravitated toward Case's side of the stage.

He gave it everything he had anyway, screaming the words into the mic, moving across the stage with something like his usual swagger. He saw a few heads nod with the music, but mostly just indifference. His confidence faltered, and the thin sound of his voice coming through the monitor speakers was another devastating blow to his ego. *This is a fucking disaster,* he thought, and the swagger went out of him.

Somehow, he made it through the song. There was applause, but it sounded perfunctory after the deafening ovations he was used to. The howling in his head stopped.

The voice in his head took on an ugly smugness. *Go on, then,* it told him. *Let's see what you got. This one's all yours.*

It stayed quiet for the rest of the set—not that that helped much. Johnny knew his voice just couldn't cut it. It came back to him shrill and tiny, barely on pitch. The band went through one song after another to an audience that seemed to Johnny to be almost completely uninterested. Johnny's Fan Club jeered and got so rowdy he wondered when they would start throwing things.

The band was tight and the beat was driving, and he knew that was all that carried the set. When it was finally over, Johnny slunk away as fast as he could, walking rapidly with his head down. Case caught his eye for one second, and he saw only pity on her face before he looked away.

Filled with shame, Johnny ran to the van.

***

"What's with him?" Case asked Danny.

"Don't know. He's not feeling well, I guess."

"Yeah. He sure doesn't look so good. I thought he was going to puke onstage. Too bad. He started strong."

"Yeah he did," Danny said. "It's hard to remember how terrified he used to be onstage."

"Wish he'd have finished stronger, but you can't have a perfect show every night."

***

From the St. Louis Riverfront Times, *July 8, 2010:*

. . . *Opening for Crashyard was up-and-coming Ragman, a hard rock quartet out of Dallas that's been getting rave reviews as the warm-up act for this tour. We found the good press to be more than justified, as Ragman blasted the room with a set of scorching rock and roll. Heavy riffs and the lead singer's raw sound imbued their set with a nice grittiness, setting the stage perfectly for Crashyard's set. . . .*

***

Johnny never saw a copy of that day's *Riverfront Times*, but he made sure to pick up the *St. Louis Post-Dispatch* before leaving town. There were no murders mentioned.

CHAPTER 29

There is darkness everywhere, and a noisome dampness thickens the air. To breathe is to pull wisps of wet air through sheets of molding gauze. Johnny can't see, but he can feel mud squishing between his toes, and the leaves and stalks of strange, fleshy plants crunch and burst beneath his bare feet. He's walking. Where? Forward. Every few steps, his foot plunges into a puddle, soaking him with stinking water up to the knee. He feels rather than hears a door open in front of him, and he walks through.

On the other side, an ocean gleams oily under moonlight. Out in the deeps, vast pale shapes move below the surface, and Johnny averts his gaze, knowing with a deep certainty that to look is to invite something *to look back. The abyss, maybe, he thinks without a trace of sarcasm.*

At the shore, the water is still, smooth as glass, like no ocean he's ever seen or heard of. The moon, too, is strange—too small, too distant, its patterns unfamiliar and foreboding. Its light is green and foul. Johnny is swept with the sense that he does not belong here, no more than a house dog belongs in the jungle.

This is the back of the world, *he thinks, and while that makes no sense from any geometric or cosmological perspective he knows of, he also knows it is true.*

"*The back of the world,*" *a voice says behind him, echoing his thoughts. He doesn't need to turn to know there is a man, or something like one, back there, cowboy hat and ironic grin masking something horrible. "Where cold and hungry things scratch to get in like scratching at the back of a picture in a frame. Watch.*"

Johnny watches the shore, careful not to look out too far. The water stirs and breaks open, and a figure, a man-shape, emerges, hunched and shuffling. Again, Johnny turns his gaze. This is not the awful presence he senses churning and roiling in the depths, but it would be similarly unwise to invite its attention.

Others follow, and soon a crowd flaps and shambles up the shore. Johnny doesn't want to look, but there are too many, and he catches glimpses. He sees pale flesh, glistening eyes, and ribs and knobbed spines punching out from their thin, almost skeletal bodies. They pass by him in their hundreds, and their stench is an atom bomb of dead fish and decaying things.

The last one passes, then stops. It turns, and Johnny is thankful that its face is buried in shadow. It gestures to him, unmistakably beckoning him to follow.

He looks down and sees his own pale flesh, his own ribs pushing out through stretched skin, and hunger fills him, hunger itself consumes him. *He has known privation before, especially at the end of the month with the bills unpaid and the cash gone. He has skipped meals for two and three days at a time, but he has never known hunger so deep or so pervasive, and he knows that he has been hungry forever. He would eat the plants from the ground if they weren't poison. He would eat the dirt if it would sustain him, grind the rocks between his teeth if it would only stop that vast, hollow ache.*

The creature beckons again, and Johnny follows. Up the beach, he can see a squat structure, no more than a dark suggestion from here, but he knows what it is. Dread coils in him, but it is a small thing next to the hunger.

He walks.

The creatures have gathered in front of the structure—a high platform, much wider than it is tall, built of wood the color of bone.

A stage.

Case stands on it, stage right as always. She's tuning up, twiddling the pegs on her guitar and tapping one foot impatiently. Danny's in back, in front of the drums. He's stamping his foot, pounding the bass drum over and over, just like a particularly slow sound check. Quentin stands at stage left, and again Johnny is grateful for the dim light that hides all detail, for Quentin is dead as can be. His eyes are sunken and dark, and tangled shapes spill from his belly, slopping over his legs.

Case stops tuning. Danny stops kicking. Quentin stands there. They are all waiting.

"They are waiting for you, Johnny," the man behind him says. "It is time for you to take the stage and call your hungry brothers forth."

Johnny turns around. The thin man in the black silk shirt is there, just as Johnny had known he would be. A wind kicks up, blowing the scent of burning metal off the ocean.

"This wasn't the deal," Johnny says.

The man says nothing, but Johnny can see the faint crescent shape of his grin widen beneath the hat.

"This wasn't the deal," Johnny repeats.

"Too bad." The man crosses his arms.

"You're not the devil," Johnny says.

"I never said I was. But you asked for fame, fortune, and a voice to move millions, and I gave it to you. Do you doubt it?"

Now it's Johnny's turn to stay silent.

"Ah. So you want to welch on the deal? Be my guest. I won't stop you. Go back to pouring coffee and scrubbing dishes. Maybe one day you'll make assistant manager. One day, when your short span of years winds itself down, you'll look back at the opportunity wasted

and weep—but that's your choice. You can always be proud of that. Making your choice.

"Those lofty goals of art and immortality? They're yours to throw away."

On the stage, the band plays a long, ugly chord.

***

"Wake up! Showtime!"

Johnny woke with a start. The surroundings were foreign yet familiar, and he remembered. Another green room. Sacramento this time, he thought. Or maybe San Diego. Somewhere a million miles away from that otherworldly beach under its baleful moon. Or a billion. He blinked, trying to clear his head.

"Jesus, Johnny, wake *up*! You can't go onstage like that." Danny shook him again.

"Knock it off, I'm coming."

He found his feet somehow, but they felt strange, and he shuffled and shambled behind Case with Danny guiding him when he started to weave. He waved Danny off when they reached the stairs. "I got it," he said, but he stopped. Dread held his feet to the floor. He could hear the crowd muttering and chuckling, and he wasn't sure he could take another show like the last one. He wasn't sure he could go up those stairs and face that indifference again, that effortless verdict from the mob that declared him worthless.

What do you say, Johnny? the voice in his head asked. It had never called him Johnny before. *Shall we give them what they came for? Something to remember?*

Unsaid was the alternative—humiliating himself onstage one more time to an audience of people that would put a finger in one ear and talk to their friends a little louder.

Letting Allen and Case down. Letting Danny down. Most of all, letting himself down.

"Yeah," he said softly. "Let's do this."

The thing *"Johnny"*—swept forward like a plague of locusts swarming through his mind. Johnny didn't resist, and he felt it in his head, spreading throughout his body, tingling in his fingertips and feet. Dark thoughts swirled elusive in his brain. His hand flexed of its own accord. He felt it move and wanted to look, but his eyes pointed ahead, refusing to obey.

That's okay, he thought, oddly calm. *Easier this way.*

"Come *on*," Danny said.

"Fuck yeah," answered something that spoke with a voice that was not quite Johnny's.

Johnny watched himself take the stage. The others followed.

***

Run, Case thought. It was the same instinct that caused her to look for exits in some of the rougher places she'd been, the same one that told her when it would be a bad idea to cut through an alley to get to her car. It was usually right—but where was the threat here? She was onstage, in full view of a thousand people. Burly security guys, bored and probably looking for an opportunity to bust some heads, stood around everywhere. The crowd wasn't even rowdy—just gratified that somebody was finally going to play some music and relieve their boredom for a few minutes before Crashyard came on.

There was nothing to be afraid of, yet her skin prickled and her heart pounded like a piston in her chest.

Fuck that. I'm here to play. Her hands, at least, weren't shaking when she started the first song. She played it automatically, fingers moving where they were supposed to with the ease of long practice while her eyes scanned the crowd. There were the familiar faces—the Fan Club, Johnny called them, and there were now more than twenty of them packed in close to the stage. They watched Johnny with an almost religious ecstasy, their expressions so like the Pentecostals she'd grown up around that she expected them to start speaking in tongues at any time. Surely they weren't the threat her body was screaming at her to run from?

Johnny sang the first line of the song. A collective shudder passed through the Fan Club, and the girl with the blue mohawk made a loud shrieking noise that sounded suspiciously like she just came, right in front of God and everyone.

Case shuddered, too, but for a different reason—she knew what she was afraid of, now.

Johnny.

His voice was deeper than ever. Deep, and commanding. It thundered through the auditorium, drawing cheers and enthusiastic screams from people in their hundreds—but it was not Johnny's voice. There was no way to fool herself about that any longer. It was the voice of an angry god cracking the sky open to bellow at his wayward flock.

Either I'm cracking up, or something bad is happening. That's what Erin had said, and Case felt it, too. She checked the Fan Club again. Sure enough, a thin man with a spiral notebook binding wound into his ear stood next to the girl with the blue mohawk. He grinned at Case, his tongue curling out to touch his lips. The girl with the blue mohawk was grinning at her now, too. Then the biker and the tattooed woman.

Case fucked up the next chord. Nobody seemed to notice, except for the Fan Club, many of whom laughed.

The biker pointed and leered. Case moved to the back of the stage. Their eyes followed her, but they all looked away when Johnny started singing again.

The whole third verse was gone, replaced with a horrifying sequence of nonsense syllables that made Case's legs weak with terror. Danny dropped one of his sticks, though he was quick enough with the spare that there was scarcely an interruption.

What the fuck is going on?

***

The sense of outright terror faded rapidly after Johnny stopped singing and Case got off the stage. Still, she remembered Erin's words: *You don't remember the bad parts very well later.* Case thought there had been some bad parts, some very bad parts indeed, but Erin was right—they seemed indistinct and unimportant, as if she'd watched them on TV or they'd happened to somebody else. That worried her. It had seemed *very* real at the time, she reminded herself.

She turned to check out Johnny, suddenly unnerved at the idea that he was behind her.

He wasn't behind her. He wasn't anywhere.

"Hey, where did Johnny go?" she asked.

Danny pointed at a side door they'd just passed. It was slightly open.

Case pushed it open the rest of the way—it was a door to the loading dock. Johnny was standing in the midst of the Fan Club. There were dozens of them, all gathered around with hands outstretched, seemingly desperate to touch him. Their faces were flushed and avid, their eyes fevered.

"We're hungry," one of them complained. Others echoed him. "Come with us."

Johnny grinned at Case and ran his hand over his greased hair. "You coming?" he asked with a sleazy wink.

"Are you insane? You don't know any of these people."

"Sure I do. We go *way* back."

Several of the Fan Club looked at Case with interest. She backed away. "Have fun," she said, and she went back inside.

She made sure the door closed behind her.

***

"Johnny has lost his fucking mind," Case said.

Danny was sitting up in the hotel bed next to her. He looked old, she thought. Even in the low light from one lamp, the lines on his face were dark and pronounced. She doubted she looked any better. The tour was taking its toll on everyone.

"I don't know," Danny said. "He's taking that alter ego of his a little too seriously, but I wouldn't say he's lost his mind." The words lacked any conviction, and Danny's eyes kept drifting to the window.

"Are you kidding? Did you see that pack of crazies he left with? They're like some kind of cult, and he just wandered off with them, happy as a pig in shit."

"Yeah," Danny whispered. "He's worked hard, and I know he likes the attention, but those people make me nervous. They've been following us."

"I know. Erin noticed them, too. They're part of the reason she left." Case thought of Erin's story about the man with the earrings, and of the bad vibe she got onstage sometimes. All the time, lately. She thought carefully before speaking again.

"Danny, I think there's something really weird going on here. Something I don't understand, but I sure know it's not normal." She put her hand on his knee. "I think maybe

Erin was right. Maybe we ought to get the fuck out of here."

Danny looked at her hand and then slowly, as though it pained him, moved his gaze up to her face. "No."

Case waited for him to say more, but none was forthcoming. "That's it? No? You don't think we ought to talk about this?"

His face stretched into a pain-streaked grimace. "Please don't go," he said.

Case got quiet. She was aware of her heartbeat and the hiss of blood rushing through her ears. In the next room, the bed thumped against the wall, and somebody swore. She didn't know if she could bear Danny looking at her that way much longer. "Why not? I can't do this forever. Not like this. Not with Johnny. Things are getting bad. The first thing you ever learn in a self-defense class is to avoid putting yourself in bad situations, and I feel like I'm hip-deep and sinking."

"Just finish the tour," Danny said. He was pleading, Case saw, breaking her heart and simultaneously disgusting her. She hated herself for the latter. "We'll talk about what happens next after we get back to Dallas, but please don't leave now. I'll talk to Johnny." He covered her hand with his own. "I've got this band, this tour, and you," he said, "and that's all. Remember what you told Erin? We've sacrificed so much for this. Can we just finish it? Please?"

Tears streamed down his face, and Case gathered him into her arms. Big, softhearted Danny.

I love you, she almost said, shocking herself as the words rose to her lips. "I'm scared," she said instead.

"Me, too."

As she held him, she wondered if they were scared of the same things.

CHAPTER 30

Two more shows, Danny told himself. Two more.

He wasn't going to last that long. He could feel it. The strain was more than he ever could have imagined. Johnny wasn't just taking his alter ego too far—somewhere, down in his mind where the dark things slithered, Danny knew that. He didn't like to think about it, though. There was enough to worry about.

There was the goddamned Fan Club, for starters. Danny had been having bad dreams and getting lousy sleep ever since that first night in the van. Nobody else seemed to notice, or maybe nobody wanted to say anything, but the bleached blonde with the leather choker that had been following them for seventeen shows and counting had been one of their visitors that night. At every show, she gave Danny a sly look, as though he were her co-conspirator. He'd started to see that face in his dreams, and in every dream she changed to something pale and reptilian and opened her jaws unspeakably wide as she came for him.

There was something else, too, something he'd been afraid to share with Case. After the last show, Johnny had tossed his journal into the nearest trash barrel like a man throwing away an empty beer bottle.

Danny didn't know what had possessed him to go after it, but he had. Maybe it was that he hadn't seen Johnny without a journal since Johnny was about twelve, or maybe it was that Johnny *had* been acting weird and Danny thought there might be a clue inside. Maybe it had been some other perverse impulse entirely, but he had waited until Johnny was gone and fished the journal out of the trash. He hadn't had a lot of time alone with it yet, but there was a whole section with show dates and grim newspaper clippings that made his stomach do unpleasant things.

It has nothing to do with Johnny, he told himself. *Johnny was with us all the time.* That was true—but why was Johnny even keeping those articles? Danny didn't know, but he thought of Quentin a lot. And the Fan Club.

He'd torched his marriage and shot a budding career in the head for this tour, but the dream was starting to show a lot of wear around the edges.

Two more shows.

***

Terror gripped Danny from the first note that came out of Johnny's mouth. Johnny's voice sounded strange, but that wasn't all—his voice always sounded strange these days. This time, though, he stepped up to the mic and opened his mouth and—

Two light bulbs exploded at the back of the room, sending a sizzling shower of short-lived sparks to the floor. The room got darker, too, much darker than it should have with just the two lights out. Case looked back at Danny with an expression that was half afraid and half I-told-you-so. Danny pretended not to see her and tried to concentrate on playing the drums, but he felt it, too. The room had dropped ten degrees and a dank odor, fish and sewage, permeated the air.

Danny muddled through the rest of the song—it wasn't hard; he could play it in his sleep by now—and at the very end he noticed the Fan Club. They hadn't sent up their usual raucous cheer at the end of the song. All twenty-odd of them stared up at Johnny, eyes wide and mouths open, as if they were about to ascend directly to heaven in some kind of bizarre rock concert micro-Rapture. The girl with the leather choker had her tongue out slightly, and she appeared to be panting. Danny shuddered.

Johnny turned around and put his hand over the mic, getting a squeal of feedback. "Come on!" he said.

"Fuck," Danny muttered, realizing he'd been spacing out for who knew how long. He started the next song.

It should have been hot under the lights, he thought. The goddamn stage lights were so horribly bright he had to squint, but there wasn't so much as a droplet of sweat on his skin. The room was getting still colder, and though he couldn't actually see his breath, he felt like he would be able to any minute. Despite the cold, the smell thickened, and now there was a hint of the ocean in the fish and shit stench.

Case and Allen had pulled back toward Danny, leaving Johnny out front to do his thing. Allen's face was pale; Case's was murderous.

They kept playing. The lights focused in on Johnny, leaving everything else swaddled in a thick, palpable darkness. Danny could see nothing beyond the stage, hear nothing above the music. They could have been playing Madison Square Garden, for all he knew. Or Venus.

Another song came to an end. No cheers came from the audience, no shouts or cries of "Freebird!" Danny couldn't tell if there was even anyone out there anymore. He felt empty darkness swirling at his back, eyes boring into his neck, and he shivered.

Johnny turned around. His grin was wide and hungry, and his eyes gleamed with a light both fanatical and predatory.

"Do 'Slipping,'" he said. "I like that one."

Danny's mouth had gone completely dry. He gaped, offering no response.

"Allen doesn't know it," Case protested in a small voice. "We didn't rehearse that one."

Allen must have seen something in Johnny's face that bothered him. "Just play," he said quickly. "I'll watch you and catch up."

"It's awfully down-tempo for this crowd," Case said.

"They'll love it," Johnny said, smiling until Danny thought his face would tear. "Trust me."

Case took an obvious glance toward the back of the stage, her eyes white and darting.

"I wouldn't," Johnny said. "The Fan Club paid good money for this show. I'd hate to see them disappointed."

Danny winced. The subtext was painfully clear, and he could only imagine how Case would respond to the threat.

This is going to get ugly.

But Case's face stayed neutral, and she played the first chord of the song, a dissonant, eerie chord that Danny had really liked—about a hundred years ago. Danny picked up the beat mechanically, following along out of habit more than anything else. It was a straightforward enough tune, and Allen picked it up after the first iteration.

Johnny nodded and went back to the mic stand.

"I felt it slipping
A little yesterday
A little bit crumbled away"

He sang, and the darkness crowded around. Danny
could see the crowd now, hundreds of pairs of gleaming
eyes reflecting the light back to the stage. The crowd
swayed back and forth with the music, making no sound.
An icy finger slid down the back of Danny's neck, and his
body stiffened. Sweat, he realized. *Now* he was sweating,
cold beads of ice water.

"I think I'm losing traction
I think I'm losing touch
I think I'm sliding away"

The Fan Club started singing with Johnny. There was no
way they could know the words, but they did. Their voices
swelled in an eerie harmony, and the darkness closed in
even tighter. Breath was hard to find, and each labored
inhalation brought the stink of decay.

Something cold touched Danny's neck again, but this
time he knew it wasn't sweat. Claws or sharp fingernails ran
down his spine, and he shivered. His mind gibbered at him:
Don't look don't look don't look maybe it will go away maybe it's
nothing don't look. He fucked up the beat and dropped a
stick.

Then the cold hand, a cold *mind* pushed against him with
a rancid and intolerable pressure. It beckoned to him,
whispered seductive things in his ear, and all the weeks of
strain and travel and fighting caught up to him. He was so
tired. He felt it push again, and he offered no resistance.

The world stopped. Case, Allen, and Johnny still moved,
but Danny's body froze, and his thoughts became strange
and alien. His limbs felt cold and dead, and he was suddenly

filled with a yawning, vast hunger, like nothing he had ever experienced.

A moment later, he was kicked to the back of his own mind, and he watched in horror his arms started to move on their own, picking up the song in the middle. Laughter filled his head.

Somewhere, buried back in his own head, Danny screamed. No sound escaped his lips.

***

That's it. I'm bugging the fuck out. Case left the stage after the last song, just as the lights came up and the crowd inexplicably burst into riotous applause. She'd make one last attempt to get Danny to leave with her, but she was done either way. *Everything about this is wrong,* she thought, even as the memory of the show drained away, losing some of its power.

Was it really that bad? she wondered as she hit the first stair. By the time she made it all the way down the stairs, all she remembered of the show was a vague unease. The Fan Club—they'd done something strange, hadn't they? And Johnny had demanded the band play—what was it? Something Allen didn't know, she was sure of that.

The specifics were gone already, but she knew she was done. *Something* had gone pear-shaped up there, and the fact that she couldn't remember it just minutes after the event was all the proof she needed.

She turned around to see if the others were coming. Allen was right behind her, a confused twist to his features. He rubbed his head and looked puzzled. Danny was in conference with Johnny. God knew what that was about, but Case doubted anything useful would come from it. Johnny was . . . not Johnny these days.

When Danny turned to her, that lingering sense of unease cranked way up. He gave her a disturbingly flat smile and patted Johnny on the shoulder. "We're going out," he said. "You wanna come?"

"Uh. Where are you going?"

Danny shrugged. "Out with the Fan Club. Johnny says they're a scream." His smile stayed fixed, like a drawing that had been stapled to his face.

Case took a step backward. "You guys go ahead," she said hesitantly. Every nerve in her body screamed. *You need to get out of here, Case,* she told herself, trying to keep calm. *Don't let them know anything is wrong, and as soon as they leave, go. Far away. It doesn't matter where. Get the hell out of here.* It didn't matter that there was only one show left—it wouldn't have mattered if there were only one *hour* left. It was time to go. "I'll see you back at the hotel," she said. The lie sounded hollow and transparent in her ears, but Danny just smiled. Johnny nodded, grinned, and touched up his hair.

"Cool," Johnny said. He led Danny past her toward the back exit. Danny didn't look back. The two of them left, and the door snicked shut.

Case counted to ten, waiting for her heart to slow down. Allen was watching her.

"I'm going back to the hotel," she said. She had four hundred bucks in the safe, and it wouldn't hurt to grab her bag and a change of clothes. "Then I'm done. I quit. I am gone. You coming?"

Allen nodded. "Oh yeah. This ride stopped being fun a long while back."

She couldn't argue with that.

***

Case punched the numbers into the safe and pulled out the four hundred dollars first. As she stuffed the wad of folded cash into her pocket, a twenty peeled free and fell to the floor. For a second, she thought about leaving it, leaving the bag, the clothes, and everything—leaving Allen, who was next door getting his own shit—and running. Time suddenly seemed very important.

That's crazy, she reminded herself. *They're out doing . . . Fan Club stuff.* According to Allen, Johnny hadn't gotten in until almost dawn the last time he'd partied with the Fan Club. Looting the entire hotel room wouldn't take more than five minutes. She snatched the bill off the floor and pocketed it. Still, she couldn't shake the idea that time was short. Her stuff and Danny's had gotten mingled over the past couple of weeks, virtually all of it ending up in Danny's bag. He insisted he'd carry everything. It had been a nice gesture, but now it was a pain in the ass.

Ah, fuck. Danny. Her heart tore at her. Danny. Could she really just ditch him? Leave him with whatever Johnny had become? She had put her ditching days behind her, or so she'd thought. *And I love him.*

That's not him, she reminded herself. She didn't know what it was, but Johnny's madness was apparently catching.

More reason to get the hell out of here right now.

But are you sure? Really sure?

She didn't know. Her eyes burned, and the light from the lamp refracted into a thousand dull shards in the prism of her tears. Big, gentle Danny. He didn't deserve what had happened to him, she thought, and a flare of righteous anger ignited in her chest.

I can't help him. And now is not the time to worry about this.

She picked Danny's bag up. Rather than go rummaging, she dumped the contents on the bed.

A notebook fell out on top, slid down the pile, and flopped open. Johnny's handwriting and newspaper clippings. Case ignored it—Johnny's crazy journal was the least of her concerns.

Then the word *Killed* in large newsprint caught her eye. She looked down the page.

Atlanta. June 17, 2010. Two Concertgoers Killed in Apparent Parking Lot Brawl.

Raleigh. June 18, 2010. Woman's Body Found Mutilated in Alley. No suspect in custody.

There was more. Every show date, every city they'd played.

The Fan Club. Where were they partying tonight? Case had a strong suspicion she knew what kinds of party games they liked. She felt fear scamper up the back of her neck, and the urge to flee amped up again. She checked the digital clock next to the bed—she'd been here for four minutes.

"Fuck this," she said aloud. Clean underwear and a backpack could go hang—she had the money, and she could replace the stuff anywhere.

What about Danny? Another pang of sadness and despair. She couldn't think about it clearly, but she knew she couldn't help him. She didn't know how.

Time to go.

She flung open the hotel room door—

And Johnny was standing there. Grinning.

Case stopped, her mouth half open, her mind spinning mad wheels with no purchase.

Johnny. Here. Not one greased hair had fallen out of its place, and his hungry smile hadn't diminished in the slightest. Nor was he alone. Danny stood next to him, his own idiot grin fixed firmly in place, and crowded around them, spread up and down the hall and stinking like a swamp, was the entirety of the Fan Club.

They all stared at Case.

"We need to talk, Case," Johnny said.

"Talk." Her mouth tasted like chalk.

"I got the impression you might be flaking out on us before the last show," he said. His face grinned, but his voice was serious as a heart attack. "You don't want to do that. Think about what you'll be throwing away. You've worked so hard to get here."

"Fuck you," Case said. Her voice trembled, but she didn't care. "I quit."

Johnny sighed. "It's not just your own career you'd be sabotaging," he said. "Think of us. Think of who you're screwing over. Erin, who spent countless hours setting this up. Me. Allen." He winked at her, so quickly it was gone before she could believe it happened. *What had he done with Allen?* "And Danny. Danny's given up a lot to be here. Are you ready to fuck him over, too?"

She acted without thinking. One moment she'd been standing there in horrified shock, and the next, her hand shot out in a vicious punch directed at Johnny's face.

He caught her by the wrist, effortlessly, stopping her hand inches from impact. She gasped in shock rather than pain. It didn't actually hurt much, but this was *Johnny*, for fuck's sake. He probably went one-thirty if he was wearing heavy shoes, and he was as skinny as a signpost. Yet he held her wrist without showing any sign of strain.

"You're not much of a team player, are you? I always knew you were going to fuck us over. If that's how it's going to be, I'll make a deal with you."

"Fuck you."

He continued as if he hadn't heard. "You play this last show, and I won't make Danny hurt himself."

"Fuck you," she said again. *That's his brother!* she thought, though some part of her wondered. *Surely he wouldn't—*

"Danny?" Johnny said.

Danny reached up, almost casually, and curled his index finger in behind the bottom lid of his left eye. Then he pulled, hard. Case heard the tearing sound clearly above her own breathing.

"Jesus Christ!" she yelled, and she pushed away. Johnny let her go, and she fell back into the room.

Bloody tears poured down the side of Danny's face while the Fan Club watched hungrily. His eyelid hung in a flap, and she could see his eye, white and wet, swiveling in its socket. "Don't leave us, Case," he said. "We'll miss you." There was a pause, and then his face changed, softened an instant before contorting into a mask of fear and pain.

"Oh God, it hurts!" he shouted.

"Danny!"

And then his face was still again. "Don't leave us," he repeated tonelessly. He wiped the blood off his face and licked it off the side of his hand.

Case jumped to her feet. "You son of a bitch!" she snarled at Johnny.

"Danny?" Johnny said again.

"No! Wait! I'm sorry!"

Danny paused. This time his index finger was stiff and straight, pointed at the same eye.

"Okay," Johnny said. "One more show."

Case looked down. Danny was still in there, somewhere. For that one awful second she had seen him.

"One more show," she said.

CHAPTER 31

Danny was in there. Somewhere. Case reminded herself of that as the van barreled down the road, bound for Dallas and the last show of the tour. She hadn't seen him since, though. The thing that was driving his body disregarded her most of the time, except for the occasional musing glance that made her feel like one of the lobsters in a tank at a fancy restaurant. At least he was wearing sunglasses now. She didn't know if he—*it*—had done anything to patch that gruesome flap of skin back in place, but at least she didn't have to look at it. It was hard enough for her to keep from replaying the moment where he'd reached in and torn his own eyelid open as casually and indifferently as opening a piece of junk mail.

Behind them trailed a caravan of more than a dozen vehicles. The fucking Fan Club. There were over fifty of them now, each with the same hungry look as Danny. Four of them had stayed in the room with her last night, just to keep an eye on her, Johnny had said. She hadn't been able to sleep under their watch, and she'd sat on the chair and glared at them most of the night.

They had spent most of that time talking among themselves about how hungry they were and grinning at Case. She had wondered if their self-control would hold out and resolved to throw herself from the window if they came for her. That decision had come naturally, a solution so obvious it needed no deliberation.

In the morning, she'd been hustled into the van with Allen, who managed a weak smile through the dazed, shell-shocked expression on his face. A cut as long as her hand zigzagged its way across his forehead.

"Rough night?" she had asked.

"You could say that."

And then they were off.

The girl with the blue mohawk rode shotgun next to Danny, and Case, Allen, and Johnny spread out in the back seats.

"Don't look so glum," Johnny said. "One more show, and then it's on to bigger and better things."

"One more show, and that's it," Case reminded him.

He shrugged. "One more show and then obscurity, if you're into that. I don't understand you, Case. Fame, fortune, and a wild rock-and-roll lifestyle are all going to be yours. Isn't that what you always wanted?"

She didn't bother answering him. If it weren't for Danny, she would have jumped for the door, never mind that they were going seventy miles an hour.

If it wasn't for Danny, I wouldn't be in this fucking van.

What was she going to do about Danny? She had no idea. As the van devoured the miles and the time before the show ticked away, her spirits sank further. She clenched her hands into impotent fists. She'd like nothing better than to knock Johnny's face in, but she didn't think her chances were good. He was faster than her, somehow, and stronger too. And it would take only a word from him and the thing inside Danny would put out Danny's eye or tear off his face or Christ knew what. How could she fight that?

She watched and waited, and the clock wound down. Her thoughts shifted from Danny to the show. Something bad was going to happen tonight. Something colossally bad. She didn't know what, exactly, but the Fan Club gave her some ideas. Johnny would make more of them—or, no. He'd *call them forth*. That felt right. He had called them forth last night. Danny had been normal before the show and something horrible had come to live inside him by the end. More of that would happen tonight, she was sure.

Maybe a lot more. Hadn't there been only twenty or thirty Fan Club members at the start of the show last night? She thought so. Now there were enough to fill a dozen or so cars. Fifty? Sixty? And the show last night had been like nothing else she'd seen before, filled with a terrible, unearthly power.

She had a feeling tonight's would be more powerful still. They were headlining, which meant a long set, and the venue packed a couple thousand people. Erin would fill it, somehow. That's what she did.

And then what?

Dread gnawed at her insides for the whole ride.

***

The green room. Just like all the other green rooms. Case had no sense of being back home, no sense of triumph at the sheer size of the show they were about to put on. She heard the pounding bass of the thrash bands that went on before them, big local names that Erin had booked for support. The place would be packed.

Erin herself came back to visit, but her stay was brief. She was clearly unsettled by the creepy grin Johnny wore, and she wrinkled her nose at the terrible smell that filled the room. The Fan Club was back here, too, and she didn't like that at all. She moved through the clot of people, trying to avoid touching any of them. Case saw the man with the spiral notebook in his ear wink at her.

She hugged Case. "Good luck," she said in a shaky voice.

"Get out of here," Case whispered. "Just get away."

Erin looked at her with wide eyes and left in a hurry.

Case checked the wall clock. Two minutes to midnight. *Just like the Iron Maiden song.*

Two minutes to showtime.

***

His people were hungry. Johnny—he liked that name, thought he'd keep it for a while—was hungry, too. So hungry.

Soon. Soon we will feed. All *of us.*

Tonight he would bring his people through. All of them. There were so few of them left in that dead world on the flipside of reality, and he was now in full command of his power. He would pull them through into this new world, pull them through into a place teeming with meat, alive and squirming on the bone, and his people would feast.

In the back of his mind, something that had once ruled this body screamed and wept.

***

"Let's go," Johnny said. Danny grinned. Case and Allen shared a terrified look.

The four of them headed for the stage.

CHAPTER 32

Somewhere deep, John sees it all, and it is as it was in those long-ago dreams. His body moves up the stairs at the back of the stage, behind the curtain, and he hears the sound of the crowd, rumbling and restless. A single voice, high and clear—a woman's voice—starts to chant: "Johnny! Johnny! Johnny!" It's only seconds before the chant is picked up by dozens more, then hundreds, then the whole room. The stamping of their feet vibrates up through the stage, up through the soles of his feet, into his belly, his heart.

His body walks out onto the darkened stage, and a roar goes up from the crowd. He stands in front of the mic, and he can feel his face twist in a sneer—the Elvis sneer from his dreams—though he never told it to move. He is powerless now, a spectator at his own moment of glory.

Case is to his right, as always, like in the dreams—and, also like in the dreams, her goldtop Les Paul has been replaced by a guitar the color of blood, the one that Kerry Buchanan gave her. The mystery bass player to his left is no mystery anymore. It's Allen, of course. Quentin is dead.

Two spotlights come on, blasting Danny and Allen with white light. As the crowd goes into a frenzy, Danny clicks his sticks together four times, and he and Allen start the song.

"Ashes and Bone."

Stop this, John thinks. *Please, God, stop this.* His only answer is laughter that echoes around his head, lashing him like a whip of barbed wire.

His head turns to the right, and his arm points. Another spotlight flicks on, pointed at Case. She is giving him an appraising, studying look, her eyes narrowed and her mouth set in a grim line. She comes in at the right time, though, following the frenetic bass part for a few bars before changing to the ugly harmony she devised for this song. The whole time, she never looks away from him, never changes her expression. The crowd claps and stomps along with the beat.

The song drops into the slow part with a sickening plunge, and John's body shivers. The guitar and bass travel in crushing unison, and then the guitar drops out, leaving the bass and drums to carry the song into the verse.

John's head swivels back to the mic. He knows something bad, something terrible is coming, and he pushes forward, hammering against the mind of his captor, the thing that has taken his body.

He catches the thing by surprise, takes control for just one second. Then he feels its heavy claws on him, pushing him back, and a crushing sense of doom collapses on him.

"Oh, God, please no," he says.

***

Case played through the beginning of the song, watching Johnny carefully. There was music going on somewhere, loud music, but her fingers were moving automatically and her mind was focused on Johnny. She thought about the beer bottle that had come whirling out of the crowd at one of the shows, right past Johnny's head, and how he'd never even flinched. She had one idea, a bad one, and probably just one chance to act on it.

Don't fuck this up.

It probably wouldn't matter—she was most likely fooling herself—but she had to do something. Even if it was wrong.

Her hand tripped easily down the fretboard, guiding the song into the slow part. She had never felt less moved by music in her life. Johnny looked at her, his face inscrutable. Her heart knocked in her chest.

Johnny turned to the mic.

Case dropped out of the song, just like she was supposed to. One hand went to the strap button at the bottom of the guitar.

A small voice came through the monitors—John's voice, quiet and terrified. "Oh, God, please no."

John, she thought. *He's in there, too. Like Danny.*

She pushed her thumb into the locking button, and it clicked. The strap came loose.

Then Johnny started singing, and the world exploded. The sound was crushing, a vast, thunderously deep voice tearing a rent in the cosmos, tearing a rent in the very concept of sanity itself, spewing a stream of syllables so vile that blood started to trickle from Case's ears. The crowd screamed, and this time there was terror in the screams.

The lights in the whole room dimmed to nearly nothing, except for the blazing white spotlight on Johnny. Darkness swirled and twisted, pouring up through the floor and the back walls like columns of smoke.

In the front row, the Fan Club howled with murderous glee and plunged into the crowd, tearing and rending. Blood spurted as far as the stage in a grisly shower.

Case came to herself as Johnny's voice swelled further. The strap was off her guitar, and she held the heavy Les Paul in her left hand.

What was I doing with this?

She looked over at Johnny as the awful sounds smashed the air around her. His eyes were closed, his mouth open wide, and both hands clutched the mic stand.

Case remembered.

She wrapped both hands around the neck of the guitar, holding it like a battle-axe or a ten-pound maul. *Sorry, Kerry,* she thought, and she charged across the stage.

The beat stopped as Danny saw her and quit drumming, but there was no way for him to get to her in time. The Fan Club was busy now that the leash had been slipped, gorging itself on the warm flesh of the spectators, and they didn't see her either.

She brought the heavy guitar down in a high overhead arc. Danny yelled, and whether it was that or the sudden absence of drums, Johnny opened his eyes.

He was too late to stop her, but he managed to jerk his head away from the blow just in time to prevent her from smashing his skull. Instead, the guitar hit high on his shoulder. Case felt the shock travel up into her arms, and even above the screaming, she heard the crack of his collarbone as it shattered. The mic stand went flying. Johnny stopped singing abruptly.

She dropped the guitar to the stage, her wrists vibrating from the shock of impact.

Johnny turned to her. His right arm hung limp, and his body seemed out of true, slumped on that side. He lashed out with his left instead, catching Case across the face.

She stumbled and fell backward, landing hard on the stage. The offstage lighting had come up some, the spotlight on Johnny gone down. In the crowd, some of the columns of darkness moved into the bodies of spectators, turning them into something awful. Other columns wavered as though caught in the throes of indecision. Still others started to fade out.

A spasm of loss crossed Johnny's face. "You bitch," he said. "You're dead. We're going to eat you slow. We're going to take turns. It's going to last a long, long time."

Then, incredibly, he turned away from her.

What the fuck? she thought, and then she understood. He was going for the microphone.

"John!" she shouted. "Don't do this!"

He whirled back to her, snarling. "I'm Johnny! Don't call me John! John's gone. John's fucking dead!"

John's in there—and Johnny doesn't like it when you get his name wrong. That she understood, rather too well. *Just like calling me Steph.* She doubted calling him the wrong name would do more than piss him off, but angry opponents made mistakes.

Like what?

More screams from the crowd she tried to tune out. From the side, she could see Danny coming around the drum kit, charging at her. Allen tried to stop him, but Danny brushed him aside like a scarecrow, hurling him across the stage. Allen hit the floor, slid, and did not get up.

Case got to her feet just as Danny reached her. He would be impossibly strong, she knew, but he didn't have any training, and his momentum was too great. She stepped toward him and dropped her body low, grabbing his arm and pivoting. A look of surprise flashed across his face, and then he was gone, sailing through the air. He landed in the crowd, in the midst of the biting, tearing frenzy that was the

Fan Club. He disappeared beneath the bodies. Beyond him, somebody fell on the mixing desk. Sparks flew.

Meanwhile, Johnny had nearly reached the microphone.

"John!" she yelled again.

He stopped, looking back and forth between her and the mic.

"Come on, John. This isn't you."

He reached a decision. "Fuck it," he said. "You're dead now. My brothers will have to settle for what's left." He stalked across the stage toward her, blood in his eyes. His right arm was useless, but she thought the left would be more than enough.

"Don't do this, John."

A vicious blow caught her on the shoulder, knocking her to the stage floor. She scrambled away, but he was too fast. His foot lashed out, catching her in the ribs, and hideous pain lanced through her body. Another kick, and she felt something break, then another.

She screamed. "John, it's me, goddammit! I know you're in there!" She clawed and scrambled, but her body barely responded. With a sick shudder, she realized she'd only made it ten feet or so—just far enough to bring John right back to the microphone he wanted so badly. *Stupid,* she thought, and then he was on her.

He landed on her body, sitting on her chest, crushing her to the floor. His good left hand reached out, and steely fingers wrapped around her throat. She scratched at his face, gouging and tearing the skin, but he didn't even defend himself. He simply didn't care.

"John," she mouthed, no sound emerging.

His face smoothed over, and the pressure at her throat eased, ever so slightly. For just a moment, she saw the skinny, uncertain kid that had approached her in the club a thousand years ago, before all this had started.

"Oh, God, I never—" he began.

She struck. Her position had shit for leverage, but she threw the punch as hard as she could. It connected with his throat, and this time she felt rather than heard the crack of snapping bone.

His mouth gaped, but no sound came out. He fell to the floor, flopping like a fish and gasping for air.

The feeding frenzy in the crowd continued. The sparks from the mixing desk had started a fire that blazed madly as people ran to the doors. Some were stopped by crazed Fan Club members, but a few others made it out.

The columns of darkness were gone.

Case dragged Johnny toward the back.

CHAPTER 33

"You okay?" Case asked nervously. "I mean, are they treating you all right?"

John scribbled something on a piece of paper and slid it across the table.

Yeah, the note said. In crayon. *I haven't been out since the funeral, but they're treating me okay.*

Case nodded. She didn't know what to say. Danny's body had been found among the burned after the fire department had finally put out the blaze. The funeral had been bad, and she had avoided John.

There had been a lot of funerals that week, but only a handful of the new inmates of the mental hospital were allowed to attend, and then only under heavy guard. All told, there had been four hundred killed that night, and another sixty-one had been institutionalized for an indefinite period while teams of doctors tried to figure out the cause of an apparent epidemic of psychosis. Sixty of those patients were still ravening maniacs, constantly raving about how hungry they were and occasionally taking bites out of hospital staff and other patients, from what Case had heard. The last patient, John, had calmed down considerably after a few weeks. He probably would have been released by now, if he didn't periodically try to kill himself.

Case had finally decided to visit John now, almost six months after the disaster. He seemed okay. Frail and thin-looking in his white hospital garb, but more or less okay. He'd never speak again, though, let alone sing. She had snapped his hyoid bone and torn both his vocal cords. She had heard that the doctors had tried to repair everything, but that they'd failed.

She thought that, on balance, that might be a very good thing.

"Bored?" Case asked, then immediately regretted it. It was a stupid question.

John shrugged. *It's not so bad. Writing a lot of poetry.*

"Yeah? Send me some when you get it done. I'd like to read it."

He nodded, but his face was still. For a brief moment, Case thought she glimpsed a hint of something ancient and awful, something horrid staring out at her, mute behind John's eyes. She didn't know if it—whatever *it* was—was still in there or not, but she knew she would wonder forever. None of the others had recovered, after all. Night after night, she lay awake listening to the noises in her apartment, wondering if all of the Fan Club had been accounted for. She was afraid she'd wonder about that all the rest of her life.

They talked for another twenty minutes or so, Case reading the notes John passed across the table and answering his questions as best as she could.

I miss Danny, he wrote toward the end, his eyes shining.

"Me too." It had been months before she could look at a pair of drumsticks without tears coming to her eyes. She missed Erin, too. Erin had listened to her, had gotten clear of the place before Ragman had even gotten onstage, but she wanted nothing to do with Case. She'd avoided Case at Danny's funeral, just as Case had avoided John. God, that had hurt. It still did. Maybe someday they'd be able to talk again, but Case doubted it. Allen had also made it, miraculously staggering out of the smoke just behind Case. She was actually doing some recording with him now, capturing a set of dark songs they'd written together while trying to cope. Case thought he might have kept her from losing her own mind—he was the one person with whom she felt comfortable talking about that awful tour, maybe the only person who understood.

There didn't seem to be much to say to John after that. She made her excuses before too long, and turned to go.

As she walked toward the door, she felt John's eyes on her, watching, contemplating—waiting.

John's eyes? Or something else's?

She turned around. John *was* watching her, but if there was any malice in his gaze she couldn't see it.

"See you later," she said.

He gave her a weak smile and waved back.

She felt him watch her all the way down the hall.

End.

ABOUT THE AUTHOR

Joseph Garraty has worked as a construction worker, technical writer, rocket test engineer, environmental consultant, and deadbeat musician, among other things. He lives in Dallas, Texas.

For news, updates, and more information, visit http://www.josephgarraty.com.